What was the sab

Did the person want to get caught?

Another sound emanated from the shadows. Something that made Michaela gasp even before the flash of the flame. She'd heard the telltale flick of a lighter.

Then a bottle rolled across the asphalt right before footsteps pounded, running away from it, from what they'd tossed: an explosive.

"Get down!" she yelled as the bottle, with a rag in it burning brightly now, rolled right near them. They were close to the building, but not close enough to open the door and get inside before the glass exploded in a fireball from the accelerant inside the bottle.

Fragments of glass flew, and the blast, as close as it was, knocked Michaela back into Charlie, whose arms closed almost reflexively around her. But he fell back, too, into the steel door behind them.

And then a moment later everything went black again when she lost consciousness.

Dear Reader,

I hope when you read this book, or any of the Hotshot Heroes books, that you feel the same way I do when I write them. I feel like I've strapped myself into a roller coaster, one that goes through tunnels so dark you can't see anything. You have no idea what surprises are coming up, what highs or lows are on the track. I hope that is how you feel as a reader, that you're as surprised as each of these hotshot heroes are when they come under attack and when they find love.

This book is my biggest surprise because it is my one hundredth book with Harlequin. I remember when, at eleven years old, I read my first Harlequin romance. I knew then that I wanted to write for Harlequin, and as determined as I was to achieve that goal, the pursuit wasn't always easy. Even after getting published, twenty years after I read that first one, I had editors come and go, lines close down, and I wasn't sure if I would make it to one hundred. But I have. And I am so thrilled that it is with this book—in which the hotshot hero is actually a heroine. She's tough and determined, and she worked hard to get where she is. She is my hero. I hope you enjoy her story and my one hundredth book.

Happy reading!

Lisa Childs

HOTSHOT'S DANGEROUS LIAISON

LISA CHILDS

HARLEQUIN
ROMANTIC
SUSPENSE

Recycling programs
for this product may
not exist in your area.

ISBN-13: 978-1-335-59412-9

Hotshot's Dangerous Liaison

Copyright © 2024 by Lisa Childs

Harlequin Enterprises ULC
22 Adelaide St. West, 41st Floor
Toronto, Ontario M5H 4E3, Canada
www.Harlequin.com

Printed in Lithuania

MIX
Paper | Supporting
responsible forestry
FSC® C021394

New York Times and *USA TODAY* bestselling, award-winning author **Lisa Childs** has written more than eighty-five novels. Published in twenty countries, she's also appeared on the *Publishers Weekly*, Barnes & Noble and Nielsen Top 100 bestseller lists. Lisa writes contemporary romance, romantic suspense, paranormal and women's fiction. She's a wife, mom, bonus mom, avid reader and less avid runner. Readers can reach her through Facebook or her website, lisachilds.com.

Visit the Author Profile page
at Harlequin.com for more titles.

I am dedicating this book to the women who made me the woman and the writer I am today. They shared their love of Harlequin romances with me as well as their wisdom and their strength. They are gone but will never be forgotten—my mother, MaryLou Childs, and my grandmother Mary Wisniewski. They will forever be my hotshot heroines!

Prologue

Sixteen months ago...

Smoke burned his nose and dried out his throat, drawing a racking cough from him that jerked him awake. He lifted his head from the leather blotter on his desk, coughed again and blinked. But the smoke burned his eyes, making them tear up and blur his vision.

What the hell is going on...?

Still half-asleep, Charlie Tillerman dragged himself up from his desk and staggered over to the door. When he wrapped his hand around the knob, the metal was warm but not too warm. Wasn't there some rule about that?

He drew in a breath, coughed as it burned his lungs and pulled open the door. The hall was all hazy, like his office. He stumbled down the hall toward the game room area of his bar, where the pool tables, dartboards and arcade games were—or where they should have been, since he couldn't see them through the smoke. But he could feel the heat coming at him in waves as the flames rose higher as he neared the front dining room area of the bar. The fire crackled, almost as if it was laughing while it consumed his livelihood, his family legacy: the Filling Station Bar and Grille. His fondest memories from childhood were of this place, of helping his grandfather out at the bar on the corner of Main Street and Lakeside Drive in Northern Lakes, Michigan.

Grandpa had died around the same time that Charlie's life had fallen apart in the big city, so he had two reasons to come home to Northern Lakes. And after inheriting the bar, he had a reason to stay.

The Filling Station once had a gas station on the property. He could smell gasoline now. It burned his nose like the smoke burned his eyes. But the pumps had been removed long ago, along with most of the soil from around where they'd been. So how could the scent be so strong?

He coughed and sputtered, his lungs and throat burning from the smoke and fumes. When had the fire started? What time was it, even? He'd left his damn cell phone in his office. But his primary concern was making sure everyone got out and none of his customers or employees were trapped inside like the local Boy Scouts—one being his nephew—who had been trapped in the middle of a wildfire in the forest a few months ago.

He blinked and wiped his eyes, trying to peer through the smoke and flames to see if anyone else was still inside the building. Because people were what was important, not possessions. If only his ex-wife had realized that…

Or if he'd realized sooner that possessions were all she cared about.

No, that hadn't been all; she cared about appearances and power just as much as her material things. When he'd lost the election for a seat in the state senate, he'd lost her. But now he was about to lose even more. He couldn't breathe, the smoke searing his lungs, and he found his legs giving way beneath him. He dropped to the floor, onto the peanuts that had been strewn across the scratched hardwood boards.

Was he dying?

Because, just before consciousness slipped away from him, the last thing he saw was the face of an angel framed with short, pale blond hair. She had the most beautiful blue eyes he had ever seen.

And then he closed his eyes for maybe the last time.

Chapter 1

Sixteen months later...

Charlie Tillerman was a dead man—or he would be if the other hotshots were right...

If *he* was the saboteur.

Michaela Momber listened to her fellow hotshots' voices rumbling around the airplane cabin as they speculated over the identity of the saboteur who'd been messing with them for way too long. The incidents had been happening for over a year now. Stupid things at first that they hadn't even realized were intentional—like equipment that had been checked suddenly breaking. But because of the nature of their jobs, those things had been dangerous. Especially when the firehouse stove had exploded, sending Ethan Sommerly to the hospital with burns. Fortunately, his beard had saved him from any significant wounds, but once his beard was gone, all hell had broken loose. He wasn't just a hotshot firefighter, he was heir to some famous family.

That situation could have been worse, like when their vehicles had been tampered with, brake lines cuts. But now the attacks had become physical, with the saboteur striking Rory VanDam over the head so hard that he was in a coma for two weeks. *Saboteur* really wasn't a strong enough word for this person.

Rory had recovered from his traumatic head injury, which happened after the hotshot holiday party six months ago. He'd also recovered from a gunshot wound he suffered when a corrupt FBI agent had gone after him. Again.

Rory was flying the plane now, so his wasn't one of the voices Michaela heard from where she sat in the back of the plane. She'd boarded first, eager to take a seat and get some much-needed rest after the two weeks they'd spent battling a wildfire. But even though she tried to sleep, the majority of her twenty-member team kept talking. It wasn't just their voices keeping her awake but also what they were talking about—or rather, whom.

"Charlie had access to my drinks," Luke Garrison remarked. "He could have been the one who drugged me. Maybe he was working with Marty Gingrich."

Marty Gingrich, a former state trooper, was the one who'd tried to kill Luke and his wife, though. Not Charlie.

But had Charlie helped? The thought had Michaela's stomach churning with dread, but she shook her head, rejecting the idea.

"It's more likely that Trooper Wells is helping Gingrich than Charlie," Michaela said, then stiffened with shock over the fact that she'd instinctively come to the bartender's defense.

"True," Hank said. "I could definitely see Wynona Wells being involved in this."

Henrietta "Hank" Rowlins was Michaela's best friend, so her quick agreement was no surprise. But did she suspect that Michaela had a reason for defending Charlie? Michaela felt a jab of guilt that she hadn't told her anything, but she'd hoped there would be nothing to tell. That it had just been a one-time thing on a night when she'd felt just too damn alone.

But it had been more than once.

"I don't trust Wells either," Patrick "Trick" McRooney said. He might have just agreed with Hank because he was engaged to her. "But Charlie definitely has easier access to us."

Damn. Did Trick suspect?

He was the brother-in-law of the hotshot superintendent, Braden Zimmer. Braden had brought in his wife's brother to investigate the saboteur, figuring that he would be more objective than the superintendent could be about his team. But then Trick had fallen for Hank and lost all his objectivity.

Michaela hoped she hadn't done the same thing. Lost her objectivity.

Not falling for anyone. That was never going to happen, she would never risk her heart again. She couldn't trust anyone, most especially herself and her own damn judgment.

"Charlie's got more access at the bar," Ethan Sommerly said. "But at the firehouse?"

Carl Kozak, one of the older hotshots, snorted. "Thanks to Stanley, everyone has access to the firehouse. Sorry, Cody."

Cody Mallehan was Stanley's older foster brother and the reason Stanley was in Northern Lakes. He had moved the teenager here after Stanley aged out of the foster care system. Cody sighed. "We're working on it."

"We're also working hard on finding out who the saboteur is and on keeping the team safe," Braden added, as if trying to reassure them. With the dark circles beneath his eyes, he looked as exhausted as Michaela felt. He probably wasn't sleeping any more than she was.

"It's bad enough fighting a wildfire," Donovan Cunningham murmured. "But to have to worry about getting hurt at home too…"

Apparently, Michaela wasn't the only one on edge right now. The stress had to be what was making her so sick. At least the wildfire they were returning from was in Ontario, so the plane ride would be short, which was good since Michaela's stomach went up and down with every bit of turbulence.

"That's why we have to investigate every possible suspect," Trick said. "Even Charlie."

"What's his motive?" Michaela found herself asking.

"You know," Cody said. "You were the one who was there when his bar burned down. You saved him."

Michaela smiled. "And he would want revenge on us for that?" He certainly hadn't seemed to want revenge on her, anyway, since he'd refused to let her pay for anything in his bar since the fire. And then they…

"He might want revenge because the arsonist who burned down his bar was really after us. He and the Filling Station were nearly collateral damage," Donovan said. He was an older hotshot, too, like Carl. Guys who'd been working as elite firefighters for a long time.

"The Filling Station is more than his bar," Braden said. "It's his home, and his family legacy."

So that did give him motive.

Even the superintendent, who was usually loath to suspect anyone, seemed to think Charlie had a motive. But…

If Charlie Tillerman was the saboteur, Michaela Momber had been sleeping with the enemy.

Had she done it again? Had she made a horrible mistake, trusting someone she shouldn't have? Not that she really trusted him. Not that she could really trust anyone…

Her stomach churned again, and she closed her eyes and

arched her neck against the headrest of the airplane seat. She didn't usually get motion sickness, but lately everything had been making her queasy. For months now, she'd been feeling so damn nauseous and bloated. So bloated that she couldn't even button her pants anymore.

If she didn't know better, she might have thought she was pregnant. But that wasn't possible. She couldn't get pregnant. But it was good that she hadn't gotten pregnant with her ex. She shouldn't have trusted him to be a faithful husband, so she certainly wouldn't have trusted him to be a responsible father.

No. She wasn't pregnant. But with as sick as she'd been feeling, she probably had an ulcer. And no matter if he was the saboteur or not, Charlie Tillerman was partially responsible for that too.

After her divorce, Michaela had no intention of ever getting involved with anyone again. Not that she and Charlie were *involved*.

But they were…

She wasn't sure what they were. But if anyone found out about them, they might think she was working with him, that she was complicit in the sabotage, too, just like so many people thought Trooper Wynona Wells might be complicit in all the horrible things her training sergeant Marty Gingrich had done to the hotshot team. Michaela really wished that it was her and not Charlie.

But she also had to be realistic and cautious, or she might wind up getting hurt, like Rory. She didn't want anyone else getting hurt, either, though. She desperately wanted the saboteur—whoever it was—caught and brought to justice.

Especially if that person was Charlie.

And if that person was Charlie, she wanted to be the one

to catch him first. With the access she had to him, she might be the only person who could catch him.

The flames sputtered and cowered, shrinking away from the water blasting from the end of the hose Charlie Tillerman held tightly between his gloved hands. After the arson fire had destroyed his bar and nearly claimed his life over a year ago, Charlie had no interest in ever going near another one. But here he was, suited up in fire-retardant jacket and pants, battling a blaze.

Sweat rolled down his back and off his face. Despite it being June, the weather hadn't warmed up much yet this year, and this late at night, it was extra cool. But the fire burned hot, especially with as close as Charlie was standing to it, just inside the open garage door.

The flames flared up, trying to reach the wood rafters of the garage, but another blast of water sent them crashing back down…below the raised hood of the vehicle inside the garage. The hood and motor were black, and the windshield and headlights had shattered in the heat. It was too late to save the car, but the battle was now to save the structure, to stop the fire from spreading any farther.

From destroying anything more.

Like his livelihood and his home had been destroyed over a year ago. He'd rebuilt the Filling Station Bar and Grille within months of the fire, working alongside the contractors and the townspeople who'd volunteered to help. While the town in the Huron Forest, with its many inland lakes, was a seasonal tourist destination, it was the locals who had been his loyal patrons.

And it was those loyal patrons—even the hotshot firefighters whom some people held responsible for the fires in the first place—who'd helped him rebuild. The arsonist who'd torched his bar and started the forest fire that had trapped the Boy Scouts six months prior to the bar burning down had been holding a grudge against the hotshot team for not hiring him. But even though he had been apprehended and brought to justice, other tragic or near-tragic things kept happening in this town. And while the hotshots seemed to be at the heart of the threats, too many other people had been put in danger as well from the violence.

The most tragic of these incidents had been a murder. But people had also been nearly run down walking across the street or, while in their vehicles, had been run off the road. There had also been shootings and explosions and fires.

Like the one he was battling now, the hose from the rig between his gloved hands, blasting water onto the flames. If only he'd had the rig and this equipment the night his bar had burned down...

If only he'd had some control over the situation and hadn't felt so damn helpless and vulnerable...

But he'd learned long ago there was no controlling anything, sometimes not even himself. At least when it came to a certain female customer.

The flames died fast, extinguished by the water, which now dripped from the blackened shell of the vehicle. While the car was a total loss, they'd managed to limit the damage to the garage it was in. This fire was probably just an accident, like the homeowner had claimed it was. He'd left the classic car running while he was working on it, and something must have sparked and started the engine on fire.

This wasn't like all those other things that had been happening in Northern Lakes. And this fire had nothing to do with the hotshots, since they weren't even in town. They were off somewhere battling another wildfire. There had been a lot of them lately, which had left the Northern Lakes Fire Department so short-staffed that they had put out an emergency call for volunteers.

Even though he'd had no intention of going near another fire, Charlie hadn't been able to ignore the call. Not after so many of his neighbors and the townspeople had helped him rebuild his business and his life. So he'd gone through training and had been out on—fortunately—just a few calls since he'd finished that training a month ago.

Maybe things were quiet because the hotshots had been gone so much. That quiet, from fires, also extended to other parts of Charlie's life. Professionally, the bar was quieter without the hotshots' business, and personally...

No. He could not risk having a personal life. He just... couldn't. After his divorce, he had decided relationships were too damn unpredictable, kind of like fires. There was just no way of knowing which way it would go, so the chances of getting burned were just too great to risk. And Charlie wasn't nearly a good enough judge of character to trust anyone with his heart again.

To trust *anyone* again. Even the angel who'd rescued him that night in his burning bar. He was actually the least likely to trust *her* because she was one of *them*. A Huron hotshot.

No. He definitely couldn't trust her. He had only seen her a few times since the night of the hotshot holiday party, which had been a private event at the Filling Station, six months ago.

Not that he wanted to see her again. It was easier if he didn't. Then he wasn't so damn tempted. But damn, he missed her too.

"Hey, you awake?" Eric asked as he stared into the back of the rig, where Charlie was sitting alone.

He didn't even remember climbing inside the truck at the

burned-out garage, much less riding back to the firehouse. But that was definitely where the rig was now, parked in one of the bays of the three-story concrete block building. That building, on the main street of Northern Lakes, was just down the road from his bar, which was too damn close, given some of what had been happening at the firehouse over the past year or so. The shootings, the explosions...

He shuddered at the memory of those things that had rattled the windows and the walls of the Filling Station, which wasn't just his business but also his home since he lived in the apartment above it.

Charlie shook his head, trying to clear thoughts of those dangers and of *her* from his mind. But that hadn't been easy to do even before they...

He definitely couldn't let himself think about *that*. So he drew in a deep breath and nodded. "Yeah, I'm awake," he assured his fellow volunteer, who was also his brother-in-law.

Eric Veltema was a big guy with blond hair that turned reddish in his mustache and beard. He had a booming laugh and a big personality, just like Charlie's sister. Valerie was the one who should have followed their father into politics, not Charlie.

Charlie had always preferred tending the bar, like their grandfather had most of his life. Charlie looked like Grandpa Tillerman, too, with dark eyes and black hair, and now that he was getting close to forty, the stubble on his jaw was starting to come in gray.

"You're the night owl," Eric said, "staying up late and closing the bar. I didn't think you ever slept."

Charlie chuckled at the misconception. "I sleep. Unlike you, I don't have kids." A pang of regret struck him, along with a sense of loss for what might have been, what could have been. His ex-wife hadn't wanted any children, though, and after what had nearly happened to his nephew, Charlie had changed his mind too. The world was entirely too dangerous to bring children into, especially in Northern Lakes.

Eric chuckled too. "Is that the reason you're staying a bachelor now? Because you want to sleep?"

"That's one of them," Charlie admitted.

But he had other reasons, and his brother-in-law was well aware of them. He and Eric had been friends since they were kids. They'd gone to school together and grown up together. Eric had been like family even before he'd married Charlie's sister, who'd always thought her younger brother's friend was annoying. Despite falling in love with him, she claimed she still found him annoying.

"Seriously, though," Charlie continued, "is Nicholas sleeping through the night yet?"

Eric's grin slid away, and he sighed. "Most nights now, but he still has the occasional nightmare about the fire."

"He's not the only one," Charlie muttered.

He'd felt so damn helpless then, when those Boy Scouts had been trapped in the burning forest and they'd had to rely on the hotshots to rescue them and put out the fire. He hoped to never feel that helpless again, but just a few months later, he'd been trapped in his own burning bar.

"That's why you have to win this election, man," Eric said. "With you as mayor, you'd have some clout to get this fire station away from the hotshot crew. Let them use someplace else as their headquarters, someplace where they don't put anyone else in danger with all their enemies and secret identities and crap."

Charlie's stomach churned with the thought of putting himself through another campaign. While he was a town council member, he hadn't had to campaign for that position because everybody had just written him into the open seat his grandfather had left behind when he died, like he'd left Charlie the bar.

But mayor was a position some other people wanted, like a local Realtor and the CEO of the lumber company that owned whatever forest wasn't state land. These two guys, Jason Cruise and Bentley Ford, had influence and money, like the people Charlie had run against before. And they would probably be just as cutthroat as his old opponents had been for that senate seat.

He took off his hat and pushed his hand through his hair. He was tempted to pull out some of the dark strands, that would probably be less painful than going into politics again. But his brother-in-law, sister and quite a few other locals had been putting the pressure on him to run. Even the incumbent mayor was offering to step down now and have Charlie assume his duties as an interim mayor, figuring that if he had the job before the election, he would have the advantage over his opponents. The deputy mayor had passed away from old age a few months earlier, so the mayor could appoint one of the town council members to take over for him.

Because Charlie wanted to protect his hometown—not just from the danger the hotshots posed but also from the danger that ambitious real estate developers posed—he was going to have to take some action. And at the moment, he could think of only one.

He uttered a weary sigh and admitted, "I know something has to be done about them."

Every time there was a shooting or someone was nearly run down or there was an explosion or a fire, everyone in the vicinity was in danger, not just the hotshots.

"And I think you're the best man for the job, Charlie," Eric persisted, like he had been doing for the past few months.

"Tillerman is the name that people in this town instinctively trust."

The election was six months away yet, but the current mayor had already publicly announced that he wasn't going to run again. Then he'd privately offered to step aside now if Charlie would agree to be interim mayor until the election. Being the "incumbent" would give him the advantage over any rival, all but guaranteeing him the win, especially if he did what the townspeople were lobbying for the mayor to do.

"You're just saying that because you want me to get rid of the hotshots," Charlie said.

"I'm not the only one who wants that," Eric reminded him. "And it's what *you* want too."

But he didn't really want to get rid of all of them. At least, not one blue-eyed, blonde beauty who made his pulse race just thinking about her.

When he finally stepped out of the back of the rig, his gaze met that blue one of hers. She was standing a little way behind Eric at the foot of the stairs that led up to the second and third stories of the building.

So the hotshots were back in town.

And from the angry expression on Michaela Momber's beautiful face, she had clearly overheard everything he and Eric had been talking about. Was she outraged for professional reasons, though, or for personal reasons?

The saboteur was feeling bold. They'd gone so long without being discovered that they felt invincible. It didn't matter who came after them or tried to find them—that person was going to fail, just like everyone else kept failing.

Braden Zimmer. The hotshot superintendent hadn't been able to figure it out. Nor had his assistant superintendents,

Wyatt Andrews and Dawson Hess. Even his smart new wife, the arson investigator, hadn't been able to figure it out.

And then Braden had brought in his brother-in-law to help find the saboteur. But Trick McRooney had failed, just like Braden had.

They had no clue.

But if, by some chance, someone started getting close to figuring it out...

Started putting it all together...

Then that person was going to have to die. The saboteur hadn't actually considered murder before—not that someone couldn't have died during one of the *accidents*. Hell, a few nearly *had* died. And because of that, because of all the things that had happened and how many people had been hurt, the saboteur would definitely face jail time if they were discovered.

And if that happened, they would lose everything that they had, everything that they were. But none of that mattered as much as the saboteur's quest for justice.

For revenge...

Chapter 2

Charlie should have been used to Michaela walking away from him. That was what she'd been doing for the past several months. No. Longer than that. She'd walked away the night she'd rescued him from the fire at his bar.

Once she'd gotten him to safety, to an ambulance waiting outside, she'd walked away from him. She'd walked back into the fire. That was a little how Charlie felt as he rushed out after her—that he was walking back into a fire.

That was how he felt every time he got close to her, like he was going to get burned by the heat between them. The passion that ignited whenever they were alone or even just looked at each other. But they'd done more than just look. Eventually, after months of him flirting with her, of trying to get her to give him a chance...

She'd given him more than that. She'd given him more pleasure than he'd ever known.

Clearly nothing like that was going to happen tonight. He was more likely to get burned by her temper because she looked really mad about what she overheard them saying. But instead of unleashing her anger, she just walked away. And he realized that beneath her anger was the vulnerability he'd found beneath her toughness.

She wasn't as tough emotionally as she was physically.

And as angry as she was about what she'd heard, she probably felt equally betrayed. That sense of betrayal was something Charlie understood all too well from the things that had come out during his campaign.

The secrets he hadn't known about his ex, the secrets she'd purposely kept from him. Like her affairs and the money she'd taken from his campaign contributions.

At the time, he hadn't appreciated how much gratitude he owed his opponent for digging up that dirt. He'd just been angry at him for humiliating him and at her for her betrayal. He'd been angriest at himself, though, for being so damn blind.

But underneath his anger there had been pain. He hoped that wasn't the case with Michaela, he didn't want her hurting because of him, thinking that he'd betrayed her.

Needing to make sure that she was okay and to explain what she'd heard, he tried to break free of his brother-in-law's grasp. When he started after her, Eric grabbed his arm before he could get past him.

"Charlie, what's the deal with you and the lady hotshot?" Eric asked. "The way she looked at you…" He shivered, then chuckled.

Michaela had a reputation around Northern Lakes for being tough—icy, even. But while she was tough, there was nothing cold about her.

"You must realize that she'd be pissed about what she overheard us saying," Charlie pointed out.

"So." Eric shrugged. "The hotshots are going to know soon enough when you're the mayor of Northern Lakes and they're looking for a new place for their headquarters. They wore out their welcome here."

"I don't have time for this now." Charlie tugged his arm

free of his brother-in-law's big hand, and he rushed toward that side door.

The last thing Charlie wanted to talk about at the moment was running for mayor. Right now he just wanted to run for Michaela, to catch up to her so that he could explain what she'd heard.

And that wasn't just because of…what they'd both agreed was a bad idea. This attraction between them, this strange and secret arrangement they had…

He stepped outside, letting the door slam shut behind him. Once it closed, it was as if someone had extinguished all the light. It was alarmingly dark without the glow of the fluorescent lights from the garage chasing away the night. Clouds must have obscured the moon, but there should have been more light.

While the streetlamps didn't quite reach the side of the building, there were light poles in the parking lot next to the firehouse that illuminated the entire area. Usually…

What had happened to them?

And more importantly, what had happened to her?

"Michaela!" Charlie called out to her now, concern gripping him, making his muscles tense. "Michaela!"

"Shh…"

The whisper from the dark raised goose bumps along his skin, despite the heaviness of the firefighter gear he was still wearing. He would recognize that husky female voice anywhere. He heard it so often in his dreams, and then he would wake up to find himself reaching for her.

But she was never there.

She never stayed, as if what they'd done was some embarrassing secret she was determined to keep. And he wasn't sure why—except that, for some reason, he hadn't been any more eager to share than she had. After his last political campaign had exposed more about his personal life than even he had known, like his wife's affairs and overspending, he was doubly determined to keep his private life private. Which was another reason he was reluctant to accept even the interim mayor position, let alone run in another election.

Lowering his voice to match her whisper, he asked, "Where are you?" And why couldn't he see her? She was still wearing her yellow hotshot-firefighter gear when he'd seen her inside just moments ago. But it was so dark that he couldn't even see her uniform.

"Shh…" she hissed again from the darkness, but she sounded closer now, and there was a strange sense of urgency or caution in her voice.

She wasn't just trying to shut him up because she didn't want to hear his explanation. There was something else happening.

"What's going on?" he asked.

Then he heard what must have drawn her attention already: the sound of shoes or boots scraping across asphalt. They weren't alone. Someone else was out in the dark parking lot with them.

He opened his mouth to call out to them, but Michaela must have been close enough to see him now, because she whispered again, "Shh…"

What was going on?

Did she consider whoever else was out there in the darkness a threat? And was that threat to their relationship she seemed so determined to keep secret? Or, given all the dangerous things that happened to and around the hotshots, was that threat to their lives?

Moments ago, when Michaela had stepped out into the darkness, she had already been reeling from what she'd just seen and heard in the firehouse. Charlie Tillerman, in the back of one of the rigs, in firefighter gear. Not yellow gear, like the hotshots wore, but black, like his thick, glossy hair and his dark eyes and apparently his soul.

He did want to get rid of the hotshots, and he and that other man had already been plotting how to do it. Her team was right to be suspicious of Charlie Tillerman. And she, once again, had been wrong about a person. On the plane ride into Northern Lakes, she'd decided to find out the truth about him, to find any evidence of him being the saboteur. She'd even intended to go over to his place tonight and look around. But maybe that had just been an excuse to see him again.

She hadn't even had to go to the Filling Station to find out the truth about him. But in that moment, she'd realized how badly she wanted him to not harbor any resentment toward the hotshots, to not want to hurt them.

But she was afraid that he had. At least, he'd hurt one of them...

So, feeling sick again, she'd rushed outside for some air, only to step into total darkness. Despite the darkness, she could feel someone else's presence. But she couldn't see who was out there. And she desperately wanted to see them.

Were they this close? The saboteur? It had to be the saboteur because she could hear the hiss of air, like tires deflating. A lot of trucks, like hers, were parked in the lot because many of the hotshots had been too tired to go home and were sleeping upstairs in the bunkroom right now. She hadn't wanted to make the drive home, either, since the firehouse in St. Paul—where she and Hank worked and lived when not out with the hotshots—was more than an hour away.

She'd intended instead to go to the Filling Station, despite the fact that the bar would have closed a couple of hours ago. Then she'd heard his voice rumbling out of the back of that rig, and after she'd heard him admit to wanting the hotshots gone, she just wanted to get away from him.

But he wasn't the one out here letting air out of tires. And if he wasn't…

Did that mean he wasn't the saboteur?

Charlie was here now, though. When he had opened the door seconds ago and light spilled into the parking lot, she glanced around the area, trying to find whoever else was out there.

But the door closed too quickly again, extinguishing that brief flicker of light and the flicker of hope Michaela had to see who was still hiding in the darkness. They must have shut off the lights somehow, or Michaela would have seen them already.

Had they seen her when she'd opened that door? And Charlie? Were the two of them in danger now, like Rory had been the night that the sound of all the engines running had lured him out into the hall?

She had no weapon, and she doubted Charlie had one either. So what had she intended to do if she actually caught the saboteur in the act?

But she wanted to see who it was so damn badly that she hadn't considered how she would actually apprehend the person. She just wanted to know who'd been messing with them for so long, putting them in danger and also doing some petty, stupid stuff like this. Letting air out of tires.

For a second, when she'd heard Charlie talking, she thought it was him. And while she'd been angry, she'd also been…hurt. But now, knowing that it wasn't him but someone else—some *anonymous* someone else, who quite possibly was a member of her team…

Fury bubbled up inside her, and she wished she had a

weapon. Or at least a flashlight. Her phone had died on the return trip from Ontario, and she hadn't had the chance to charge it yet. Or she would have used that to not just see the person but take a picture of them in the act of sabotage.

Maybe Charlie had his phone on him. When he'd opened the door, she'd started back toward the building. Toward him, drawn to him, as she'd been for too damn long. She'd tried to resist the attraction, but he was just so good-looking and so charming. But those were the very reasons she should have resisted him, because she knew those traits were her weakness and made it as hard for her to see clearly as it was for her to see in the dark parking lot right now.

But as she moved closer to him, she could see him a bit in the faint light seeping out from under the door of the firehouse. She needed to find out if he had his phone on him, but she didn't want the sound of their voices to draw the saboteur's attention or to send the person running before they could see who it was.

So she moved even closer to him and whispered near his ear, "I need your cell."

His body moved in a slight shiver. And he nodded and pulled out his phone. "Call the police."

The police wouldn't get there in time to stop whoever was out in the dark with them. And neither would anyone inside the building because she had no doubt that if the door opened again, the person would run off.

Why hadn't they done that already, though? When she'd walked out or when Charlie had?

What was the saboteur waiting for?

Did the person want to get caught?

Another sound emanated from the shadows, something that made Michaela gasp even before the flash of the flame. She'd heard the telltale flick of a lighter.

Then a bottle rolled toward them, right before footsteps pounded across the asphalt, running away from what they'd tossed: an explosive.

"Get down!" she yelled as that bottle, the rag inside burning brightly now, rolled right near them. They were close to the building but not close enough to open the door and get inside before the glass exploded in a fireball from the accelerant inside the bottle.

Fragments of glass flew, and the blast, as close as it was, knocked Michaela back into Charlie, whose arms closed almost reflexively around her. But he fell back, too, into the steel door behind them.

And then, a moment later, everything went black again when she lost consciousness.

Braden Zimmer was in his office on the second floor of the firehouse. He'd just intended to take care of a few things on his desk before heading home. Sam, his wife, wasn't home right now. She'd just wrapped up an arson investigation out west and was staying in Washington for a couple of days to spend time with two men who were both nicknamed Mack: her dad and her oldest brother. The younger Mack had mysteriously shown up in Northern Lakes four months ago, just in the nick of time to save the life of another hotshot, one he'd known from their military service.

Mack Junior was back, but nobody really knew from where or what he'd been doing while he was there. Sam was determined to find out, but Braden wasn't sure she would get much information out of her oldest brother.

That wasn't all she was going to ask Mack, though. She wanted his help. Because even as good an investigator as she was, she hadn't been able to figure out who the saboteur was either.

Mack had already helped out once, when he'd shown up in town all those months ago. If he hadn't, Braden would have wound up burying another member of his team. Rory VanDam or whatever his real name was. Like Ethan Sommerly, Rory insisted on keeping the name he'd assumed five years ago when he and Ethan, who was really Jonathan Canterbury, had survived a plane crash.

A member of your team isn't who you think they are...

Braden had received that anonymous—and ominous—note more than a year ago, but he was no closer to finding out who'd sent it or whom they were referring to. At least two people on his team weren't who he'd thought they were.

They were even better. Really good guys, and Braden would have lost one if Mack hadn't shot the FBI agent trying to kill Rory VanDam. Mack knew who Rory really was from serving in the military together.

While neither Rory nor Ethan Sommerly was who they'd said they were, neither of them was the saboteur. They'd both been victims of the saboteur instead, as well as victims of the enemies from their own pasts. With the danger they'd been in, they were lucky to be alive.

The saboteur hadn't killed anyone yet, but Braden was worried that it was only a matter of time before one of the "accidents" that the saboteur kept staging caused fatal injuries for another hotshot.

And then Braden felt it.

The slight shudder of the building, as if something had struck it. He jumped up from his chair and rushed around his desk to pull open the door to the hall. He barely made it to the top of the stairs when he heard the yelling.

"Help! We need help!"

Braden didn't recognize the voice, but there were some new volunteers in the local fire department. The new crew had a rig out when he and his team had returned from Ontario earlier that evening. Maybe they'd struck the building trying to drive it back into the garage.

"Call an ambulance!" another voice shouted.

That voice, Braden recognized: Charlie, the bartender and owner of the Filling Station. He was one of the new volunteers, much to Braden's surprise. He hadn't shared that news with any of the other hotshots yet because they were already suspicious of Charlie. And he didn't want any of them trying to investigate on their own and getting hurt. It was bad enough that he'd put his brother-in-law Trick in danger by having him help investigate and protect the others.

But Braden would have to check out Charlie now. He'd known him and the Tillerman family for years, but he knew, after what Marty had done, that anyone was capable of being dangerous. And Braden couldn't deny that Charlie volunteering at the firehouse gave him easy access to it.

Of course, Carl had pointed out that, thanks to Stanley—the nineteen-year-old who helped out around the firehouse—frequently forgetting to lock the doors, pretty much anyone had access to the building. Maybe someone else—or some-*thing* else—had caused that disturbance he'd just felt.

"What happened?" Braden asked, running down the stairs to the garage area. Once he hit the bottom step, he gasped, and he could see why there was such urgency in Charlie's voice because of what he held in his arms: Michaela's limp body. Her head lolled back, blood dripping from her temple, staining her pale blond hair red. "Oh my God!" His hand shook as he pulled out his cell.

The other man, who'd yelled first for help, was on his phone, speaking to a 911 dispatcher from the call center.

But Braden called Owen. The paramedic was closer than

the hospital since he was probably just a street over at his girlfriend's apartment. "What happened?" he asked Charlie again.

"Something blew up—a bottle. There's glass and something...gasoline...and fire," he said, his deep voice vibrating with concern and confusion.

It was clear that there had been another explosion of some kind and Michaela had been injured in it. Braden relayed those details to Owen, who assured him that he was already on his way. One of the paramedic rigs was parked in the garage, though, so Braden pulled open the doors to it. "There's a stretcher in here we can lay her on, and we can get something for her wound..."

And hopefully, Owen would be there as fast as he'd promised.

As Charlie carried Michaela toward the open doors of the rig, Braden stepped forward to help, but the bar owner's arms tightened around her as if he didn't want to let her go. "She's breathing. I think," he said, his voice gruff. "And she has a pulse but..."

He was scared.

And so was Braden.

Charlie was also hurt, blood running down the side of his face like it did from hers. Maybe that was why he seemed so confused. He could have a concussion.

"Help's on the way," the other man—the new volunteer—said, and he shuddered as he stared at Michaela too. Then he looked at Charlie and gasped. "You're hurt, too, man!"

Ignoring him, Charlie jumped up into the back of the rig, and finally, he released Michaela's limp body onto the stretcher. The side door opened again, and Owen rushed inside and across the garage toward them.

"The asphalt's on fire," the paramedic said. "What the hell happened?"

"Some kind of explosive again," Braden said. "Michaela's still unconscious."

But then she moved slightly, shifting against the gurney as she started to regain consciousness. And her jacket fell open. Unlike the rest of the team, she hadn't changed out of all her gear yet. She wore the yellow pants, but they were unsnapped and straining over the slight swell of her belly.

And Braden, whose wife was expecting a baby within the next few weeks, realized that the female hotshot was pregnant too. She'd never said anything to him. Hell, he hadn't even known she was seeing anyone.

But from the way Charlie was sticking so close to her side, even as Owen started treating her, Braden had another suspicion about the bar owner: that maybe he was the father of Michaela's unborn child.

But none of that mattered as much as making sure that Michaela and her baby survived the saboteur's latest attack. Or Braden's fear might be realized, he might be losing another hotshot.

Chapter 3

Charlie couldn't stop pacing the ER waiting room. If he stopped, his shaky legs might fold beneath him like they had that night the bar had been on fire. The explosion in the parking lot had literally knocked him off his feet, but that wasn't what was affecting him now.

He was scared, but not for himself. He was scared for Michaela.

"She has to be okay," he muttered beneath his breath. "She has to be."

She'd saved his life over a year ago when she pulled him out of the fire, but he hadn't been able to do anything tonight to protect her or to help her. He felt like he had when his nephew had been trapped in the forest fire and when he'd been trapped in his own burning bar—so helpless that he couldn't draw a deep breath because of the pressure, the panic, nearly crushing his chest.

He wasn't alone now like he'd been in that bar fire before Michaela found him. Most of the hotshots had shown up at the hospital, too, rolling in behind the ambulance that had transported Michaela here. He would have ridden with her, but he'd wanted Owen to focus on her and not on the stupid cut on his head.

His brother-in-law had insisted on driving Charlie. And

fortunately, Eric's truck had been one of the few in the lot that the tires hadn't been slashed. Maybe he and Michaela had prevented that from happening with their sudden interruption of the vandal's plan.

"You're bleeding, man," Eric said. "You need to get someone to look at you too."

Maybe that was why he'd driven him to the hospital: he thought Charlie needed medical attention too. But all Charlie needed was Michaela, to make sure that she was all right.

"He's right," Braden Zimmer, the hotshot superintendent, said. "You probably need stitches."

Charlie raised his hand to his face, to where the blood had slowly been trickling down from his forehead like a trail of sweat. His hand was already stained with blood, but that was probably Michaela's, from the wound on her temple.

She'd been bleeding more than he was. How bad was the injury to her head?

She'd lost consciousness. Even though she'd started moving in the back of the ambulance, she hadn't opened her eyes. She hadn't totally regained consciousness.

Yet.

"How is she?" he asked, his voice gruff.

Braden shook his head, his jaw tense, as if he was clenching it. "I haven't heard anything yet."

Charlie followed the trickle of blood on his face up to just above his left eyebrow, and he flinched from a sudden jab of pain. Then he jerked his hand back, and his fingers came away with fresh blood. He hadn't stopped bleeding yet.

"You need to see a doctor," Eric insisted. "You need stitches."

And the hotshot superintendent must have thought so, too, because he rushed up to the waiting room desk clerk.

Seconds later, the door opened to the interior of the ER, and a nurse came out for Charlie.

He didn't protest getting treatment now because this way, he would be closer to Michaela, to wherever she was being treated. And he would, hopefully, be able to find out how she was doing.

If she was going to be okay…

"We need to irrigate and stitch that wound," the nurse was saying as she led him down a short hall to an open area. She guided him toward one of the gurneys lined up between pulled-back curtains. All the beds were empty except for one, in which an older man was sleeping, his curtains open so the nurses could keep an eye on him.

Where was Michaela? Why wasn't she back here?

"Sit down," the nurse said.

"I…" He cleared his throat of the emotion rushing up on him. "I need to know how Michaela Momber is."

The nurse's brow furrowed a bit as she studied his black uniform. "Are you one of her coworkers? Were you hurt the same time she was?"

He nodded. Even though he technically wasn't a coworker, he had been hurt with her. Which was ironic, given that, for the past several months, he'd been more worried about getting hurt *by* her.

"She's in radiology," the nurse replied, "getting a head CT and an ultrasound."

He nodded again. "That's good. They'll be able to see if she has a concussion, then."

The woman nodded now and smiled. "And make sure that her baby is okay."

"Baby?" Finally, his shaky legs gave out, and he dropped down to sit on the edge of that stretcher.

The woman's mouth dropped open, and she shook her head. "Forget I said that. I assumed you knew…"

No. He'd had no idea that Michaela was pregnant.

Had she ever intended to tell him?

And was he the father?

"Pregnant?" Michaela snorted at the ridiculous claim. And they thought *she* was the one with a concussion? "I am not pregnant."

Or maybe she was still unconscious and she was just dreaming about the impossible, about something she had once wanted so damn badly. If so, this was a cruel dream, and tears stung her eyes. She shook her head again and winced at the pain that jolted her.

"You're definitely pregnant," the doctor said and pointed to the monitor of the machine pulled next to the bed in which Michaela was lying.

She blinked to clear the tears from her vision and focused on that screen. There were arms and legs and a head with the perfect little profile of a small nose and rosebud lips. She reached up to touch her aching head, and her fingers skimmed across a bandage. "I do have a concussion?"

That had to be what was going on, why she was seeing and hearing things.

When Rory VanDam had been struck over the head a couple of months ago, he spent two weeks in a coma because of the severity of the concussion. And when he'd finally woken up, he'd been so confused.

Like she was now. Because nothing was making any sense to her…

Like what she was seeing…

She had to be hallucinating…because that just wasn't possible.

"Your CT scan showed that you have a very mild concussion," the doctor said. "I think it was more likely you passed out because you were severely dehydrated and anemic. You must have horrible morning sickness."

Michaela shook her head. "I have an ulcer..." From all the stress. From the danger. From how gruesomely she'd lost one friend and how close she'd come to losing so many others, including her best friend.

Where was Hank? Probably with Trick McRooney. Ever since Hank had fallen for the new member of the hotshot team, Michaela had kind of lost her best friend. She'd felt so alone that she finally let Charlie's charm get to her and undermine her determination to stay single and uninvolved. Given her judgment, it was safest for her and for anyone she might get involved with.

Had Charlie gotten hurt too? He'd been behind her, though, in the parking lot. So he had to be okay...since she was. But she really wasn't okay.

The doctor chuckled and pointed toward the screen. "That is not an ulcer."

"But I can't be pregnant," Michaela insisted.

"Why do you think that?" the doctor asked, her expression serious now as she met Michaela's gaze.

The woman, with her blond hair bound up in a high ponytail, looked very young. The name tag, with her photo, attached to her pocket proved that she was an MD. Dr. Brooke Smits. She had to be just a resident, maybe even an intern. That was probably why she didn't know what she was talking about, what she was seeing on that screen.

"I'm infertile," Michaela explained. "I don't even get periods."

"Well, you probably haven't had one for the last five months, but you must ovulate occasionally."

Michaela shook her head. "Ever since I was a teenager—from how hard I work out and how physically active I am—I stopped menstruating."

"Very low body fat, like you have, would affect your periods," Dr. Smits said. "But that doesn't mean that you're infertile. You would just have a little more difficulty getting pregnant."

"I tried for years with my ex-husband," Michaela said. "But his mistress had had no problem getting pregnant." She waited for the jab of pain she usually felt when she thought about him—about *them*—but she felt nothing now but the throbbing in her temple. A sound echoed that throbbing, and she could see it on the monitor as a little flutter across the screen. A heartbeat.

"I am *really* pregnant?" she asked. Was it actually possible?

The doctor smiled brightly at her. "You really had no idea?"

Michaela shook her head, then tensed. "I had *no* idea. I've been working wildfires. The smoke…" Her voice cracked with fear for her child. "And I inhaled some carbon monoxide in the firehouse six months ago when all the trucks were started up. How much damage did I do?"

She couldn't blink the tears away now as they streamed from her eyes, overcome with fear that she might have already harmed the dream that she'd thought for so long she would never realize. A child.

"The carbon monoxide incident probably happened before you got pregnant. You look to be around twenty, maybe twenty-two weeks."

So, after the holiday party…

"And your baby's heart is strong and steady, and the lung development looks good. I would say the baby is healthy.

Now, the mother—" the young doctor gave her a stern look "—needs to take better care of herself. You need prenatal vitamins and rest, or you're going to be passing out again, and you'll wind up on bed rest."

"I didn't pass out because I was tired," Michaela said, and she touched the bandage again.

Dr. Smits sighed. "I know there was another incident at the firehouse."

Another. Of course the doctor would be aware of how many people she'd treated in the ER who'd come from the firehouse. There had been way too many *incidents* involving the hotshots getting hurt.

"You're going to have to be extra careful," the doctor advised. "On your job and with your prenatal care. I'm going to give you a referral to an ob-gyn, and you should make an appointment as soon as possible."

Michaela sucked in a breath as a horrible thought occurred to her. "Am I going to be able to keep working?"

"The ob-gyn will be better able to answer your questions about restrictions and such," Dr. Smits replied.

Restrictions? There was no such thing as light duty as a hotshot. Michaela's job was so important to her—as her ex had said, maybe too important. It had taken her away from him so much, and it had taken away her chance of ever conceiving.

Or so she'd thought.

She hadn't been willing to give it up for her ex-husband. She focused on the screen, on that perfect little profile, and warmth flooded her heart.

But for the baby...

She moved her hands to her stomach, running them over it, and she felt a little flutter inside her, a little movement, and on that screen, the baby kicked. She gasped. "That's what I've been feeling? I've been feeling her or him?"

"You want to know?" Dr. Smits asked.

"Yes," she answered. Not that it mattered. "Mostly I just want to know that he or she is healthy."

"I promise you that your baby really appears to be strong and healthy," the doctor reassured Michaela. "But you have to make sure *she* stays that way."

"She?"

The doctor smiled that bright, happy smile again. "Yes. You're having a daughter."

While Michaela wanted to know so that she could connect more fully with her child and so that the baby would seem more real to her in what was such a surreal situation, she didn't really care what the gender of her child was. But she knew *who* would have cared: her father. Her daughter's grandfather would have been disappointed, like he'd been when his only child had been a daughter. But Michaela had no intention of telling her father about her pregnancy.

But the *baby's* father...

Charlie deserved to know, even though Michaela felt sick all over again at the thought of telling him. They had both agreed that this—whatever *this* was—was not going to be anything serious or lasting. Both had been burned before and had no intention of trying marriage again or even a relationship. What they had wasn't supposed to lead to anything.

But it had...

To a baby girl.

While Michaela was happy, would Charlie be? Or would he be like her father had been: resentful of her and her mother?

The dangers of her job weren't the only things that Michaela needed to protect her baby from...

* * *

Trick McRooney stood just outside the police tape, which had been strung around the firehouse parking lot right next to the building.

Another attack on their home turf.

By one of their own?

Trick nearly chuckled at the irony of him thinking that way, of being possessive of a place and of a team. For years, he'd avoided forming any sort of attachment to a job location and especially to people. His and his siblings' mom taking off when they were young had made it hard for him to trust people.

But that had changed when he joined the Huron hotshots several months ago. Because he knew that he belonged here in Northern Lakes with his fiancée, Henrietta "Hank" Rowlins, and with his sister and brother-in-law.

But if these attacks kept happening, Braden was bound to lose his job. And Trick would probably lose his too. But he cared less about the job than about someone losing their life. Michaela was in the hospital. He and Henrietta had been at the cottage she'd inherited from her grandfather when they got the call. Henrietta was on her way to the hospital but had insisted that he come here to find out what he could about what had happened to her best friend and the only other female on the twenty-member team of hotshots.

But Trooper Wells had ordered him to stay outside the crime scene tape. On the outside of the firehouse. And out of her way.

As if he couldn't be trusted, when *she* was the one nobody trusted. She was the only suspect they had all agreed on when they discussed the saboteur on the plane ride home. Wynona Wells had worked too closely with the trooper who was in jail for trying to kill one of the hotshots and for his role in the death of another hotshot. Trick had taken Dirk Brown's place on the team, and it was his job to ensure that nobody else lost their life.

"C'mon, Trooper Wells," he called out to the officer again, as he had a few times prior, only to be ignored. "I need to know what happened here tonight." And if he could get inside the damn firehouse, he would be able to access the footage from the cameras Braden had had installed after Rory was hurt so badly. The cameras were mostly on the main level, though, to catch people going in and out the doors and up and down the stairs. There were none out in the parking lot. But maybe they would have some installed there too.

She finally turned toward him. "You probably have a better idea what happened here than I do," she said. "None of you have been forthcoming with me about anything that has been going on with the hotshots."

Because they weren't sure they could trust her. Hell, they weren't sure they could trust each other. It almost had to be one of them. Didn't it?

Unless…

Trick had considered Charlie Tillerman a suspect. There had been a couple of times when people—himself included— almost certainly had to have been drugged while they were at the bar. And who would have had the easiest access to do that other than the bartender?

But Charlie had been with Michaela when she got hurt tonight, and he had possibly been hurt too. So that ruled him out as a suspect. Probably. Trick couldn't be sure, since he really had no idea what had happened tonight or how badly anyone had been hurt.

And the only light in the parking lot came from the ones the state police crime techs had set up. What had happened to the lights on the parking lot poles? And there was a motion light on the building by that side door that was supposed to automatically come on. But it was dark, too, even with Trooper Wells standing right in front of it.

Someone had obviously planned what had happened tonight. They'd extinguished all the lights so that they could slink around in the shadows like they'd been doing for over a year. That damn saboteur...

Some of the things they'd done were petty—messing with equipment, like the trucks that had flat tires sitting in the lot right now. There were a few of them. Braden's. And Donovan Cunningham's. He lived close enough that he probably should have gone home. But maybe he'd still been showering when the saboteur had struck.

Carl Kozak's truck tires were flat, too, and he lived close enough to have gone home as well. Trick was glad that he and Henrietta had gone to her grandfather's cottage to shower and sleep instead of sticking around here.

There were a couple of other trucks in the lot that he didn't recognize. Maybe the new volunteer firefighters' rides. They'd had a call tonight and had one of the rigs out when the hotshots returned from Canada. And when he and the other hotshots had returned to the firehouse, the parking lot lights had been on then. All of them.

So whoever put them out could have been someone on their hotshot team who'd either thrown the breaker to shut them off or had somehow broken the bulbs. The only broken glass on the asphalt seemed to have come from that bottle, though—the one that had been rigged like a Molotov cocktail.

What had that been intended to do? Had it been meant for Michaela or for one of the vehicles? Or to start the firehouse itself aflame?

"We can't tell you what we don't know," Trick pointed out, his frustration overwhelming him.

Michaela better be okay. She was one of the toughest people he knew, though, so she had to be.

The trooper narrowed her eyes and studied his face. "But none of you will tell me what you do know either."

"Have you tried talking to Michaela already?" he asked. If she had, then the hotshot was awake. When Braden had called them, he assured Henrietta that her best friend was already coming around, that she was going to be okay.

But Trick wondered if the hotshot superintendent had been speaking the truth or just saying what he wanted to be true. Braden desperately didn't want to lose another member of his team. Trick didn't want to either.

"I was told she was unconscious still," Trooper Wells said. "But then, I've been told that before…"

"Rory was in a coma for two weeks," he said. But to protect the injured hotshot, Braden had held her off for the extra week that Rory had been kept in the hospital for observation and for his memory to return completely to him. He'd been so confused when he'd awakened.

And given his previous career as an undercover DEA officer, it was no wonder he'd been so disoriented. Trick hadn't lived the life Rory had, and he was confused.

Why did someone keep coming after them?

What the hell was the motive?

Chapter 4

A butterfly patch and some liquid bandage sealed the wound over Charlie's eyebrow. He had opted for that instead of stitches—not that he was afraid of needles. What he was afraid of was losing track of Michaela.

He needed to see her, to talk to her, to make sure that she and the baby were okay.

Baby...

His baby?

He didn't think she was seeing anyone else. Not that she was really seeing him. He wasn't even sure what they'd been doing. They hadn't been dating, since they'd never actually gone out anywhere. She hadn't seemed to want anyone to know about them. Why? Because she'd been seeing someone else, too, like his ex-wife had been?

But Michaela was nothing like Amber. Even back when they met in college, Amber had been focused on the future, on all the money they would make and power they would have. Michaela seemed to focus only on the present.

But with a baby on the way, she was going to have to think about the future now. And talk about it.

No matter what he and she were doing—dating or otherwise—Charlie definitely needed to see her now. So once the doctor medically cleared him to leave, he pulled back the curtain of his area and looked for her. But again, there was only the older man, sleeping on one of the many stretchers.

Had Michaela been admitted to a room upstairs? The ICU?

"Where is Ms. Momber?" he asked the nurse who'd treated his wound.

"Are you family?" she asked him. "Or just a coworker?"

He wasn't really even a coworker. He was only a volunteer, and he wasn't sure that was a position he wanted to keep any more than he wanted to take on the new position as mayor, interim or otherwise. Just having a seat on the town council was bad enough. The lumber company's CEO and the local Realtor had seats, too, and he often clashed with them over their agendas for the town.

The nurse cleared her throat, prompting him to answer her question.

But he wasn't sure what Michaela considered him, let alone what he considered her. His guardian angel, at least once. And then...

"I'm..." he murmured, "a friend..."

"I have to respect the privacy issues with health care," she said, her face flushing. "And I already told you too much."

That Michaela was pregnant.

"I need to see her," he said, his heart pounding heavy and hard in his chest. "I need to see that she's okay." Her and the baby.

The nurse leaned closer and pitched her voice lower. "She's already left."

"What?" Sure, he'd had to wait awhile for the doctor to check out his wound and for the nurse to actually treat it, but how had Michaela gone from unconscious to walking out of the hospital in that limited time frame?

But at least that meant she hadn't been hurt too badly. This time.

But with all the trouble that kept happening with the hotshots, how long would she be able to stay safe? Especially if he and the other townspeople pushed to move the hotshot headquarters somewhere else?

Then he wouldn't be able to protect her. Not that he'd been much protection tonight. But after tonight, he wondered just how much danger she and the baby were in—and not just from fires but because she was a hotshot firefighter.

Michaela had spent too much time in the hospital over the past year, usually in the waiting room while another hotshot was being treated. She'd been poisoned once, but that had been long before she was pregnant. Because she hadn't succumbed yet to her attraction to Charlie at that time. They'd just been flirting then, like he'd flirted with her since the fire in his bar.

At first, she'd figured he flirted with everyone in order to bring in tips and business. But she'd never seen him flirt with Hank or even with Tammy Ingles, and every man with a pulse flirted with Tammy except for Ethan. And Tammy had wound up with Ethan.

Charlie definitely hadn't flirted with Michaela for business or tips because he'd always refused to let her pay for anything.

"Your money is no good here," he'd claimed every time she tried to settle up her tab. He'd sworn that he was forever in her debt because of that night…

Of the fire.

The memory of that, of finding him on the floor of the burning bar, filled her with the fear and dread she'd felt then. But he'd survived that fire.

And this time, he hadn't been hurt that badly—at least, that was what some of the other hotshots had told her when she walked out into the waiting room just moments ago.

But what about next time?

And it seemed that there was always a next time with the hotshots. Most of her team—not just Hank—was in the waiting room. They'd all been there for Michaela, to make sure that she was all right. And warmth should have flooded her heart with love for them, but she couldn't help but wonder… was it one of them who'd hurt her tonight and who could have hurt her baby as well?

Was the saboteur a member of her team who was with her in the waiting room right now? Pretending to be concerned about her?

Charlie wasn't the saboteur. Despite what she'd overheard him saying earlier tonight, he'd been with her when that bottle was rolled in their direction. He wasn't responsible for that Molotov cocktail.

But he was for…

She touched her stomach. That was actually all on her, though. She'd been so convinced that there was no way she would ever conceive that when he'd run out of condoms one night, she assured him it was fine. That there was no chance of her having any illness, since she hadn't been with anyone since her last medical checkup, and that there was no chance of her getting pregnant.

But somehow, miraculously, she had.

Would Charlie think that she'd lied to him? That she was trying to trap him?

Into what?

She never intended to get married again. And she was pretty sure he felt the same way, because the few times he'd mentioned his ex, he sounded as bitter and burned as she'd been. But then, she really didn't know him very well, because, until tonight, she hadn't had a clue how he really felt about the hotshots.

Maybe if what she'd overheard hadn't rattled her so much, she would have been more alert when she stepped outside, and she would have caught a glimpse of whoever had been in the parking lot.

The saboteur. He or she had struck again. Michaela had the stitches to prove it. And what had Charlie gotten?

Finally, he stepped through the doors into the waiting room, and a dark-haired woman launched herself at him. "Oh, thank God, you're all right!"

Heat rushed to Michaela's face. She'd been such a fool for thinking that she might have been the only woman he was seeing. Just because she hadn't really seen him flirting with anyone else didn't mean that he didn't. With as busy as the hotshots were, it wasn't as if she spent all that much time at the Filling Station or with Charlie.

But maybe this woman did, since he clearly meant a lot to her. She hugged him tightly while tears streaked down her face.

Tears stung Michaela's eyes then, too, but she furiously blinked them away. Then she cleared her throat and told Hank, "We can go home now."

While Hank technically still lived with Michaela in the rooms above the firehouse in St. Paul, an hour north of Northern Lakes, she spent most of her time with Trick McRooney.

And Michaela was alone.

Maybe that was why she'd given in to her attraction to Charlie. But it was just an attraction. She wasn't in love with him. She was never falling in love again.

But then she felt that little flutter inside her belly again, and she now knew that wasn't an ulcer. It was her daughter. The minute she'd seen her perfect little profile on that ultrasound screen, Michaela had fallen deeply in love with her baby.

She needed to do whatever was necessary to keep her child safe from harm. At the moment, she was too tired to contemplate what she was going to have to do and all the changes she was going to have to make and what she would have to give up.

"You want to go up to St. Paul?" Hank asked her with an understandable trace of reluctance.

That hour drive seemed interminable right now. But Michaela didn't want to go back to the firehouse here in Northern Lakes either. Moisture rushed to her eyes again, and she closed them to hold in the tears. "I just want to go someplace safe," she said.

"Then come home with me," a deep voice murmured.

She flashed back many months ago to the first time Charlie had said those words to her.

It had been a night like this, when she felt so alone. Dirk Brown had died. Hank had gotten involved with Trick McRooney and was hardly ever around, and so many of the hotshots had nearly lost their lives, either because of someone from their pasts or because of the saboteur. She was overwhelmed and scared and didn't know whom she could trust when danger was all around her.

While she'd been attracted to Charlie, she hadn't known if that attraction was mutual. She'd never taken his flirting seriously. Her fellow teammates goofed around like that with each other, teasing—sometimes inappropriately—as a way to relieve the stress and tension of their careers. And of the current situation they were in…

With someone making their jobs even more dangerous than they already were.

That night, when Charlie had invited her home with him, she walked out of the restroom to find the corner booth, where the hotshots always sat, empty. They'd all left while she was in the bathroom. A pang struck her heart because she felt like she wasn't important. Like nobody cared about her.

And for a painful second, she flashed back to her childhood, which was something she rarely liked to revisit. So, to drown out those horrible memories, she walked up to the bar and asked for a drink.

Charlie cocked his head and studied her face. "You just missed last call, Angel."

"Stop calling me that," she said. That had been his nickname for her since the fire at his bar.

"But you're my guardian angel," he said, and his mouth curved into that sexy, lopsided grin that never failed to quicken her pulse. "And because of that, I will make you a drink."

"I thought I missed last call," she reminded him. "Isn't giving me a drink after hours going against the rules of your liquor license?"

He nodded. "Yeah, if I gave you the drink here at the bar."

"Where else would you give it to me?" she asked, and she was smiling, too, in response to that wide, wicked grin of his. "In the alley?"

"My place," he said. Then he leaned across the bar and, in a husky whisper, added, "Come home with me, Angel."

Warmth spread throughout her body, and her pulse quickened even more. She knew that he was offering more than a drink. And she had never been so tempted to accept.

She should have been immune to guys like him, good-looking and charming, not just because she worked with so many but also because she'd once been married to one. But her husband hadn't reserved his charm, or any other part of himself, to just her. That was why she would never get married again. With as much time as she'd spent away from home, fighting wildfires, she couldn't trust that her next husband wouldn't get lonely, too, and feel so neglected that he would cheat. Her ex had found his hookups in bars. Charlie, owning the bar, probably had the option of taking a different woman home every night.

Tonight, he wanted it to be her. And tonight, feeling abandoned and vulnerable, so did Michaela...

That night had been long ago, and there had been some other nights in between then and now. Tonight might have been one of them if she hadn't heard him say what he had earlier at the firehouse. She'd told herself that she was only heading to his place to do some amateur sleuthing, to find out if the suspicions about him being the saboteur had any merit. But she knew what would have happened, what always happened when they were alone together.

But then she'd heard what he said, what he really thought about the hotshots. And then that damn improvised explosive device had gone off and injured them.

She opened her eyes now to make sure that he was okay. He had a bandage above one of his dark eyebrows, like the one she had on her temple but a little smaller. Otherwise, he looked good. Too good, like he usually did, with his chiseled features and that sexy black-and-gray scruff on his square jaw.

"Please, Michaela," he said, his deep voice made gruff by a strange urgency. "We *need* to talk."

And she realized, because of his intensity, why he

wanted to talk. It wasn't about what she'd overheard. Or about what had happened in the firehouse parking lot.

Somehow, he'd figured out that she was pregnant. Hell, maybe he'd figured it out before she had. And he obviously wanted to talk about that, to find out if he was the father.

She'd intended to tell him the truth, but she glanced behind him to where that woman stood. But now she was leaning against the other volunteer firefighter. And Michaela could see the woman's resemblance to Charlie. They had the same dark hair and deep-set eyes and chiseled features. She was probably his sister. And she was watching them as intensely as Charlie was watching her. As everyone else was watching them, and they were probably all wondering the same thing, wondering what was going on between them.

Michaela hadn't told anyone, not even her best friend, that she was seeing Charlie—or whatever it was she was doing with him when she went home with him from time to time. And from the way his sister and maybe brother-in-law were staring at them, too, apparently he hadn't told anyone either. But what they had was never supposed to be serious, so it made sense for them both to keep it secret.

But they probably wouldn't be able to keep it secret much longer. Not with her being pregnant with his baby.

Secrets. The hotshot crew seemed determined to keep them from Trooper Wynona Wells.

Too many secrets. Like where the hell the "victims" of tonight's incident had disappeared to. They weren't at the hospital. She'd checked the ER. They'd been released, and the few hotshots who were still in the waiting room wouldn't tell her where they'd gone.

If only they would actually trust her…

She glanced into the rearview mirror of her state police

SUV. Just wearing the hat and the uniform should have been enough to inspire confidence in her integrity.

And probably would have, if not for the actions of other officers.

Because of those actions, she couldn't necessarily blame them for not being able to trust her. Her former training sergeant, Martin Gingrich, had betrayed everyone's trust, including hers. And he had put her in a difficult position with everyone in Northern Lakes. Because now no one knew whether she was friend or foe.

Marty Gingrich had definitely been a foe. He'd tried to kill one of the hotshots and his pregnant wife. He'd also helped his lover kill her husband, and both of them had almost gotten away with it.

But his former lover had wound up dead.

And Marty had been caught. Eventually. Marty hadn't been the only one she'd arrested because they'd gone after the hotshots, though. Around the holidays, someone had tried to kill Trent Miles and the Detroit detective he was seeing, but the detective had mostly, and rightfully, taken the credit and the suspect for that arrest. And the FBI agent who'd tried to kill Rory VanDam had gotten killed instead. There had been others too. A woman after Trick McRooney and the greedy brother-in-law who'd hired killers to take out Ethan Sommerly, aka Jonathan Michael Canterbury IV, after he'd learned he was still alive.

But for as many people who'd been caught or killed for hurting hotshots, there were other things that had happened, for which all of them had denied responsibility, making it apparent that there was someone else after all the hotshots.

That could have been what tonight had been about, or maybe there was someone else specifically targeting Michaela Momber or Charlie Tillerman, like some of those other hotshots had been specifically targeted.

Would the person, the one who kept coming after the hotshots, get caught? Or would his or her identity forever remain a secret?

Chapter 5

Since taking on the role of volunteer firefighter, Charlie had to count on his employees to cover the bar for him and to close and lock it up at night. He'd thought he had employees he could trust, but as he approached the back door that opened onto the alley, he could tell that it wasn't even shut tightly, let alone locked.

"Did you tell someone to wait for you?" Michaela asked, her voice a whisper again, like it had been in the parking lot earlier. She must have noticed the almost open door too. Hopefully she wasn't assuming that he had a girlfriend waiting for him.

She didn't trust people any more easily than he did. She hadn't said a lot about her divorce, but he suspected it had been for some of the same reasons he'd gotten divorced. That her spouse hadn't been any more faithful than his had been. That was probably the only thing he and Michaela actually had in common: failed marriages due to their spouses' infidelities. Two, if Michaela was as bad a judge of character as he had been. And three...

If that baby was his...

And it probably was since she had agreed to come back to the bar with him. Or maybe she'd left the hospital with him to escape from the questions her fellow hotshots had seemed ready to ask. Questions that had probably been about them.

Or maybe she'd left with him in order to escape from the trooper who Trick McRooney, via a text to Hank, had warned them was about to show up at the hospital to take their statements. While the hotshots clearly didn't like or trust the woman, Charlie wanted to talk to Trooper Wells about what had happened and make sure that she found who was responsible for hurting Michaela.

But he wanted to talk to Michaela first. Yet they hadn't said a word to each other on the short ride from the hospital just outside of town to the bar. He wasn't sure how to ask what he shouldn't have even known yet, not until she told him she was pregnant.

But he needed to know if that baby she was carrying was his. And since she'd agreed to come back here with him, he suspected that it probably was.

Fortunately, his brother-in-law had loaned him his truck. Since Charlie's sister had driven her car to the hospital to check on him, Eric had a ride home with his wife. Valerie had left their kids home alone in her mad rush to get to the hospital, so they'd been eager to get back to them before they woke up. The oldest, Charlie's niece, was thirteen, so she was old enough to watch her younger brothers, who were eleven and eight. Unless Nicholas, the eleven-year-old Boy Scout, woke up with one of the nightmares he'd been having since that disastrous camping trip.

After tonight, after that flash explosion in the firehouse parking lot, Charlie was probably going to have more nightmares of his own. But the night wasn't even over yet.

And there was something odd about the back door. It wasn't just that it was partially open, but part of the metal looked a bit warped or bent. What the hell had happened?

In reply to her question, he shook his head. "Nobody should be here."

Everyone on his staff was usually really good at getting even the most reluctant-to-leave customers out and the bar shut down at closing time. So, at nearly three in the morning, the place should have been empty, with his staff gone for the night too.

But inside, something dropped to the hardwood floor and shattered like that burning bottle had shattered earlier. Startled and afraid, he turned to Michaela, who stood behind him in the alley. "Go back to the truck," he whispered. He'd parked it in the alley near the dumpster.

He hadn't wanted her to have to walk far—not after how she'd passed out earlier. Had that been because of her head wound or because of the baby? Now he wished he'd parked farther away. He wanted to keep her and that unborn baby safe…because he had a feeling that they weren't right now. That whoever was inside the bar posed a danger.

"What are you going to do?" Michaela whispered back at him.

"I have to see what's going on in there," he murmured. He'd lost the bar once—his grandfather's legacy—because of that arsonist. He didn't want to go through having to rebuild it and his home all over again. He had to protect it, just like he had to protect Michaela and the baby.

She shook her head now and tugged hard on his sleeve as if trying to hold him back. "No," she hissed at him. "Come with me, and let's call the police to check it out."

He'd intended to do that back at the firehouse when they'd heard someone sneaking around out there, probably vandalizing vehicles. But there hadn't been time to even call the police, let alone for them to arrive in time to help.

Inside the bar, more glass shattered. And Charlie cursed. He couldn't let anyone destroy his place.

Not again.

He jerked open the door and rushed inside. While the door hadn't been shut, the bar was pretty dark but for the small beam of a flashlight that someone held behind the bar.

"Hey!" Charlie yelled.

And the light moved as the shadow holding it vaulted over the bar. Charlie started after him but slipped on something on the floor, nearly falling. It wasn't peanuts, since the staff would have swept them up before closing. The Filling Station was one of the few bars that actually still allowed patrons to toss the shells on the floor. It was a tradition Charlie was determined to carry on from his grandfather's legacy—one of the best memories from his childhood.

Glass, not peanut shells, crunched beneath his boots, and the soles slipped on the liquor that had spilled from the broken bottle. His arms flailed as he tried to keep from falling.

Then the front door opened as the shadow barreled into it, shouldering their way out into the night. Charlie recovered his balance and rushed out after the intruder, desperate to see who it was. To see who must have broken into his place…

Just like Michaela had been desperate in the firehouse parking lot.

And they'd both gotten hurt.

He was going to get hurt.

Again. And maybe this time, it would be worse than a cut above his eyebrow.

"Stop!" Michaela had already yelled it once just as he'd rushed through that partially open door into his bar. If he had heard her then, he'd ignored her, as he'd run down the hall toward the bar area.

She'd ignored him too. She hadn't gone back to the truck like he'd advised her to do. She wasn't even sure the vehicle was unlocked for her to be able to get inside for her protection.

She stood in the alley, peering through that open back door to the bar, trying to see what was happening. She would have called the police, but her cell was still dead. And Charlie probably had his on him.

"Charlie?" she called out louder, her voice cracking with fear for his safety.

Through the open door, she could see the beam of the flashlight bouncing around behind the bar. Charlie must have seen it, too, because he ran toward it then, his boots pounding on the hardwood floor before he seemed to slip.

Then the front door opened to the main street, where the streetlamps sent more light spilling into the bar. It sparked off the shards of glass littering the hardwood floor like peanuts usually did.

That door opened again as Charlie went charging out after the intruder without a thought for his safety, even after what had just happened to them earlier. How they had already been hurt at the firehouse...

Had whoever had thrown that bottle at them come after them here too? Maybe a hotshot hadn't been the target of that parking lot attack, maybe Charlie had been. And now he was off in pursuit of his would-be attacker.

But would he be the pursuer?

Or had the whole break-in just been another attempt to get to him?

"Stop!" she yelled at him again, and panic rushed through her.

They'd already made one mistake earlier that night in the firehouse parking lot—they should have hurried back inside the building right away. Once she'd noticed that all the lights were out in the lot, she should have gone back inside, but she hadn't wanted to see Charlie after what she'd overheard.

But that was nothing in comparison to what had happened to them and what could have happened to them...

But she'd stuck around, hiding in the darkness like whoever was out there, giving Charlie the chance to catch up with her. And giving that person the chance to light the "fuse" on the bottle bomb. Michaela had wanted to see who it was, who the saboteur was, just as Charlie must want to see who the intruder was.

But was it the saboteur who'd been at the firehouse, or had it been whoever had broken in here? Had they been after Charlie then too?

Without him standing between her and the building, she could tell that the door to the alley had been pried open. The jamb was splintered, and the metal was mangled.

The intruder must have used a crowbar or something to force the door open, twisting the dead bolt and breaking the jamb. Maybe they still had that crowbar and would use it on Charlie if he caught up with them.

She stepped through the damaged door and started across the floor toward the front door through which he and the intruder had disappeared. But as she passed the bar, another bottle dropped and glass shattered.

She gasped at the sudden noise and the splash of alcohol and the spray of shards of glass. Maybe the bottle had just accidentally fallen, but she doubted that. And that doubt had her heart racing with fear of the very real possibility that she was not alone.

Something else moved in the shadows. Was it just another bottle rolling around? Or was it a person moving toward her?

While Charlie had run out after one intruder, there must have been another one still in the bar.

And now she was in the dark with that intruder, uncertain of where or if she should run. Or if it was already too late for her to get away...

Braden should have been home in bed. But he couldn't sleep, and not just because his wife—his very pregnant wife—wasn't home.

He wasn't worried about her, though. She was safe—probably safer than she would be in Northern Lakes—where she was in Washington with her dad and her oldest brother.

And her younger one was here with him in his office, where Braden had been spending way too much of his time lately. He needed a vacation, but the last one he and Sam had taken had been more harrowing than relaxing. That was just the way everything seemed to be lately for the hotshots: harrowing.

Michaela hadn't even been able to leave the firehouse without coming under attack just outside the door, on her way to her vehicle. He was going to have to get some damn cameras installed in the lot too. He really should have already done it. But he'd thought that having them inside would be protection for his team and would also reveal which of the team members might have been on the move last night.

But he and Trick had watched all the footage. Too many people had been coming and going last night. The hotshots. And the volunteers. Which was why he hadn't installed a security system and special locks as well, because there were always too many people coming and going around the firehouse who would have had to know the code and some who, like Stanley, probably would have kept setting it off.

With all the hotshots and volunteers in the firehouse last night, it really could have been any of them except for Michaela and Charlie, because they hadn't thrown that Molotov cocktail at themselves.

Had they been the targets, or would whoever had stepped outside the door have come under attack? Just like Rory had that night he stepped out of the bunkroom...

Braden had installed the cameras after that, but he'd wished so many times since that night that he'd installed them before. That he had some idea who was going after his team and why.

"What the hell is going on?" he murmured, more to himself than to his brother-in-law. It was a rhetorical question, he knew neither of them had an answer to it.

"Henrietta says that Michaela left the hospital with Charlie Tillerman," Trick said as he glanced down at the cell phone in his hand.

Hank must have sent him a text.

"I didn't even know she was seeing Charlie," Braden remarked. But then, he clearly didn't know everything about all his hotshots, or he would have some idea which of them was the saboteur, if any of them were.

He hoped like hell that none of them were.

But he couldn't figure out how so many things had happened unless the saboteur was one of them—or at least, very close to one of them.

Like Charlie...

But he'd been hurt out there, too, with Michaela. So maybe Michaela was in no physical danger from the bar owner. But that didn't mean she wasn't in danger emotionally, especially if that baby was Charlie's.

Braden couldn't protect her from the emotional danger, but he had to try to protect her from the physical danger. "We need to step up our investigation," he said. "We need to narrow this—" he gestured at the video footage on his computer monitor "—down and find some viable suspects."

But this wasn't his area of expertise or Trick's. If only they could trust Trooper Wells...

But this attack had happened outside the firehouse, so the suspect probably wasn't even on the footage. So really, whoever had pulled the dangerous stunt in the parking lot could have been anyone.

And could have been after Charlie or Michaela...which put them both in even greater danger.

Chapter 6

Charlie rushed out into the street without a plan, his boots pounding against the asphalt as he ran in the direction he'd seen the intruder go.

But what was he going to do if he actually caught the intruder? He didn't have any handcuffs to hold the person. And he didn't have any weapon to defend himself if that person had something on them. And they could have anything.

A gun.

A knife.

An accomplice...

He stopped so abruptly that he nearly tripped over his boots. He hadn't considered that the intruder might not have been alone.

That there could have been someone else back in the bar. And Michaela was there too. Hopefully she'd gone to the truck and locked herself inside. But if she hadn't and something happened to her...

Panic gripped his heart, squeezing it tightly. He turned to head back toward the bar, but it was farther away than he'd realized. He couldn't even see the neon sign that was always lit up and angled so that it was visible from both streets of the corner on which the building sat.

He must have crossed a few streets in his pursuit of the

intruder. And he hadn't even gotten close enough to get a good look at the person.

All he'd seen was dark clothes and a vague outline indicating that the person was probably as tall as he was. But a hoodie had been pulled up over the person's head, and he'd never seen their face. Yet he'd seen more of this person than he had the one in the parking lot at the firehouse. Could it have been the same person?

Or was there a sudden and random crime wave sweeping through Northern Lakes tonight? Either way, everyone was in danger, especially Michaela, who was already hurt.

Desperate to make sure she was all right, he ran even faster now. The neon light came into view with a few letters either burned-out or broken. He ran up the couple of steps to the front door and pushed on it, but it refused to budge. It must have locked when it had closed behind him.

To get to the unlocked door in the back, he had to run around the block because the two-story buildings were side-by-side, with no space between them until the alley. His lungs burned for air from his panting, and his legs ached from running in heavy boots. But he had to make sure that Michaela was safe.

As he neared his brother-in-law's truck, he slowed down. He could see through the windows that it was empty. Michaela hadn't locked herself inside like he'd advised.

He shouldn't have been surprised she hadn't listened to him. Michaela was tough and independent. But she was already hurt, so she was especially vulnerable right now. And if that intruder hadn't been acting alone in the bar...

He drew in a breath, trying to control the panic overwhelming him. Then he stepped through the damaged door into the back hallway of the bar. He tilted his head and listened. But there was no sound of breaking glass this time.

There was nothing but silence.

He flipped on the lights, like he should have earlier. But they revealed nothing but the broken glass and spilled liquor.

"Michaela?" he called out, and his voice echoed hollowly inside the place.

Had she gone upstairs to call the police? Hoping that she had, he rushed through the kitchen toward the stairwell at the back of it that led up to his apartment. But that door to the stairwell was locked, like he'd left it when he'd rushed out for the fire call earlier that evening. She wouldn't have been able to get inside without a key.

Why hadn't he ever given her a key?

She probably wouldn't have taken it, but he should have at least tried. Because now he had no idea where she was.

He searched the entire bar, yet there was no one but him inside. If there had been another intruder, that person was gone now too.

With Michaela? Had they taken her with them?

Was that why he couldn't find her?

When she heard that noise, Michaela knew not to stick around again like she had in the firehouse parking lot. There was no telling what the person was capable of doing to her. So she turned and ran like Charlie had.

But she wasn't running after anyone. She was running away. Once she was on the street, though, she wasn't sure where to go. Back to the firehouse?

Was anyone still there? Were the police?

And where was Charlie?

Was he all right?

Had he caught the other intruder, or had that intruder caught him?

She needed help. If only she had a phone that was charged, she would have called for help.

At this hour, all the other businesses she passed were closed, like the bar. Courtney Beaumont's dress shop. Tammy Ingles's salon and spa.

The businesses were closed, but like Charlie, both Courtney and Tammy had apartments above their businesses. Maybe one of the hotshots who dated those women were with them. Owen with Courtney or Ethan Sommerly with Tammy.

Owen and Ethan had both been at the hospital while she was there, waiting to find out how she was, but they would have had time to return to their homes by now, like she and Charlie had had time to return to the bar.

The bar that someone had broken into…

Why?

To try to hurt him or her again? Maybe that hadn't been a random attack in the parking lot at all. Maybe someone was specifically after one of them…like so many of the other hotshots had had an enemy after them as well as the saboteur.

Worried about Charlie and her and her baby's safety, she doubled back toward Tammy's salon and started across the street to it. Ethan would help her find Charlie. And if they found the intruder instead, Ethan was a big guy.

But he could still get hurt—just as he had a short while ago when helping protect Trent's sister from the person who'd been threatening her so she would stop investigating the plane crash Ethan and Rory had been in five years ago. That person, a corrupt FBI agent, had really been after Rory, though, and had shot him.

It seemed like everybody Michaela knew kept getting hurt. Was Charlie hurt right now?

Was that why she hadn't found him yet? Had that person just lured him out of the bar in order to hurt him? Or worse? To kill him…

But why? What possible enemy could Charlie have?

He wasn't an heir to a fortune like Ethan Sommerly really was. Or a former undercover agent like Rory had been. But then, nobody had known that Ethan and Rory were those things. They'd had their secrets.

Maybe Charlie had secrets too.

Or maybe he'd made an enemy he had no idea he'd made, like Trent Miles had for being unable to rescue someone from a fire in Detroit.

Or Trick McRooney, who'd attracted a stalker he had no idea was after him.

Anybody could be in danger for any reason. She'd realized that a long time ago when she was just a kid. But over and over, she'd seen how that danger had affected her friends and coworkers.

And now Charlie.

He was neither of those things to her, but yet he was more.

And she didn't want anything to happen to him.

Her heart was beating fast—so fast that it made her light-headed again. Her legs weakened, and she dropped down to one knee in the street. As she did, bright lights suddenly appeared, shining directly at her. Blinding her.

Then tires squealed, and she couldn't tell if the vehicle was speeding up or stopping. She jumped up and lunged toward the sidewalk, desperate to get out of the street, to save herself and her child.

But the vehicle stopped, the brakes squeaking in protest of the abruptness. Then other lights flashed, blue and red, just a few times before they flashed off again. A door opened and closed, and a woman asked, "Are you all right?"

Michaela looked up at Trooper Wells, and relief poured through her, draining some but not all the tension from her body. "Oh, thank God it's you," she said. "Please, you have to help me."

"Are you hurt?" the woman asked.

Michaela scrambled up. "I'm not. I'm fine, but we need to find Charlie Tillerman."

"I'm actually looking for both of you," the trooper replied. "I need to take your statements about what happened earlier at the firehouse."

That felt insignificant now. "We just got to his bar and found that someone broke into it," Michaela said. "And Charlie ran off after them."

The trooper nodded. "Get into my vehicle," she said as she held open the door for Michaela, "and we'll look for them."

Anxious to find him—to help him—Michaela scrambled inside. She didn't realize until the door closed that the trooper had helped her into the back. Not the front.

She reached for the handle, but it didn't budge. She was locked in the back, with a partition between her and the front.

The trooper opened the driver's-side door and slid behind the wheel.

"What's going on?" Michaela asked her. "Why did you put me in the back?"

Was she under arrest?

And for what?

"None of you hotshots trust me," the trooper replied, "and I realized that I shouldn't trust any of you either."

Michaela wanted to argue with her, but she wasn't sure who she could trust on her hotshot team either. Not anymore.

Not after all the things that had happened.

But she could trust Charlie, at least with her life. But not with her heart. She'd learned long ago that she shouldn't trust anyone with her heart. Because as a kid, she'd learned that the people who were supposed to love you the most were the ones who could hurt you the most. Not that she thought Charlie loved her…

Or that she loved him…

She just wanted to make sure that he was all right. That he wasn't hurt.

But she realized, as the trooper shut off all the lights and drove through Northern Lakes in the dark, that she shouldn't have trusted her either. What if the female officer was the saboteur, and maybe she was worried that Michaela had seen her back at the firehouse?

Maybe instead of helping her, Trooper Wells intended to get rid of her for good.

Trick was worried about the team and about his brother-in-law. Clearly, the man was exhausted, he was barely able to keep his eyes open as he played through the video footage. Trick was standing beside Braden's desk because if he sat down, he would have probably fallen asleep. After getting back from fighting that wildfire in Canada for the past two weeks, they should have been resting. That was what he and Henrietta had intended to do when they'd gone to her cottage.

But, alone again for the first time in a couple of weeks, they hadn't wasted any time sleeping. And then the call had come from Braden.

Another incident.

They weren't even staged to look like accidents anymore.

The saboteur wasn't even bothering to try to hide their misdeeds anymore.

They were getting bolder, with attacks happening more and more frequently and at the firehouse. Which was another reason he and Henrietta hadn't stayed. Even with the cameras Braden had installed, it wasn't safe to be here.

Even now, in the small confines of Braden's office, Trick felt a chill race down his spine. It wasn't that sixth-sense thing that his brother-in-law got when fires were about to happen.

It was just dread.

Because he knew that something else bad would happen soon and would keep happening until the saboteur was finally caught. That was why he was still at the firehouse going over that footage from the cameras. Not many people were aware that they'd been installed, so maybe the saboteur slipped up and revealed him- or herself.

A knock sounded at the door before it was flung open, and Henrietta rushed into the room. She threw her arms around Trick's neck and hugged him, her body shaking.

He grabbed her shoulders and stared into her beautiful face. "What's wrong? What happened?"

If that son of a bitch had gone after Henrietta...

"I don't know," she replied, her voice cracking slightly with fear. "I should have taken Michaela home. I shouldn't have let her leave with Charlie."

Braden jumped up from his desk. "Why? What happened to Michaela?"

Now.

Braden didn't say it, but it was in his voice. That fatalism. Once something happened to a hotshot, it never stopped with one event. Bad things just kept happening to them.

Henrietta stepped back and shrugged. "I don't know.

Charlie just called me, asking if I had picked her up from the bar. He can't find her."

"They were together," Trick said. "You texted that she left the hospital with him. How can he not know where she is?" And why the hell had Michaela trusted him enough to leave with him? She was smarter than that.

Henrietta shook her head, and her long hair whipped across her back and swirled around her shoulders. Usually, she wore it in a thick braid, but he'd taken that out when they'd gotten to the cottage, and the long tresses rippled like waves of rich brown. She was so beautiful, but on the inside as much as on the outside. She was also very concerned about her friend.

"I don't know…" she murmured. "Charlie said something about finding his back door open and he ran inside the bar, and then she…just…disappeared…"

People didn't just disappear. They either ran away…

Or someone took them away.

Which was the case with Michaela?

Chapter 7

Where the hell is she?

Charlie had already called her best friend, the first person Michaela would have called if she'd wanted someone to pick her up. But Hank hadn't heard from her.

Where could Michaela have gone? She hadn't taken the truck, so she would have had to walk. It wasn't like Northern Lakes had cabs or many Uber drivers. Until tonight, he'd liked that about the place and had vowed to keep the town as small and personal as it had always been, despite the protests of other members of the town council who wanted to overdevelop the area to make it more commercial.

This was the first time Charlie regretted fighting some of those plans. If it was more commercial, there would have been places open tonight. Fast-food restaurants or all-night party stores, some place Michaela could have gone so that she wasn't alone, like he'd left her in this place.

His stomach churned with self-disgust. She was already hurt. And pregnant...

And he'd left her alone and unprotected. No matter that she'd been released from the hospital, she'd still been hurt. Vulnerable.

After he'd called Henrietta, he'd called 911 too. The dispatcher hadn't sounded as if the break-in at the bar was an emergency, though, at least not until he'd told her that the person who'd been with him when he found the intruder inside was now missing.

The dispatcher had asked if there were signs that some-one had been hurt. While there was broken glass and spilled booze, he didn't see any blood on the floor.

But that didn't mean that Michaela hadn't been hurt again. With as feisty and independent and strong as she was, he doubted she would have left with someone without a fight. Unless it was someone she knew, like Hank.

Or another hotshot.

But could she really trust any of them?

Could he really trust her? Maybe she didn't care about him at all. And she'd taken the opportunity of him running after the intruder to leave because she really didn't want to talk to him.

A siren pealed out for a second before cutting off. He rushed to the front door and pushed it open. Blue and red lights flashed, blinding him for a moment. He blinked to clear his vision, then focused on the figures walking toward him.

A trooper with a hat on and a gun holster strapped to her side. And Michaela.

"Oh, thank God, you're all right," he said, relief making his body shudder.

But then she got closer, and he noticed how pale and shaky she was as she passed him to step inside the bar. He lowered his voice to a whisper and, with concern, asked, "Are you all right?"

She glanced warily back at the trooper, who followed her inside, but then she slowly nodded. "Yes, are you?" she asked, and her voice cracked a bit.

He didn't know if it was with concern for him or exhaustion, though. She looked so pale and uneasy.

"You shouldn't have gone off in pursuit of a suspect," Trooper Wells admonished him. "You could have been shot. Once you saw that the door had been forced open, you should have called me right away."

"Fortunately, I haven't had a break-in before," Charlie said. Even the arsonist hadn't broken into the bar, and after he was arrested, Charlie had seen no need to install an alarm system. His grandfather had never had one. And he'd wanted the bar to be just like it had been when his grandfather owned it. But he should have realized that once it burned down, nothing would ever be exactly the same, and he should have installed an alarm. "When I saw that open door and that someone was still inside, I just let instinct take over..."

"You wanted to catch them," Michaela said. That had probably been her intention at the firehouse, to find out who'd been skulking around in the dark parking lot.

The trooper glanced around the bar. "And I take it that you didn't?"

He shook his head. "No."

"Do you know what they took?" she asked.

"The night bartender would have taken the cash receipts to the bank for a deposit right after he closed up and left," Charlie said, walking around the bar to the cash register. With all the marks and scratches and dents on it, whatever had been used on the back door had been used on it as well. But it had withstood the assault better than the door had, because the bottom drawer was still closed.

He glanced around the bar area. There were far fewer bottles than there had been earlier that night. And he doubted that it had been all that busy on a Wednesday night. "A substantial amount of alcohol is missing, though."

"There are a lot of broken bottles," Michaela said. "Another one broke after you left." She shuddered.

"What happened? Was there someone still in the bar?" he asked, his fears confirmed that he shouldn't have left her alone. He wanted to put his arms around her, to hold her close and comfort her and to reassure himself that she was all right now. But when he approached her, Trooper Wells stepped between them.

"I need to take your statement, Mr. Tillerman," the officer said.

He nodded. "Sure. But I guess you can pretty much tell what happened here tonight."

"A robbery," she said with a nod.

But was that all it was? After what had happened earlier, he couldn't be certain about anything right now. Not even about Michaela…

"Is that why you left? Was there someone else still in here?" he asked Michaela again.

She shrugged. "I don't know. I heard some noise, and that bottle fell on the floor…"

And must have reminded her of that bottle rolling across the parking lot toward them earlier in the night. She'd probably been scared, and he hadn't been here. She'd been alone…except for whoever else had still been in the bar.

He mentally smacked himself for taking off, for not thinking about the possibility of there being more than one intruder. And for assuming that she wouldn't follow him inside, that she would do as he'd advised and lock herself in the truck. But she was a hotshot, they were trained to head toward danger, not away from it.

"It looks like some of these bottles might have just rolled off the bar top," the trooper remarked. "So it's possible that there was only one intruder. But that's a chance that neither of you should have taken. I will say it again—you should never confront an intruder on your own."

He nodded heartily. "Yeah, I know it was stupid." The stupidest part had been leaving Michaela alone and unprotected, especially with her being pregnant and already hurt. "I'm glad you went for the police," he said to Michaela.

But she shook her head. "*She* found *me*." And she shuddered again.

Was she afraid of the trooper? Did she suspect her of being involved in what had happened to them tonight, in some of the things that had happened with the other hotshots?

And if so, then he should be afraid of Trooper Wells too. Because she wasn't like him and Michaela. She was armed.

Within minutes of Michaela and the trooper returning to the bar, Braden, Trick and Hank had shown up to look for her. She could have left with them.

The trooper had already interrogated her while driving around town, supposedly in search of Charlie and that intruder. But she wasn't sure the woman had even really believed her about the bar until the call had come through Dispatch about the break-in. And even then, she hadn't called in techs to process the scene until she'd seen it for herself.

Once the techs had arrived, Michaela could have left.

She probably should have left.

But instead, she'd urged Trick, Hank and her boss to go home and get some rest. Hearing that, Charlie had handed her his keys so that she could go upstairs and rest, too, while the police finished processing the bar for evidence regarding the break-in. Now she sat in the living room of his apartment over the bar. When his bar had burned down over a year ago, he'd lost his home as well as his livelihood.

While he'd rebuilt the bar below to look exactly like it had when his grandfather owned it, the apartment above it was very updated and modern, with tall windows and high ceilings with exposed rafters. The main area was all one room, the big living room open to the kitchen, with its state-of-the-art appliances, quartz countertops and custom-made cabinetry. And she knew it had been well insulated, too, so that there was no noise from the bar below.

The only way she heard anything now was because she'd left the door to the stairwell open. And the rumble of voices drifted up from the bar.

Wells's voice and Charlie's deeper one.

Wells obviously wasn't finished with him yet either. She was bombarding him with questions like she had Michaela. And he had no more answers than Michaela had. Neither of them had seen anything in the firehouse parking lot or in the bar. They had no idea who was after them or why.

Did the trooper have more answers than they did? Did Wells know more about what was going on than she claimed? Was she the saboteur?

After getting locked in the back seat of the police SUV, Michaela trusted the trooper even less than she had before. She wasn't entirely sure what would have happened if Dispatch hadn't called about the break-in at the bar and Michaela's disappearance from the scene.

Would she have brought her back to the bar or to jail or to somewhere else?

Somewhere else was exactly where Michaela should have been now. But that look Charlie had given her at the hospital made Michaela suspect that he knew about her pregnancy. Maybe because she was already showing and hadn't realized it. How had she been so stupid that she'd had no clue, that she'd thought her morning sickness was an ulcer?

And why was she continuing to do stupid things, like stay here and wait for Charlie? It wasn't as if she expected him to be happy about the baby and want to help her raise a child. Michaela knew she should leave, but before she could even get up from the chair, she heard footsteps echoing in the stairwell.

Charlie stepped into the living room with her, closed and locked the door. He even checked the knob, making sure that it had locked. If he was doing that for their protection, the back door to the alley had proved that a lock wasn't enough to keep out someone who really wanted in.

He wasn't safe. And neither was Michaela.

He leaned back against that door and released a long, shaky sigh. "What a night…"

Except it wasn't night any longer. Outside the many windows of his apartment, the sky was lightening with the approach of dawn.

"I should go…" she murmured, and she finally managed to scramble up from the overstuffed leather chair. But as she did, her weak legs nearly folded beneath her like they had earlier, in the street.

Charlie jerked away from the door and rushed toward her, closing his arms around her as he pulled her close to him. "Are you all right?"

She wanted to push him away, but instead she found herself wrapping her arms around him and just holding on for a moment. So much had happened that day—hell, the last two weeks at the wildfires and the last several months with the hotshots. And she was so damn tired. Too tired to fight the feelings rushing through her, the relief that he was okay and the joy that she was pregnant…with his baby. For the moment, she really didn't want to think about anything else, like what could have happened to both of them and their baby.

"I should take you back to the hospital," he said. "You're not okay."

She found enough energy then to put her hands on his chest and lever herself away to get some space between them. Beneath her palm, his heart beat heavy and fast. Like hers…and like that heartbeat she'd seen on the ultrasound screen.

"I'm fine," she said. "Just tired. And a little dehydrated…" And anemic, according to Dr. Smits.

She wished now that she hadn't refused the IV the doctor had wanted her to have before releasing her. But she'd just wanted out of the ER, to check on Charlie. To make sure that he was all right.

He moved again, this time swinging her up in his arms. She remembered another time he'd done this and what had happened once he'd carried her to where he was taking her now, through one of the open doors off the living room, to his bedroom. But this time, he just laid her onto the king-size four-poster bed, and then he rushed off instead of following her down onto it, his mouth fused to hers, his hands everywhere…

She let out a soft gasp of surprise and disappointment at finding herself alone in his bed in his room, with its brick exterior wall and darkly paneled interior wall. On those nights when she hadn't been able to ignore the desire she felt for him, she'd experienced so much pleasure from his kisses, from his touches and from his body.

Her body tensed, her nipples tightening at just the thought of how he'd made her feel, of how incredible sex with him had been. More incredible than any other experience she'd had. Just thinking about those nights had her flushed and even thirstier than she'd been.

Then he was back, pressing a glass of orange juice against

her lips. "Drink this," he said. "It'll help if you have low blood sugar too." He had a packet of crackers and a container of yogurt in his other hand.

"I'm not diabetic," she said. "I'm—"

"Pregnant," he finished for her.

She'd suspected he knew, but hearing him say it doused the desire she'd been feeling for him. Had he sounded disappointed? Upset? Angry?

Stalling for time, she took the glass from him and drank all the orange juice. She even ate the crackers and the yogurt too. She did it more because she needed to gather her thoughts than because she actually wanted the juice or the snacks. But surprisingly, it did seem to give her a little boost of energy.

"How did you figure it out?" she asked. Was it that obvious and she'd missed all the signs? But even if the possibility had crossed her mind once or twice, she'd rejected the thought because she didn't even get periods. How could she have ovulated and not even noticed? Because she was so busy and so stressed...

"One of the nurses assumed I knew because she also assumed we were coworkers," he explained. "But please don't be upset with her."

It was sweet of him to defend the nurse. But Michaela was still irritated with her. "I hope she didn't tell any of my coworkers," she muttered.

"Were you ever going to tell me?" he asked. "Or did you think it was none of my business?"

"Is that your way of asking if this baby is yours?" she wondered. She hadn't been with anyone else since they'd started whatever they'd started, but she hadn't told him that. She hadn't wanted him to think she was looking for something exclusive and permanent.

"I don't know what I am allowed to ask," he said and released a shaky sigh like he had earlier after locking the door. "I know it's your body and your—"

"I'm keeping the baby," she said, moving her hand over the small swell of her belly. "And of course it's yours. I never intended—"

"To tell me," he finished for her again.

She shook her head. "I didn't know I could get pregnant. In fact, I was convinced that I couldn't."

"That's why you told me not to worry about protection that one night."

A couple of weeks after the hotshot holiday party, they'd been together again. But he'd started to pull away because he'd run out of condoms. And she'd assured him that as long as he was healthy, there was no way she could get pregnant. She'd been so wrong.

"My ex-husband and I tried for years to have kids, but I don't ovulate—or I didn't think I did." She sighed. "I don't know what my fertility issues really were now. And I didn't know until tonight that I was pregnant."

He leaned back then and stared at her, his dark eyes wide with disbelief.

"I know. I'm an idiot," she said before he could. "I thought I had an ulcer and my stomach was just bloated." She shook her head in self-disgust. "And I've always wondered before how a woman couldn't know…"

"Now that you know, what do you intend to do?" he asked, as if he was choosing his words carefully.

"I already told you that I'm keeping her," she said defensively—but of her child, not herself. She didn't want *anything* to harm this baby that she'd wanted for so long, least of all herself. But with her job, the way she lived, the risks she took, she wasn't sure how she could carry this baby to term unless she quit her job and maybe even left town.

"Her?" His voice cracked with the question.

She nodded. "Yes. They did an ultrasound in the hospital. Despite my not knowing that I'm pregnant, she seems healthy, according to the doctor."

He pushed a shaking hand through his thick hair. "A little girl…" he murmured, and his voice cracked again.

She bristled with defensiveness now that maybe he wasn't happy about the baby being a girl. That like so many other men, including her father, he wanted a boy instead. That he considered a girl useless.

"You don't have to do anything," she assured him. "I'm not expecting anything from you. Not child support and definitely not a commitment. So don't go thinking that I did this to trap you."

That was what her dad had always accused her mother of doing, of using her unplanned pregnancy to trap him into a marriage and into roles that he hadn't wanted: husband and father.

Especially to a little girl.

Her macho firefighting father had only wanted sons. But Michaela was the only child he'd had, which had been unfortunate for both of them but probably a good thing for any siblings she might have had. They'd been spared his idea of parenting.

"I know this…" She didn't know what to call what they were. They weren't in a relationship. They weren't even really casually dating. She shrugged off all the possible labels. "Actually, I have no idea what this thing is between us," she amended. "But the one thing I do know is that neither of us intended for it to last."

Relationships rarely lasted with hotshots because they

traveled too much and were sometimes away for weeks at a time, with little contact with the loved ones they left behind. So she had gone into this *situation* with Charlie knowing that it was only temporary.

"And this pregnancy isn't going to change that," she continued. "It isn't going to change anything."

He laughed then.

And she braced herself for the bitterness, the resentment and recriminations.

But he just smiled at her, almost as if he pitied her. And then he said, "It changes *everything*, Michaela."

Lights glowed behind the blinds in the windows on the second floor of the building for the Filling Station Bar and Grille. It was a surprise that anyone up there would still be awake.

Charlie Tillerman and the female hotshot had had a busy night.

First, the thing at the firehouse. And then the break-in at his bar…

But those events were trivial—inconsequential—compared to what was going to happen next.

What *had* to happen next…

Charlie Tillerman had to die.

Chapter 8

Charlie didn't have to open his eyes to know that he was alone. He always woke up alone. Michaela never stayed the entire night, not even when they...

Fell asleep together, like they had last night. But last night, they'd done nothing but sleep. And his body ached in protest.

Or maybe it ached from what had happened in that firehouse parking lot. With just that one scratch over his eyebrow, he hadn't been hurt too badly. Not like Michaela had been. She should have stayed at the hospital. And last night, after they'd talked, he'd pleaded with her to stay with him.

She'd arched her dark blond eyebrows then, like she thought he was asking for something more. Something that his body cursed him for not asking for, for that mind-blowing release that he'd only experienced—with that intensity of pleasure—with her.

But because she'd clearly been exhausted, he'd assured her that he just wanted her to rest. And he'd also wanted to make sure that she was safe. He'd intended to stay awake, to watch over her, but he'd probably fallen asleep before her. Had she even stayed?

Some bodyguard he'd proved to be.

With a weary sigh, he opened his eyes. While he hadn't

been sleeping long, according to the clock beside his bed, he had to get up. He had to clean up the bar, not just from the mess the intruder or intruders had made but from the fingerprinting and evidence collection the crime scene techs had done as well. Last night, he'd called the new bar manager he'd hired when he started his volunteer-firefighting training, and the guy was coming in early to help with cleanup and to call the insurance company and restock the bar. Hopefully, they wouldn't have to close for any longer than the morning. He wasn't letting the criminals affect him or his business any more than they already had.

And Michaela…

He had no hope of her not affecting him. And her pregnancy.

A baby girl. Would she look like her mother, with blond hair and bright blue eyes that twinkled when she was teasing him? The way Michaela's eyes twinkled when she was teasing him?

Warmth flooded his heart. After his ex-wife had finally admitted that she never wanted to have a baby, he had convinced himself that he hadn't wanted one, either, that it was better not to have one. But now that his daughter was on her way, he realized how badly he had really wanted a child and that he'd just been lying to himself because, like Michaela, he hadn't thought it was going to happen.

And it still might not, if those horrible things that kept happening to the hotshots kept happening to Michaela now. She had to stay safe. But she'd already been hurt last night. He needed to check on her. He reached for his cell next to the bed and saw all the missed calls and voice mails that had come in.

He must have inadvertently shut off his ringer, or he'd been sleeping so soundly that he hadn't heard his phone at all. His hand shook as he picked up the cell and looked through the messages.

And then his heart pounded fast and hard. Someone he knew—someone he cared about—was in the hospital now.

Michaela hadn't been able to sleep much, not with Charlie lying so close to her. She'd wanted to be with him in every way, but she knew that he was right when he'd laughed at her naive assumption that nothing was going to change.

He was also right that everything had changed.

Last night, that stupid little improvised Molotov cocktail had blown Michaela's world apart. Nothing was the same anymore, and it would never be.

So she'd given up on trying to sleep and had headed to the firehouse. Crime scene tape fluttered in the morning breeze, looped around that patch of asphalt scorched from the fire. The tape also wound around several trucks that sat, with deflated tires, farther out from the burned area.

Was one of those vehicles Charlie's? Had he been the actual target since his bar had been broken into as well? But then, why damage so many other vehicles, most with the US Forest Service decal on the door?

The owners of the trucks were lucky that they hadn't caught on fire too. Maybe that had been the intent with that bottle. Maybe it hadn't been thrown at her but toward one of those vehicles. She hoped that was the case, because she didn't want to be the target of the saboteur.

He'd nearly killed Rory about six months ago. After turning on all the fire engines, the saboteur had struck Rory over the head with an axe handle as Rory had rushed out of the bunkroom to shut off the trucks. He'd been trying to stop the building from filling with fumes. Rory had nearly died trying to save the rest of the hotshots, who'd still been asleep in the bunkroom. She'd been one of them.

Even though her head pounded now, it couldn't be nearly as bad as what her fellow hotshot had gone through. Rory probably hadn't been the target, either, just collateral damage in this person's war on the hotshots.

She felt that little flutter inside her again, and she knew it wasn't nerves giving her an ulcer. It was her baby. She had to make sure that her daughter didn't become collateral damage too.

Or Charlie…

That was why she'd left him. And why she hadn't reached for him last night. Life was too complicated for any more complications right now.

And Charlie, and her attachment to him, was becoming a complication. One she couldn't emotionally handle at the moment.

She also didn't know what she could physically handle.

So she ducked under the crime scene tape and reached for the handle of the side door. The knob turned easily, it hadn't been locked.

Stanley, the teenager who kept the firehouse and the equipment cleaned, often forgot to lock it. That was why so many people persisted in believing that anyone could be the saboteur, because anyone can get inside an unlocked firehouse.

Many of the hotshots suspected that Charlie was that person. Maybe it was easier to imagine him as the saboteur than to believe that one of their own team members was the person hurting them.

It wasn't hard for Michaela to believe that, though. She knew not to trust the people closest to her. She'd learned that as a child. She touched her stomach. That was something she hoped her child would never learn and that her little girl would always trust Michaela to do the right thing as her mother.

What was the right thing to do for her now?

She pushed open the door and stepped inside the firehouse. Annie, the firehouse dog, bounded over to her. Half sheepdog and half bullmastiff, the firehouse mascot was enormous, with a huge head and big paws and a lot of fur. She didn't jump up on Michaela like she usually did, almost as if she knew that Michaela was pregnant.

"Why didn't you tell me?" Michaela asked as she petted the dog's big head.

Annie stared up at her with her soulful dark eyes. And maybe it was because Michaela was thinking of him so much that those eyes reminded her of Charlie's, of his soulfulness. He was that typical bartender who listened to everyone's problems and offered sympathy and a drink and the wise advice that came from having an old soul. Like that first night he'd invited her to come home with him— he must have realized how alone she'd felt and how hurt she'd been that everyone had taken off and left her behind. And at first, when she'd gone upstairs with him, he'd just let her talk, about herself, about her job. She'd been the one to make the first move and had kissed him. And even then, he'd hesitated, making sure that *she* was sure before he kissed her back.

She wished she could trust her judgment, which told her that he was a good guy. But she'd been wrong about her ex, and she could maybe be wrong about Charlie too. Even though all the locals insisted that he was exactly like his late grandfather, from whom he'd inherited the Filling Station, and was the kind of guy you could trust with your secrets and maybe your life…

But what about your heart?

"Are you okay?" Stanley asked as he came around one of the engines, a polishing rag in his hand. "I heard about what happened last night." He shuddered, and his curly blond hair fell into his eyes.

He was a sweet kid and the former foster brother of one of the hotshots, Cody Mallehan. When Stanley aged out of the system at eighteen, Cody had moved him up to Northern Lakes and gotten him the job at the firehouse. Stanley had been with them over a year now, and he was as much the firehouse mascot as Annie was in some ways. He was always around, always happy to see them and always happy to help.

"I'm fine," she assured him.

But he pointed to the bandage on her temple. "That looks like it probably hurt."

He'd been hit in the head—horribly—once, and like Rory, he'd suffered quite the concussion from it. The arsonist, Matthew Hamilton—who Stanley had thought was his friend since Matt wasn't much older than him—had done that, though, not the saboteur. But if the saboteur wasn't caught and stopped soon, the kid could get hurt and his faithful sidekick, Annie, could too.

"I'm glad you weren't here last night," she said.

"Me too," Stanley agreed with a vigorous bob of his curly-haired head. "That foster kid who was allergic to Annie has been placed with some other family, so we can stay at Serena and Cody's again. And they said they'll make sure all the new kids they take in don't have any dog allergies."

She smiled. "That's good." Serena and Cody had recently gotten licensed as a foster home, caring for kids like

Cody and Stanley who had no family. But they were now each other's family.

The hotshots had felt like family, too, once, but not anymore. There was always an undercurrent with them now, a certain level of mistrust, that shimmered just beneath the surface of all their interactions.

Hell, that made them feel more like family to Michaela, that she couldn't trust any of them not to hurt her. She couldn't trust anyone, though.

Not even Charlie.

Maybe most especially not Charlie. Because he could hurt her the most, even if he was as nice a guy as all his patrons thought he was.

"Is Braden here?" she asked. His truck was in the lot, but that was probably because its tires were all flat.

Stanley shrugged. "I don't know for sure. All those trucks need air in their tires again."

But the air hadn't just been let out, some of the tires had gouges in them too. In the daylight, Michaela had been able to see that. If only it hadn't been so dark last night…

Maybe she would have seen who'd done that damage. There had also been damage done to Charlie's bar. It seemed unlikely that the two incidents were connected, though.

Because what could the saboteur have against Charlie Tillerman? Unless they'd heard what she had the night before…

That if he became mayor, he would make the hotshots find a new headquarters. He wanted them all gone from Northern Lakes. Even her?

Or maybe most especially her.

Last night, she should have talked to him about his plan to get rid of the hotshots and about those two incidents. But they'd been too tired and too shocked over the baby news to discuss anything else. Still, they hadn't really talked much about the baby either. He'd said everything was going to change, but he hadn't shared how.

"Sam's out of town, so Braden probably is here," Stanley replied. He knew the superintendent well.

She smiled at the kid again, petted the dog once more and then headed toward Braden's office. She knocked once. But nobody replied.

Maybe he had gone home. Trick could have dropped him off at his house, or it was close enough that he might have walked, like she had walked over from the bar. But just to be sure, she knocked once more, and then she heard something drop onto the concrete floor behind the door.

"Are you okay?" she called out, and she turned the knob. Like the side door, this one was unlocked, too, so she pushed it open.

Braden blinked bleary eyes at her before reaching down to pick up a thermos from the floor. "Oh, hey. I must have fallen asleep." He rubbed his hand over his face, which had lines in it from the leather blotter on his desktop.

She resisted the urge to laugh—not just because he was her boss, but because it was probably partially her fault he'd stayed here instead of sleeping last night. And she felt a twinge of guilt for causing him concern. If only she'd gone immediately back inside, then she wouldn't have gotten hurt. And then, when she'd disappeared from the bar last night and Charlie had called Hank, Braden and Hank and Trick had been worried about her all over again.

"Everything all right?" he asked her.

She nodded even though it was a lie. Everything was not all right. But he knew that, too, after everything that kept happening to the hotshots.

"I just wanted to tell you something…" She closed the

door behind her so that nobody else would overhear their conversation. She wasn't sure whom she wanted to tell yet about her baby, but her boss deserved to know.

"You're pregnant," Braden said before she could even find the words.

Shocked that he knew, she choked on her saliva and coughed. Then she cleared her throat and asked, "How did you know?" Had the nurse assumed he knew, like she'd assumed Charlie must have known?

He smiled. "I noticed when Charlie lifted you into the back of the paramedic rig," he said. "I don't know why I hadn't noticed before."

"Don't feel bad about that," she said as she dropped into one of the chairs in front of his desk. "I didn't know I was, either, and I still couldn't believe it until I saw her on the ultrasound."

"Congratulations?" He arched a dark brow, making it a question.

She released a shaky sigh and nodded. "Yes, and thank you. For years, I believed I couldn't get pregnant. I didn't think it was possible…"

"You've done a lot of things that haven't always been possible," he said. "Like becoming a female hotshot."

"Hank is one too," she reminded him. And there were more than just the two of them now. But the ratio of women compared to men was still lower than it should have been. While the physical requirements for the job were probably easier for a man to meet, Michaela had met them. Other women could, too, but she suspected that a lower number of women were hired because there were still more men like her dad in positions of power than like Braden Zimmer.

"It was easier for Hank than for you," her superintendent said.

She would have been offended if she didn't know what he meant. Hank was as tall as the biggest guys on the team, and as strong as them too.

Michaela was shorter, and she had to work out longer and harder than the others in order to be strong enough to do the job. And for the others to trust her to do the job. And she suspected some of the guys still didn't believe she should do it, like her dad.

And now that she was pregnant…

"I'm not sure how long I can do the job," she admitted to him.

Braden nodded. "Talk to your doctor."

"I don't have one, but the ER doctor recommended an ob-gyn that she likes."

"Ask Willow. She might have some recommendations too."

Willow, hotshot Luke Garrison's wife, was a nurse, and she had just had a healthy baby boy. Finally. She'd suffered some miscarriages before carrying this child to term. Willow had thought that was because of the stress of being married to a hotshot, of worrying about him all the time when he was out on a fire call. And they'd been separated for a while before finally reuniting as a family.

If just being married to a hotshot made a pregnancy risky, what chance did Michaela have of continuing to be a hotshot herself?

"Unless you don't want *anyone* to know yet," Braden added.

"I don't, not yet," she admitted. She wasn't sure why she wanted her pregnancy to be kept secret, though. For the baby's sake or for hers? She felt so protective of her child. Was that why she'd wanted to keep her relationship with Charlie secret? Because she'd wanted to protect it?

Or had she been protecting herself in case it hadn't lasted, just as her marriage hadn't? She and Charlie had pretty much agreed that it wouldn't last, since neither wanted to ever get married again.

"I'm sure Willow, being a nurse, would keep whatever you asked her confidential," Braden assured her.

She snorted. "Her coworker let the truth out to Charlie last night."

"So he knows?"

She nodded. And she could see the question in his dark eyes, the one he was too professional to ask her. She smiled and said, "He is the father."

"I didn't know you two were even seeing each other."

"I like to keep my private life private," she admitted. She protected herself that way, as much as she could protect herself from speculation.

"Charlie Tillerman's a good guy," Braden said, as if she needed an endorsement of his character.

And she snorted again.

"What? Didn't he react well to the news?" he asked, his dark eyes wide with shock.

She wasn't really sure how Charlie had reacted, how he actually felt about the baby or about her. But he'd been sweet, carrying her into the bedroom and bringing her the orange juice and especially with acknowledging that any decisions were hers to make. She didn't have to worry about him telling anyone about the baby. But maybe she should make sure about that.

"I wasn't talking about the baby," she said. "I was talking about how some of the hotshots—like even your brother-in-law—suspect he's the saboteur."

Braden sighed and shook his head. "I don't believe that.

I've known the Tillerman family for a long time. They're good, civic-minded people."

She snorted again. "Yeah, civic-minded. That goes with what I overheard him and another volunteer talking about last night, and that made me think that Trick and the others might be right about him," she admitted. And for those horrifying moments, she'd been outraged and devastated. Then she'd stepped outside into the darkness...

Braden shrugged. "I don't know if I need to hear gossip..."

She shook her head. "You need to hear this. That other volunteer—I think it's his brother-in-law—is trying to get Charlie to run for mayor. And the reason he wants him to, and that Charlie is considering it, is to get rid of us."

"What?" Braden asked, and he rubbed his forehead as if he had a slight concussion too. "Get rid of us *how*?"

"They, and apparently some other townspeople, don't want the hotshot headquarters in Northern Lakes anymore," she explained.

Braden let out a little sigh. "Can you blame them? Charlie lost his bar and his home because of the arsonist. But then the trouble in town didn't end with Matt Hamilton's arrest. Because there's that damn saboteur..."

Fury coursed through her as she remembered all the horrible things the saboteur had done to everyone. And now her, too, if that was who had thrown the Molotov cocktail at her. She touched the bandage on her temple, where there was a dull throb and an itchiness to the healing stitches.

"Do you really think the saboteur is one of us?" Michaela asked her boss, wondering where his head was at. "That one of us could be hurting the others?"

"I don't want to believe that one of our team is capable

of doing that," Braden said. "That one of us would betray the rest of us that way..."

She didn't want to believe that either. "The only way we're going to know for sure is if the son of a bitch ever gets caught."

Braden shook his head. "Not 'if'—when. We have to stop him, Michaela, and soon. We have to make sure nobody else gets hurt. And I'm sorry that you were—"

"That's not your fault, Braden," she assured him. "I know you've been trying to catch the saboteur for a long time now."

Unfortunately, he hadn't been successful. But that hadn't been for lack of trying on her boss's part. He had his wife helping him investigate, and then her brother Trick and other team members had tried to figure out who it was too. Michaela blamed the reverse karma that she'd seen all too often as the reason why the saboteur had avoided getting caught, that some people just seemed to get away with the bad things they did. Like her dad.

He'd never lost his job or his freedom or even his wife. Michaela's mother had stuck with him despite all the verbal and sometimes physical abuse he'd doled out to his family.

But maybe he'd lost a little bit of his enormous ego when Michaela had proved to him that his job wasn't as hard as he'd claimed, because despite not being the son he'd wanted, she'd carried on the *family* tradition. She'd become a firefighter. No—she hadn't just become a firefighter, she'd become a hotshot, something her dad had never been able to do despite all the years he'd tried to become one. Of course, instead of blaming himself for not working out enough or eating well enough to be in peak physical condition, he'd blamed his family for holding him back.

She'd proved to him that hard work paid off and that a

female could be stronger and tougher than even he thought he was. But she didn't feel as much satisfaction as she once had over that now. In fact, despite the baby fluttering inside her, she felt a bit empty.

Hollow. Like it was a hollow victory to her now. Now that she knew what mattered.

Her child. She had to do whatever necessary to protect her child. So Michaela hoped her boss was right, that it wasn't a question of *if* the saboteur would be caught but of *when*.

Soon.

It had to be soon. And maybe the best way to make sure that happened was to do a little investigating of her own...

Had Braden just lied to a member of his team? Had he made a promise to Michaela that he wouldn't be able to keep? He stared at the door she closed behind herself moments ago, and he wondered if he should call her back. If he should reiterate how important it was that she be careful until the saboteur was caught. *If* the saboteur was ever caught...

He'd been so determined to find out who it was for so long, but all his efforts hadn't produced any results. Sure, he'd eliminated a lot of people on his team as suspects. Wyatt. Dawson. Cody. Owen. Luke. Hank. Ethan. Trent. Rory and now Michaela. That still left almost half of them as viable suspects, which made him feel as sick as Sam had in the early days of her pregnancy.

His cell rang, startling him nearly as much as Michaela's knock on his door had earlier. "Zimmer," he answered without looking at it.

"Zimmer here too," a female voice said. "McRooney-Zimmer."

"Sam." His heart swelled with love. "Tell me you're coming home soon." He missed her so damn much.

"Soon," she promised.

But then he wondered if that was a good thing, with how dangerous it was in Northern Lakes. Maybe it was better that she stayed in Washington with her dad and her brother, especially with the baby coming in a few weeks. Then both she and the baby would be safe and protected.

But his heart ached at the thought of not being with them and of not being the one to protect them.

"And when I come back, I might be bringing reinforcements with me," she said. "I just have to do a little more convincing."

"Do it fast," he pleaded with her. "We need all the help we can get to catch this bastard." He told her about last night, about the stupid stunt in the parking lot that had injured Michaela and Charlie Tillerman. And how after that, Charlie's bar had been broken into, but a break-in didn't feel like the work of the saboteur. Like it had happened so many times in the past, it seemed that the saboteur striking gave someone else the motive or the courage to go after a hotshot—or in this case, maybe after a bar owner. But who was the target? Charlie or Michaela?

"I don't want anything else to happen…"

For *anyone else* to get hurt.

Chapter 9

Was this his fault?

The reason that his friend was in the hospital?

Charlie moved closer to the mayor's bed, concern gripping him over how pale and old Les Byers looked. The man was younger than Charlie's late grandfather but older than Charlie's dad. He should have retired long ago, but the town kept reelecting him, mostly because nobody ran against him, knowing that they would lose. He was a smart and, more importantly, honorable man who put the best interests of everyone else above his own. So, naturally, everyone loved him.

Like Charlie's family did. Like Charlie did. And after losing his beloved grandfather just a few years ago, Charlie didn't want to lose anyone else he cared about.

"Les?" He called the man's name softly so as not to startle him, but he wanted to make sure that he was all right.

The old man's eyes opened and blinked. "Ah, good. You came…"

"Of course, as soon as I got the messages," Charlie said. And he had rushed out so quickly that he hadn't even told the bar manager who he was going to see. But he probably wouldn't have shared the news even if he hadn't been in a hurry, because he wasn't sure that the rest of town should know that the mayor was in the hospital. "How are you, Les?"

"Lucky to be alive," the mayor murmured. But he didn't look lucky. He looked exhausted.

Even more so than Michaela had looked the night before. "You should get some rest," Charlie said. "We can talk more later, when you're feeling better." He had to get better, but Charlie didn't even know why he was here, what his medical condition really was.

The mayor shook his head. "No. We have to talk now. You need to take over for me."

Charlie's head bobbed. "Sure, of course, until you get back on your feet."

Les shook his head again. "No…"

Panic struck Charlie's heart. "What is it?" Was it terminal? "Cancer or…"

"Poison," the mayor replied.

"What?"

"They think it's a heart attack or something, but my heart is fine," Les insisted, and he weakly thumped his hand against his chest. "There's nothing wrong with it. Somebody had to have slipped me something. I made them take my blood to test it, to see what it was."

Charlie hoped Les hadn't been drinking in the Filling Station the night before. Since he'd been on that volunteer fire call, he wasn't sure if Les had been there or not. But over the past year, a few other people had insisted something must have been slipped into their food or drinks at the bar. And he had a feeling that those hotshots seemed to suspect he was the one who'd done it.

"Why would anyone slip you anything?" Charlie asked. The mayor wasn't a hotshot, like the other people who'd been drugged or were in danger.

Like Michaela had been the night before. Had she been the target of that bottle bomb thrown in the parking lot?

Panic hit him again, so hard this time that he nearly gasped. Was she okay? Or would whoever had hurt her the night before try to hurt her again?

He should have stayed awake last night, he should have made certain that nothing happened to her. And what if she hadn't left on her own?

Someone had broken into his place once, maybe they had again. But when he'd left, the door to the stairwell had been locked and undamaged.

No. Michaela had left on her own, like she had every other time she'd been in his place. And probably for the same reason: because she just hadn't wanted to stay.

Why?

Was she just not as into him as he was her? Or was it because she struggled to trust as much as he did due to the failed marriages in their past?

That wasn't the only reason Michaela had not to trust people, though. Too many things had happened to the hotshots over the course of the last year or so. Too many dangerous things, like last night.

Les's eyes were closed. Had he drifted off to sleep or…

The machines connected to him hummed steadily along, though, as if everything was all right.

"Les?"

The older man's eyes blinked open again, and he stared up at Charlie as if surprised to find he was there. Maybe Les had had a stroke. But his speech wasn't slurred, and once he blinked some more, he seemed to focus. His blue eyes were bright and intense. "You have to step in," he said, his voice sharp with urgency. "With no deputy mayor, it has to be a town council member. I can't trust anyone else."

Charlie knew that feeling all too well. "Why not?"

"Someone tried to kill me," Les said. "Someone is desperate and deranged enough to kill to get what they want."

"What do they want?" Charlie asked.

"What does anyone want?" Les asked, and he leaned back against his pillows again as if he was about to fall asleep. But he murmured, "Money. Power."

That was what Charlie's ex had wanted. But Charlie wasn't like that. His sister and Eric weren't either. They just wanted to be happy and raise their kids without worrying about something horrible happening to them again, like that fire. So he shook his head, rejecting what the mayor was saying.

"Not everybody wants money and power. I don't. I just want to be happy." And to raise his daughter without worrying about something horrible happening to her.

What did Michaela want? He'd wanted to ask her that last night. He'd needed to talk to her more, but she'd already been shaky. Dehydrated. Tired.

But he was the one who'd fallen asleep. And she'd left, like she kept leaving.

"You have to be careful," Les said. "You can't trust anyone."

Charlie was already well aware of that. But had Les really been poisoned? Or was he just paranoid? Had he had some kind of break with reality?

Or had he been affected by what seemed to be a crime wave suddenly sweeping through Northern Lakes, threatening the lives of everyone in its path?

He had to find Michaela and make sure that she and their baby were safe. But what was the best way to protect her? To accept the interim mayor position? To get the hotshots moved out of town?

Or would accepting the position put him, and maybe her,

in even more danger? Because if the mayor had been poisoned, whoever took over the position could be next. And had what happened last night been about the hotshots at all, or was someone targeting him? Then Michaela was in danger because of him, not because of the hotshots. In wanting to protect her, he might put her more at risk.

After a nap at the firehouse—during which, she'd charged her cell phone—Michaela called the obstetrician that the ER doctor had recommended. Unless another patient canceled, Michaela wouldn't be able to get an appointment for a couple of days, so she would have to wait at least that long before learning her limitations regarding her career, which was also her life.

Or at least, the job had once *been* her life. She'd worked so hard to become not just a firefighter but a hotshot. But if she had been able to get pregnant during her first marriage, she would have taken a leave of absence. However, once she'd learned that it was unlikely she would ever conceive, she threw herself into her job even more. And when her marriage had ended, it was all she had.

But now...

She patted her belly. Now she had the baby. After leaving the firehouse, she stopped at Courtney Beaumont's boutique, and she purchased some loose, flowy kind of clothes for comfort and for camouflage. And she left the shop in one of them, a long yellow sundress that swirled around her in the early-summer breeze.

She wasn't ready to tell anyone else about her pregnancy—not until she knew what she would have to do, how soon she would have to stop working or if she should even be working at all as a hotshot.

Despite grabbing some breakfast at the firehouse and

cookies at Courtney's boutique, her stomach rumbled as she headed down the sidewalk with her shopping bags clasped in one hand. The bar was on the corner between Courtney's shop and the firehouse, and even on the street, she could smell the scent of grilling burgers. Her stomach rumbled louder, and she felt that little fluttery feeling again.

Her daughter wanted a burger too. Or did she want her father? To hear his voice? To be near him?

She wasn't the only one, Michaela wanted to see Charlie too. Just to make sure that he was all right, that the bar would be fine and...

That he was fine.

Even as angry as she should be with him for wanting to get rid of the hotshots, she understood why the townspeople would want to move the headquarters out of Northern Lakes. There had been so much trouble, so much danger, around the hotshots for too long now. After what had happened last night, Michaela should probably start her leave immediately and not take any more chances with her life and, most especially, with her baby's life. But running away wasn't going to stop the saboteur. After the break-in at the bar, she wasn't even sure last night had been the work of the saboteur or someone else.

Braden had a plan for catching the saboteur and seemed to believe he could apprehend the culprit soon... But maybe Michaela could help him. At least she could investigate a bit more about what had happened at the bar the night before—and during the course of her investigation, she could get that burger.

She could also check in with Charlie at the same time. She pulled open the door and walked into the bar. A few hotshots were gathered in the big corner booth in the back, which was "their" seat. A quick glance confirmed it was

Bruce Abbott and Howie Lane, the youngest two of the hotshots, but they were no less sexist than the older guys, Donovan Cunningham and Carl Kozak. The four of them openly treated her like she didn't belong, no matter how much she carried her own weight and sometimes theirs too. Or even that night she'd carried Charlie from the bar...

All the other hotshots who'd been here that night had come to respect her after that rescue except for those four. She wouldn't have put it past one of them to have pulled some of the more harmless of the sabotage just to give her a hard time. But she hadn't been the only victim.

So many other hotshots had gotten hurt. And some of them, like Rory VanDam, very badly.

Howie and Bruce didn't wave her back to the booth—not that she would have headed their direction anyway. She barely spared them a glance. Instead, she took a seat at the bar, but her pulse didn't quicken at the sight of this dark-haired bartender. It wasn't Charlie.

"Hello," Will, one of the backup bartenders, greeted her with a grin. "What can I get you? Beer? Chardonnay?"

She flinched, wondering if she'd had any alcohol while she was pregnant. But thinking that she had an ulcer, she'd stopped drinking a while ago. She'd actually stopped after a bottle of wine at her and Hank's place had been poisoned about eight months ago. The poison had just knocked her out, to get her out of the way because Hank had been the real target. And Hank could have died because Michaela, incapacitated, hadn't been able to help her or even warn her that a madwoman had broken into their apartment.

"Don't serve her," a woman said now, her tone sharp with bitterness. "She shouldn't be allowed to drink here. None of them should."

Michaela turned her head to find the woman from the

hospital the night before, the one who'd run up and hugged Charlie, standing beside her. The dark-haired woman fairly bristled with outrage. Michaela hadn't met her before, so she didn't know Charlie's sister's name. And he'd whisked her out of the hospital last night without introducing them.

Michaela should have asked Charlie her and her husband's names. But they hadn't had much time to talk the night before—not after finding the bar broken into and with at least one intruder still inside it.

Until Charlie had chased one of them out. Like apparently this woman wanted to chase Michaela out of the Filling Station now.

"I'm sorry, Mrs. Veltema, but Charlie has strict rules about when and who to cut off," the bartender replied, and then he winked at Michaela. "And he would never let me cut off his favorite customer."

Did Will know about them? Or was he just referring to the way Charlie always brought up her saving his life and refusing to let her pay? Assuming that was probably why Will thought she was Charlie's favorite customer, she smiled back at the young bartender. "Thanks, Will, and I actually don't want a drink. I would love the Gouda-bacon burger and fries, though."

Will winked again and nodded. But before he could turn toward the kitchen, Mrs. Veltema reached across the bar and grabbed his arm.

"Where is my brother?" she asked.

Will shrugged. "He was already gone when I came in this morning to help clean up. But the new manager was here." He turned toward an older man, who appeared to be counting bottles behind the bar. "Jerry, do you know where Charlie is?"

Jerry sighed and nodded. "He's at the hospital."

Michaela gasped in unison with his sister. "Is he okay?" she asked before the other woman could.

Will nodded. "Yeah, he's not there for himself but because a friend of his is there. Someone close to him isn't doing too well."

Mrs. Veltema's dark eyes flicked from Michaela to Will again. Then she glanced around the bar, as if everyone she considered close to him was there.

Did she know about him and Michaela?

The woman let the young bartender tug his arm free and duck back into the kitchen. Then she whirled on Michaela again. "He could have been there because he's hurt again. He could have been there, like he was last night, because of *you.*"

"I didn't hurt him last night," Michaela said. But if she'd warned him the minute he stepped out the door, he might have been able to get back inside before that little makeshift firebomb rolled toward them.

"You might not have personally done it," Mrs. Veltema said, though she sounded doubtful of Michaela's claim, "but you're still responsible. You and the rest of your damn hotshot team. You're responsible for him getting hurt last night and for him getting hurt here when his bar burned down. The Huron hotshots are the ones who've brought all the danger to Northern Lakes. And you need to leave. Now."

"You're throwing me out?" Michaela asked, and her lips twitched with a slight smile. The other woman was taller than her, and probably heavier, but Michaela was stronger. She had no doubt about that.

"Someone needs to throw you out," Mrs. Veltema said, and she started reaching for Michaela's arm like she intended to drag her off the stool and out the door.

Michaela opened her mouth, but before she could utter the word on her tongue, another voice said it: "Don't."

Charlie's deep voice rumbled out, low and angry. "Don't you dare touch her, Valerie."

The woman instinctively jerked her arm back, but then she snorted and shook her head. "What's wrong with you? Are you still grateful to her for pulling you out of the fire? Grandpa's bar wouldn't have burned down in the first place if it wasn't for the hotshots."

"Michaela had nothing to do with that arsonist," Charlie said, and he stepped closer to Michaela, sliding his arm around her shoulders as if he was protecting her now. "Or with anything else that's happened around here."

Michaela felt that little zip of electricity she felt every time Charlie touched her—even last night, when she'd been so exhausted after the wildfire and what had happened in the parking lot and bar. She'd been too tired then to act on that feeling, and maybe that was why it was even more intense now. So intense that her pulse quickened and her heart beat faster.

Charlie must have felt it, too, because his arm tightened around her, and his face flushed slightly as he stared down at her.

Valerie narrowed her dark eyes and studied them. "What's going on with you two?"

So he hadn't told his sister about them. Why? Because he'd been honoring Michaela's request for privacy, or because he didn't think whatever they had was serious enough to talk about?

"She's pregnant with my baby," Charlie said.

Michaela again gasped in unison with his sister. Then she glanced quickly around, wondering who else might have overheard. If Howie and Bruce had…

She shook her head and lowered her voice to a whisper to point out, "This isn't the time or the place for this discussion."

"No discussion is necessary," Charlie said. "It's a fact, and my sister is going to have to deal with it and treat you with the respect you deserve. You did save my life."

And now she wondered if he was just talking about the fire. But he had to be. He hadn't been miserable and suffering when they'd started seeing each other. He'd just been lonely, like she'd been. She touched her stomach where another little flutter rippled through her.

She wouldn't be lonely anymore.

But that was because of the baby, not him.

Valerie just continued to stare at them, her mouth slightly open in shock.

Will cleared his throat. "Uh, Michaela's lunch is ready."

"We'll bring it upstairs," Charlie said. Then he used his arm around Michaela to help her down from the barstool and around the bar and through the door to the kitchen.

And he just left his sister standing there, staring after them. Michaela didn't know whether to feel sorry for the woman or to laugh at her.

Charlie unlocked the stairwell and guided Michaela in front of him while he carried up her lunch plate with the burger and fries, which smelled so good.

But Michaela was hungry for more than the food right now. She'd missed Charlie. She'd missed him during those two weeks she'd been gone, and she'd wanted so badly to see him again. But last night had been chaos, with so many things happening and so many revelations and so much danger...

And it was all still there, the chaos—but now in the chaos,

she wanted to reach out and hold on to the only thing that had ever distracted her and made her feel better: Charlie.

"I'm sorry about my sister," he said. "Her son was one of the Boy Scouts trapped in the wildfire the arsonist set back before—"

"Before he set your bar on fire," she finished. Valerie Veltema had a couple of reasons to resent the hotshots. Three, including last night when her brother had gotten hurt again. And now Michaela did feel sorry for her because she totally understood.

"Like I told her, you had nothing to do with any of that," he said.

"But she still wants the hotshots out of Northern Lakes."

"She's not the only one," Charlie admitted.

"You do too?"

"The only thing I really want is for nobody else to get hurt," he said.

"How is your friend? The one in the hospital?"

"I hope he'll be all right," Charlie replied, but his forehead furrowed as if he was doubtful.

"I'm sorry," she said.

His mouth curved into a slight grin. "Nobody can blame a hotshot for what happened to him," he assured her while also maintaining his friend's privacy. That was his reputation, the reason so many people confided in him, because he kept their secrets. Except for hers...

She should have been angry about that, but the way he'd announced it actually made her happy. He hadn't done it with shame and resentment but with pride and protectiveness. And Michaela couldn't remember the last time someone had so hotly defended her or taken care of her like he had last night with the orange juice and the food.

"Go ahead, eat your lunch," he said now, trying yet again to take care of her.

As good as the food smelled, she wanted something else more: him. It had been too long since she'd kissed him, since she'd touched him. And if they'd been hurt worse last night, she might not have had the chance to kiss him and touch him again. When Will had said he was in the hospital, she'd been so afraid, so worried that she wouldn't see him again. Let alone be with him...the way she needed to be with him.

With a bar full of people downstairs, there should be no threat of intruders breaking in or someone throwing explosives. There was no threat except for the risk of her falling for him.

The way he'd stuck up for and defended her warmed her heart, had it beating even faster and harder than it usually did around him. She'd worry later about whether or not anyone else had overheard what he'd said.

The truth was going to come out eventually. As her ex-husband had learned, it usually did.

Hopefully, the saboteur would learn that soon too. Or it might not be safe for Charlie to be around her. But if she needed to step back from him, she wanted at least one more memory.

So she took the plate from his hands and set it onto the countertop. "I'll eat that later," she said. "I had a bunch of cookies at Courtney's boutique." She had the bags wrapped around her wrist, and she dropped them to the floor now next to the counter.

"Shopping spree?" he asked, and his dark gaze skimmed down her body. Then he released a soft whistle of appreciation. "Beautiful..."

He always made her feel beautiful from the way he

looked at her and touched her. Usually, she didn't want to think about her looks at all, just about her strength and capabilities. But Charlie made her feel beautiful and appreciated in the same way that he made her feel cared for.

But her ex had made her feel beautiful, too, with all the charming things he'd said but hadn't really meant. So she didn't trust her judgment when it came to men. But even if she was wrong about Charlie, he'd still given her more pleasure than anyone else ever had.

And he'd given her something she'd never thought she could have: a baby.

At the moment, she wanted the pleasure, though. She grasped his forearm and tugged him through the living room to the bedroom. The blanket and sheets were still rumpled from the night before, as if he'd been in too much of a hurry to make it this morning.

Because of his friend?

She wanted to ask more questions. But before she could say anything, his arms closed around her and he leaned down to kiss her. And, as always, the second his lips touched hers, passion ignited inside her, burning hotter than any fire she'd ever fought. But just like a fire, sometimes it threatened to consume and destroy her.

He pulled back, though, panting for breath, and shook his head. "This isn't a good idea."

"It never was," Michaela agreed. She didn't know why she'd ever thought it was, but they'd seemed to be on the same page, wanting nothing serious, no strings.

And now they were going to have a child…

It definitely hadn't been a good idea, but she had no regrets. Because she was finally pregnant with the baby she'd wanted for so long.

And because of how Charlie had made her feel those times they'd succumbed to passion…

So much pleasure.

Her only regret would be not experiencing that again.

"You're hurt," Charlie said.

She touched the bandage on her temple. "This doesn't hurt." Then she touched the one above his eye. "Does this hurt?"

His hand covered hers on it, as if he'd forgotten it was there. "No. It doesn't hurt."

She trailed her other hand down his chest, over the buttons of his shirt, until she reached the button at the top of his jeans. "You're not hurting anywhere?"

He groaned and closed his eyes. "Michaela…"

"I'm not hurt," she assured him. "And this is fine…" She wasn't totally certain about that, not until she talked to the obstetrician. But she knew enough pregnant women, like Willow, and some of the other hotshots' wives, and had overheard and been part of enough conversations to know the mother having sex didn't harm the unborn baby. And that, thanks to TMI, some women had a stronger craving for sex than they did for pickles or ice cream. They'd laughed and blamed the hormones. And Michaela had envied them, thinking she didn't have the right hormones.

She was a mess of hormones now. That she'd thought, incorrectly, had been due to an ulcer. But they were due to her baby.

And to Charlie.

He was more than a craving. He was almost an addiction. She had to have him.

She trailed her fingers lower, over the fly of his jeans, and he groaned again. "Michaela…" And his arms closed around her, lifting her off her feet.

This time when he laid her onto the bed, he followed her down, his mouth fused to hers as he kissed her hungrily. Just as hungrily as she kissed him, nipping at his lips while she unbuttoned his shirt and unzipped his jeans. She was desperate to feel his leanly muscled body naked against hers. It had been too long.

She'd been away at the fire for so many weeks. And for the first time ever, she'd missed someone who wasn't there. She'd missed him.

Or maybe she'd just missed this.

"Slow down..." he murmured against her lips, then pulled back just enough to slide his down her throat. He undressed her with just a bit more patience than she'd had. And every inch of skin he exposed, he caressed and kissed... especially the soft swell of her belly.

Then he moved lower, between her legs, and drove her out of her mind. She clutched at him, dragging him up. Desperate to feel him inside her, she wrapped her legs around his waist. And then he was there...

Filling her.

Bringing her to the brink of madness, with that tension winding so tightly inside her that she thought she might burst like that bottle had in the parking lot. That she might just catch fire and explode.

He kissed her again, deeply, sliding his tongue into her mouth like his erection slid inside her, driving deep. And he reached between their bodies, stroking first a supersensitive nipple before he moved lower, stroking the even more sensitive part of her body.

She came, crying out his name from the intensity of pleasure he brought her. But what had she brought him? A baby he might not want.

And danger...

Chapter 10

So many of Charlie's experiences with Michaela seemed more like dreams than reality. Like some hot fantasy he'd dreamed up.

Because could anything really feel as incredible as her mouth against his, as her body wrapped around his or as the passion that burned so hot between them, as the pleasure that was so intense that it overwhelmed him?

Maybe the reason that it seemed like a dream, though, was that every time he woke up afterward, she was gone, leaving him to wonder if she'd ever really been there or if he'd just imagined it all.

Still, he could smell her on his sheets and on his skin, but there was also another smell in the room: the lingering odor of her burger and fries. Was she still here?

He jumped up from the bed and hurried out to the kitchen. The plate was on the counter, with just a few of the fries and a bite of the burger left. But after a quick glance through the open doors to his spare room and the bathrooms, he confirmed that she was gone.

Like usual.

His phone, sitting next to the empty plate, buzzed. Probably with a text from his sister. Or his brother-in-law. He glanced at the screen and saw unread messages from both of them. But they weren't the only people who'd texted him. The rest of the town council members had as well.

The deputy mayor had passed away a year ago, so one of the council members would have to assume the interim mayor position until Les got better. *If* he got better…

Charlie needed to check on him, like he needed to check on Michaela too. Was she all right? She'd seemed so when they made love. Hell, she'd been so passionate and, as always, had inspired such passion in him that he'd lost his mind.

Maybe that was the problem with them. The passion took over every time they were alone, leaving them no room to talk, to find out what the other really wanted. Or was that all that Michaela wanted from him?

Since she'd been so determined to keep their relationship— or whatever it was—secret, he'd assumed that was all she wanted. But had the baby changed that?

And what did he want?

He needed to figure that out, too, and not just about Michaela but also about that interim mayor position. Another text came in.

From Will: Can you come down here? Some people want to see you.

He sighed. He doubted that Michaela was "some people." Maybe her fellow hotshots, if any of them had overheard what he'd said about her being pregnant with his baby. He'd expected her to yell at him because he'd told his sister, but instead, she'd led him to his bedroom. He never knew what to expect from her or if he could even expect to see her again.

But he expected to see his sister again, probably with his brother-in-law as her reinforcement. So maybe they were "some people." He could have asked, but he didn't really care who it was, since it wasn't Michaela.

He dressed quickly and headed down to the bar, where Will pointed to a table with two people sitting near the door. He wouldn't have expected them to be at the same table when they could rarely handle being in the same room, at least not without him and Les Byers keeping them in neutral corners.

"Gentlemen," he said as he greeted them.

The term was ironic, though, as he considered neither the CEO of the lumber company, Bentley Ford, nor the Realtor, Jason Cruise, to be gentlemen. Bentley was in his late fifties, with iron gray hair and a stocky build. Jason was in his thirties with slick blond hair and a slick, fast way of talking, like if he talked fast enough, he could talk the listener into doing what he wanted.

"Take a seat. We've got a lot to discuss right now." Bentley kicked out the chair across from him, the one that was so close to Jason that it probably hit his leg from the way he flinched. Or maybe he just didn't trust Bentley to not try to hit him. While Jason just talked, Bentley Ford wasn't above using other means to get what he wanted.

"We should have called an emergency meeting at town hall," Jason said. "We should have followed protocol."

Charlie doubted that the Realtor wanted to do things by the book, he probably would have just felt safer there than he did here with Bentley. Bentley was the kind of man who was used to getting what he wanted, no matter how hard, mentally or physically, he had to fight for it.

"You heard about Les, then," Charlie mused.

"His wife called me," Jason said with a smug smile.

"He's going to be fine," Charlie insisted—because he wanted to believe that, not because he knew it was true.

Bentley shrugged. "It doesn't matter. Les Byers is an

old man. He's not going to recover quickly. He needs to be replaced."

Charlie bristled over Bentley's callousness, but he clenched his jaw to hold back the names he wanted to call the heartless son of a bitch.

"Yeah, and we know who Les Byers wants in his position," Jason said.

"Not you," Bentley said with a snort.

"Not you either," Jason said. "He wants Charlie."

"But Charlie doesn't want it," Bentley said. "What Charlie can do, though, is convince the mayor to appoint someone else, or Charlie will be the deciding vote for either you or me if the mayor isn't able to appoint anyone."

A pang of concern and guilt struck Charlie's heart. "What do you mean? Have you heard an update? Is he doing worse?" Was that why he was acting like Les wasn't going to recover? And while his friend had been getting worse, Charlie had been sleeping…after incredible sex.

It was like he was addicted to Michaela, like he couldn't get enough of her. Not that he'd been with her nearly enough yet—not with as busy as her life was.

"Worse?" Bentley said. "He's already not doing very damn well. He's an old man. He probably won't recover from this stroke or heart attack or whatever it was."

"His wife thinks it was a heart attack," Jason said. He sighed and shook his head. "With the way he eats, it's no wonder."

Bentley snorted. "He eats a lot of meals here. He's your pal, Charlie. You can talk some sense into him, or you will be the one who's forced to choose between me and Jason."

Charlie wasn't sure that talking some sense into his old friend was possible right now, not with how paranoid Les had seemed at the hospital earlier. Thinking he'd been poisoned...

Was it possible that had actually happened? Les seemed pretty certain of it, that he was too healthy to have had a heart attack or stroke.

If Les had been poisoned, Charlie was probably sitting with the prime suspects right now. But while both of these guys wanted what they wanted, they wouldn't hurt an old man to get it. They wouldn't have to. Since Les had already announced he wasn't going to run again, all they had to do was wait until the election, which wasn't that many months away.

Unless, for some reason, they weren't willing to wait. Maybe Les hadn't been willing to wait, either, and he wanted to step down now. He'd been trying to convince Charlie to take his job for several weeks now.

Charlie grinned at Ford and lightheartedly warned him, "My idea of sense and yours might not be the same."

Bentley chuckled. "You and I might be more on the same page than you think."

"Yeah, neither of you want any improvements to the town," Jason said. "You're determined to keep Northern Lakes in the Stone Age."

"There's that," Bentley said. "And we might even be on the same page about the hotshots."

Jason shook his head. "Charlie wants them out of here, and you want them to stay."

"Charlie might have changed his mind, according to some gossip going around..."

Apparently, Ford had heard about Michaela.

"What gossip?" Jason asked the question before Charlie could.

Bentley just grinned. "Not my news to share."

"How did you hear it?" Charlie asked. He would have noticed if Bentley Ford had been around when Charlie had gone off on his sister. The way Valerie had been reaching for Michaela, like she'd been about to physically throw her out of the bar, had infuriated him. He'd been so damn mad that she was about to hurt the woman he…the woman carrying his child. And so he'd let the words out without meaning to.

Without thinking of how mad Michaela might get at him or who else might overhear. Michaela hadn't been mad—at least, she hadn't mentioned it. But then, as usual, they really hadn't talked much.

But were other people already talking about them? That was what he'd hated about politics, how there had been no way to keep his private life private. But if Bentley had heard about Michaela, that was Charlie's fault for losing his temper and running his mouth in the bar.

"I have sources everywhere," Bentley said.

Charlie just about shivered at the ominous tone. Bentley Ford was a powerful man who was used to getting his way, so a lot of people were on his payroll. Maybe even some of the people who were on Charlie's payroll too.

Maybe Bentley wasn't as patient as Charlie had thought. Maybe he wanted the mayor's job too badly to wait for it. Maybe Les wasn't paranoid or delusional. Maybe someone really had poisoned him.

But if that was true, then what would that person do to Charlie if he took the mayor position? Would they try to get him out of their way? And what if Michaela was close to him, like she'd been last night in that parking lot and again in the bar—would she get hurt, too, because of him? Had she been hurt last night because of him?

* * *

Maybe she should have woken Charlie up before she left his place. Maybe she should have even invited him to go along on the appointment.

But Michaela still didn't know how involved he wanted to be with their daughter or if he even wanted to be involved at all. So when the ob-gyn's office texted her that another patient had canceled and the doctor could see Michaela today, at her office in the hospital, Michaela had rushed off to meet her. Fortunately, Owen had been in the bar when she'd come downstairs and he'd given her a ride to the hospital. He'd even offered to wait around for her, but she'd told him she would call someone to pick her up.

Feeling like a pincushion between the blood draws and the iron infusion she'd received to treat the anemia, she was happy to escape from the doctor's office with a bottle of prenatal vitamins and a prescription for more. Or she *had* been happy, until she ran into Trooper Wells as she crossed the hospital lobby. She swallowed down the groan rising up the back of her throat and tried to sidestep around her. But the trooper stepped right in front of her again.

"I already gave you my statement last night," Michaela said. "So I hope you didn't come here looking for me." And how the hell had she known to find her here?

The trooper shook her head, and a lock of red hair slipped out from beneath her hat. "No. I was called here to take someone else's statement."

A little chill chased down Michaela's spine at the almost ominous tone to the woman's voice. "Well, I'm sure that has nothing to do with me." And she tried sidestepping around the trooper again.

But Wells matched her step once more, like they were doing some odd dance or like that bully on the playground who refused to let the kid he was tormenting get around him. To get away from him.

Michaela had learned long ago how to handle bullies, after growing up with one in her own house, as her father. She definitely could have gotten around the trooper, but she wouldn't put it past Wells to arrest her for assaulting an officer. And the doctor had just warned Michaela that she needed to get some rest. She doubted that a jail cell would be very comfortable for sleeping.

She wasn't even sure now where she was going to go to rest. Maybe she was tired, because the drive to St. Paul seemed too far right now. And the firehouse hadn't been particularly safe lately, even though Braden had confided to her that he'd installed some cameras inside and was going to add even more. It still made her uneasy to stay there. She could go back to the bar and to Charlie, but she wasn't likely to rest much if she went back to him. And last night, the bar hadn't been very safe either.

"Is there some reason you're not letting me leave?" Michaela asked the trooper.

Wells's face flushed slightly, making her skin just a soft pink instead of the translucent paleness it usually was, which was in stark contrast to the bright red hair that slipped out from beneath her hat. "I have some questions for you, Ms. Momber," the trooper said. "And I think you need to be aware of the danger you could be in…"

Michaela snorted and touched the bandage on her temple. "'Could'? No wonder the…" She stopped herself from saying the rest—that no wonder the saboteur hadn't been caught, especially since Wells clearly had no idea how much danger they were in. But was that the trooper's fault or the hotshots', since none of them could bring themselves to trust her with all the information they had?

Even now, Michaela couldn't bring herself to trust her. Wells's strange demeanor unsettled Michaela and sent that chill of uneasiness sliding down her spine.

"No wonder what?" Wells asked.

Michaela just shrugged. "I take it you haven't caught whoever slashed the tires and threw that bottle or broke into Charlie's bar last night?"

"That's kid stuff compared to…" And now the trooper trailed off.

Michaela didn't have to know what she'd stopped herself from saying to know that it was significant. "I'm not Brittney Townsend," Michaela said, referring to the ambitious reporter who was also Trent Miles's sister. She had exposed a couple of the hotshots' big secrets, but in the process, she'd fallen for Rory VanDam. "I'm not going to go public with whatever you tell me."

"It's going to get out soon anyway," the trooper said with a sigh. "The mayor is in the hospital."

Michaela nodded. "Charlie said he had a friend in the hospital."

"Are they friends?" Wells asked.

Thinking of all the times she'd personally seen Les Byers in the Filling Station, sitting at the bar and talking and laughing with Charlie, she nodded. "Yes, they are. Good friends."

No wonder Charlie had rushed off to the hospital like Will and the new bar manager said he had.

The trooper made a strange, almost disparaging, sound.

Michaela nearly sighed. "Why don't you think they are?" she asked.

"I'm just thinking of suspects, and Charlie Tillerman is the prime one in this since he's the one tapped to take over as the interim mayor now."

Michaela's head began to pound. Her weariness was definitely catching up with her. "Suspects for what? What are you talking about?"

"The mayor thinks he was poisoned. And even though we're still waiting on blood tests to confirm, the doctor thinks it's possible as well."

Michaela sucked in a breath. What the hell was going on in Northern Lakes? Under her breath, she muttered, "At least that has nothing to do with the hotshots."

"That remains to be seen," Wells remarked. Obviously, she'd heard Michaela.

"But if Charlie's your prime suspect—which is ridiculous, by the way—then this has nothing to do with the hotshots," Michaela pointed out. She couldn't think of any reason why anyone would hurt Les Byers, though. He was as revered in Northern Lakes as Charlie's grandfather had been—as Charlie himself was becoming.

Wells tilted her head and stared at Michaela as she asked, "Doesn't Tillerman want to become mayor so that he can get rid of the hotshots?"

That chill raced over Michaela again. Obviously, the trooper knew more than they'd suspected. Or she'd heard more somehow. "Did the mayor tell you that?" she asked. "And does he suspect Charlie of poisoning him? And do you know for certain if that even happened?"

"We're running tests to confirm his suspicion," she said. "And he doesn't suspect his friend. But…"

"You obviously do," Michaela said. "But you haven't even confirmed that any crime really happened to the mayor. He's an old man." Maybe he was getting dementia and that was why he believed he'd been poisoned.

But what if he was right and someone had wanted him out of the way?

She couldn't believe that would be Charlie. But what did she really know about the man who'd fathered her baby? They didn't talk nearly enough. Because every time they were alone, the passion between them overwhelmed her. And she hadn't really wanted to talk to him either. She hadn't wanted to open up about her past or even her present, not with the hotshots all under threat.

All she'd wanted was a break from the danger and the drama. But she'd wound up creating more for herself. She'd wound up creating a baby too. And now she had to protect that baby from the danger and the drama.

While eating her burger and fries, she'd done a little investigating of her own as Charlie slept. But he'd had nothing around his apartment that was in any way incriminating of anything. In fact, he hadn't had much at all around his place but his furniture and other essentials. That was probably because he'd lost everything in the fire.

"I've looked into Charlie Tillerman," the trooper confided. "He's not just the friendly local barkeep that his grandfather was or the dedicated town council member that his father was. Charlie was big in politics in Detroit. He has ambitions, Ms. Momber, and it doesn't seem like he's willing to let anything get in his way."

Michaela snorted now. "Ambitions? In Northern Lakes? If that's the case, why rebuild his bar after the fire? Why even keep it after he inherited it? Why wouldn't he take the money and go back to Detroit?"

"His marriage fell apart," the trooper said. "It was public and messy, and maybe he needed some time away for that bad press to die down. A way to rebuild his image like he rebuilt his bar after the fire."

Michaela shrugged off the trooper's suspicions and her words. "None of this has anything to do with me," she insisted. They weren't really even seeing each other. But they were going to have a child together.

If he wanted to be involved…

"I wouldn't be so sure about that," Wells said. "And you better make sure that Charlie Tillerman doesn't consider you in the way of what he wants…" Her green-eyed gaze flicked down Michaela, over the soft swell of her belly in that loose-fitting dress.

Michaela swallowed another groan. Despite all her best efforts to keep her life private, it didn't seem that anything ever stayed that way in Northern Lakes.

She was going to have to announce her pregnancy to more people than Braden and Charlie. She was going to have to tell the others.

Hank first, though.

Henrietta Rowlins was her best friend. And Michaela had a feeling she was going to need a friend, especially if Wells's suspicions about Charlie were correct. And if they were correct, she might need more than a friend.

Maybe a bodyguard.

But with everything that had been happening to the hotshots, she probably already needed a bodyguard. Not just for her life but also for her heart…

The vibrating cell had Trick's stomach muscles tightening with dread. What was it now?

Who was hurt?

It seemed like every time a call came in, it was bad news. Swallowing a groan, he rolled over in bed and reached across Henrietta toward the bedside table. Because they hadn't gotten much sleep the night before, they'd gone to bed early tonight. Not that they'd gotten much sleep yet.

In fact, they'd just fallen asleep when he heard the buzz

of the vibrating cell. But when he reached for his phone, he found it lying still beside Henrietta's. Hers was the one with the call coming in on it.

"Hey, sweetheart," he murmured. "It's your phone."

She groaned, then shot up in bed, suddenly wide awake, and concerned too. Her hand trembled as it closed around her phone. She glanced down at the screen, and her forehead furrowed with concern. "It's Michaela…"

The cell stopped moving then. She'd missed the call. But before Henrietta could call her back, a text lit up her screen. Can you pick me up?

"Maybe she just wants to go home," Henrietta murmured.

But Trick had a bad feeling.

Then Henrietta texted back: Where are you?

Three dots lit up the screen, but no words came. Then the phone vibrated again with Michaela's call.

"Where are you?" Henrietta asked as she answered.

And Michaela's reply confirmed Trick's bad feeling. "I'm at the hospital…"

What had happened now?

Chapter 11

"Some people" hadn't been just Bentley Ford and Jason Cruise. Charlie's instincts had been right about his sister and brother-in-law because they showed up at the bar, too, shortly after the town councilmen left. Too shortly after, because Charlie was still in the bar instead of where he wanted to be—looking for Michaela.

Had she gone back to the firehouse?

And which one? The one here in town or the one in St. Paul? She and Hank worked in St. Paul as firefighters when they weren't off with their hotshot crew, working wildfires all around the country and Canada too. She traveled a lot. Would she keep doing that? And for how long?

What about the baby?

He had so many questions he wanted to ask her, questions he should have asked her earlier. But she'd distracted him with her kisses, with her touching him…and he'd lost all control, as he always did around her.

Which was why they were having a baby…

But while he tried to get out the door, his niece and nephews wouldn't let him. They wanted to tell him about school and their sports and their friends. He loved them too much to brush them off, which was probably why Valerie had brought the kids for dinner with her and Eric, so he wouldn't ignore her like he wanted to.

Or so he wouldn't do what he really wanted to do, and that was tell her off, tell her to stay out of his life, that he didn't need his big sister meddling like she had in the past.

But she kept the kids around during dinner so that he couldn't do that. Then she must have decided that she wanted to talk, because she sent them and Eric off with a bunch of quarters to play the video games that were in the back room with the pool tables and dartboards.

"Were you serious earlier?" she asked, her voice a low and furious whisper. "Are you really having a baby with that female hotshot?"

Through nearly gritted teeth, he warned her, "Valerie…"

"What is it? Do you feel indebted to her because she pulled you out of the fire?" she asked. "You have to know that they were responsible for it."

He groaned. "The arsonist was responsible for setting my bar on fire," he said, repeating what he'd told her earlier. Then he glanced toward the back room, where Nicholas was playing a pinball game next to his younger brother, little Charlie—his namesake. Eric was teaching Olivia how to play pool. The teenager looked so much like her mother— like him—with her thick dark hair and dark eyes. Would his daughter look like him? Or like Michaela? And would she be as close to him as Olivia was to Eric? *Daddy's little girl*, Valerie called her, even now that Olivia was nearly as tall as he was.

Remembering what he'd been about to say, once he'd made sure Nicholas couldn't hear, he added, "And the arsonist was responsible for the fire near the Boy Scout campsite. Not Michaela. None of that was her fault."

Valerie sighed and shrugged. "It doesn't matter. She's still obviously in danger. She got hurt last night and got you hurt too."

"Again, she didn't throw the bottle at herself and me. She wasn't responsible. In fact, she pushed me back and probably saved me again from being hurt worse," he said. "And before you try blaming her for the break-in, too, that wasn't her fault either. She was with me, so she wasn't prying open the back door to the alley."

Valerie gasped. "Break-in? There was a break-in here? I don't ever remember anyone breaking in when Grandpa owned it."

He sighed. "Neither do I." That was why Charlie had been determined to keep the place like Grandpa had, free of cameras and security systems. But after last night, he'd finally conceded to Jerry, the bar manager, that it was time to get them installed. It was actually past time. And it was possible it had happened before and Grandpa hadn't told them. Grandpa had been independent. He liked to handle things on his own. Kind of like Michaela.

Did she think she was going to handle their child on her own? Was that her plan? To be a single mother? She'd said she didn't want child support from him. Or a commitment…

But she hadn't asked what he wanted. Maybe it didn't matter to her.

"Are you okay?" Valerie asked.

He nodded. "Yeah, though that's probably just because I didn't catch the guy I chased out of here."

Valerie reached out then and grabbed his arm. "You chased the robber out?"

"It was stupid." Mostly because he'd left Michaela behind and unprotected. That had been the stupidest thing he'd done, even stupider than the fact that he kept falling asleep and letting her slip away without having any idea where she was or if she was safe.

"Yes, it was stupid," Valerie said. "What is happening to Northern Lakes? We want to keep the town safe, a small town like it always was. But there's that nightclub on the outskirts of it and more cottages open for short-term rentals. And outsiders are taking over the town."

"Maybe you should run for mayor," he said.

She smiled. "Between raising three kids and working at my in-laws' trucking business with Eric? Yeah, I have all kinds of free time."

"Enough to get in my business," he said with a pointed glare.

"I'm sorry," she said. "I had no idea you were involved with anyone, let alone a hotshot. Why would you keep that from me?"

He sighed. "Because I didn't want *anyone* in my business. I had enough of that when I was in politics."

"I know," Valerie said. "But your opponents did you a favor, letting you know who and what your ex-wife really was."

"Yes, they probably did. But it was even more humiliating to find out that way."

"What do you know about this hotshot?"

Not enough. "We weren't serious," Charlie said. "That's another reason we weren't telling anyone."

"Well, I think it's serious now," she said.

But was it?

"You're having a baby together," Valerie said, and now she smiled. "That's wonderful. I was so disappointed when, during and after your first marriage, you said you weren't ever going to have kids. It would have been such a waste because you'll be a wonderful father."

He hoped so, and he hoped that Michaela would give him a chance to be a father. But if she didn't, he could force the issue, take her to court for visitation or custody. But he didn't want to force himself on her, he wanted her to want to co-parent with him. He wanted her to want him in her life.

And for her to be in his. But was that safe for either of them? Physically or emotionally?

"I didn't mean to worry you," Michaela said. She suspected Hank had broken every speed limit between her cottage and Northern Lakes Memorial Hospital with as quickly as her truck appeared at the curb outside the lobby doors.

"Are you all right? Why are you here?" Hank asked. "Did something else happen?"

Michaela shook her head. "No. Like I told you when you finally picked up your phone, I'm fine."

"Then what are you doing here? Just getting your stitches checked?" Her dark-eyed gaze slid to Michaela's arm and the bandage in the crook of her elbow. "You needed blood tests? Are you okay?"

She was better than the mayor, according to Trooper Wells. But she wasn't entirely certain she believed her. Who would have poisoned sweet Les Byers, and why?

"I'm fine, really," she insisted. She drew in a deep breath, bracing herself to make the announcement. Then she released the breath, which was ragged now, and said, "I'm just pregnant."

Hank laughed. "Yeah, that's funny, smart-ass."

"I'm serious."

"You must have a concussion," Hank said, and her smile slipped away now. "You told me you can't get pregnant. And even if you could, how the hell did it happen? Immaculate conception?"

Michaela laughed. "No, definitely not that." Even now, her body hummed with the pleasure Charlie had given her.

Fortunately, the doctor had confirmed that sex was not going to affect her pregnancy. In fact, there'd even been some talk of it helping right before delivery or something. Her face heated with the embarrassment she'd felt then, talking so frankly with the doctor.

And probably needlessly. She really shouldn't keep seeing Charlie, for so many reasons. She was getting too addicted to him, to being with him. And she knew better than to trust him not to lose interest in her, like Phil had lost interest. She'd made a mistake with her first husband, just like her mom had made a mistake with her dad. And that mistake had been much worse than Michaela's. Good judgment definitely didn't run in her family, so it was better not to risk falling in love.

Hank reached across the console and grabbed her shoulder. "Who is it? Who are you seeing?" Then her eyes widened. "Oh my God, it's Charlie. Charlie Tillerman."

Michaela nodded.

And now moisture rushed to Hank's dark eyes, but she blinked it away. "Why didn't you tell me that you were seeing him?" she asked, her voice cracking with emotion.

A pang struck Michaela's heart, too, as she felt like she'd betrayed her best friend. "It wasn't really anything…"

"You made a baby with him," Hank said as if awed.

"But I didn't think that could happen," Michaela reminded her. "And it was just this dumb thing…"

"He always flirted with you, but you seemed more annoyed by that than taken in," Hank said. "I thought he reminded you of your ex."

She cringed at the thought of Charlie being anything like him. He seemed like such an honest person, but he hadn't told her everything that Trooper Wells just had.

"I don't know what I was thinking…" When she'd re-sisted him or when she'd given in to her attraction to him.

"I just wish you would have told me," Hank said, still seeming hurt.

"Like you and Trick didn't keep your relationship a se-cret in the beginning?"

"Trick and I weren't supposed to have a relationship. It was against Braden's rules, until you all lobbied to change them," Hank reminded her. "There's no rule against *you* having a relationship."

"But there is," Michaela said. "My rule."

Unamused, Hank frowned. "You can't keep using your failed marriage as an excuse to not give anyone else a chance. Not every man is a dick like your ex."

"More men than you'd think," Michaela mused.

Hank shook her head. "I know more good men than bad. My grandfather. Even my ex-fiancé. And all the members on our team, Michaela."

But Michaela shook her head then. "No. One of those members might be the saboteur."

"Or the saboteur could be someone else entirely."

"Charlie," Michaela said. "That's who some of the team has suspected. And Trooper Wells is suspicious of him too."

"Is that why you didn't tell anyone that you were see-ing him?" Hank asked, and her voice cracked again with the question, betraying her hurt. "Do you have your doubts about him?"

"I have doubts about me," Michaela said. "I don't have the greatest judgment when it comes to men, especially charming men. But I don't agree with Trooper Wells that he had anything to do with the hotshot sabotage or the mayor's poisoning."

Hank gasped, and her eyes widened with shock. "The mayor was poisoned?"

"I don't know for sure. That's what he's claiming," she said.

"And he claims it was Charlie?"

Michaela shook her head. "Oh, no, not at all. Trooper Wells—"

"Of course Trooper Wells would try to pin it on someone who's close to a hotshot," Hank said. "She's probably framing you as an accomplice."

"That would be crazy even for her," Michaela said. "I barely know the mayor or Trooper Wells. I don't know what anyone would have against me. Not even this damn saboteur. Unless..."

"Unless what?"

"It's someone trying to point out that I don't belong as a hotshot." And now she was going to have to take medical leave. Her doctor had warned her that it was just too risky for her pregnancy, with as far along as she was now and with being anemic, to battle any big blazes.

"You're one of the best hotshots on the team," Hank said. "One of the strongest and the hardest working. Don't let some occasional misogynistic comments from some of the guys bring you down."

Michaela squared her shoulders. "You know me better than that. They don't hurt my feelings."

Hank chuckled. "No. They piss you off and make you even more determined to show them up."

"What's wrong with that?" Michaela asked.

"I wish you didn't care what they thought," Hank said. "That you didn't let their comments affect you one way or the other. That you were confident in who you are and that was all that matters."

Michaela flinched like Hank had struck her. Sometimes her best friend was too insightful. She released a shaky breath. "Well, I thought you would understand."

"I do," Hank said. "I get it. Sam McRooney-Zimmer gets it. Trent's new girlfriend—the detective, Heather—gets it. We've all had to deal with chauvinists in our chosen professions. But we shouldn't let them affect how well we do our job or why we do our job. We should just be doing it because we love it. No other reason."

Michaela might have flinched again, but she was too stunned to feel whether her face moved. Had she chosen her profession just to get back at her dad?

Was she more concerned with proving herself strong enough and smart enough that she wasn't doing what she loved just because she loved it?

What did she love?

She felt that flutter inside her and pressed her hand to her belly as warmth flooded her heart. She knew what she loved: her daughter. To protect her, she would have to take that leave, and maybe while she was off, she could figure out if she wanted to go back.

Like right now, she couldn't figure out if she wanted to go back to Charlie.

"Where do you want me to take you?" Hank asked. "St. Paul?"

Michaela shook her head. "I need to get my truck tires fixed so I have it up there with me."

"Trick told me that Braden and Stanley were working on getting the ones repaired that could be repaired and the ones replaced that had to be replaced," Hank said. "Yours might be ready to go." She pulled away from the hospital then, heading toward town.

And if the truck wasn't ready to go, Michaela would

just stay at the firehouse until it was fixed. She couldn't go back to Charlie's place right now, since she was a little embarrassed over how she'd pounced on him earlier. She was also a little afraid—not because of Trooper Wells's suspicions of him, but because Michaela was starting to care about him more than she wanted to, more than it was safe for her to care about anyone.

Tillerman was going to be a problem. In more ways than one. And problems had to be dealt with in the only way that made sure they never became a problem again. They had to be permanently eliminated.

And as soon as the bar cleared out and Tillerman was alone, he would be eliminated.

Chapter 12

Charlie hadn't intended to fall asleep again, but he'd had another long day. With getting called to the hospital, with Michaela, with the councilmen and his family...

But because of Michaela, he wanted to stay awake, in case she came back. Or maybe he should go out to find her and make sure she was safe.

In order to protect her, though, he needed to be more alert than he currently was. So after closing down the bar and going upstairs, he intended to shower—probably in frigid cold water—to wake himself up. But once he was in his bedroom, he couldn't stop himself from dropping down onto the bed. The sheets were still tangled from their earlier adventure, and they smelled like Michaela. Sweet. Musky. Sexy.

He breathed in deep and closed his eyes. He should get up. He needed to get up. But it was as if the air was heavy or something, like it was weighing him down, smothering him... And he could hear some kind of beeping noise, like a fire alarm.

But there was no smoke. No flames. No heat.

It wasn't like last time. But he awoke the same way he had in the fire, with Michaela standing over him, peering down into his face while she lightly rocked his chin back and forth in a tight grip. Unlike last time, she was wearing a mask, but she pulled it aside to yell at him. "Charlie, Charlie!" She coughed. "You have to wake up!"

Even his dream knew he was dreaming…

He smiled at her. "I want to go back to sleep," he murmured, his words slurring like he'd been drinking. But he couldn't remember the last time he'd even had a drink. So that wasn't the case.

He had to be just dreaming. That was the only way she would have stayed with him—in his dreams.

"No, no, you have to stay awake." She coughed again. "Someone tampered with the gas. This place is full of fumes. You have to get out of here."

The gas.

That was the reason for that heaviness, the reason he felt like he was suffocating.

She smacked him lightly on the face, but he felt the sting against his skin. "Come on, Charlie. You have to help me. I don't think I can carry you this time." She started coughing again.

And he woke up more. She was pregnant. She shouldn't be inhaling the gas. She shouldn't be trying to save him again. He should be trying to save *her*.

But when he tried to stand up, his legs folded beneath him, and his consciousness began to slip away. He had to stay awake, though. He had to help her and their baby so that they could all get out. Otherwise, they all might die.

Especially if someone tossed a burning bottle into the bar like the bottle that had been thrown at them the other night.

If the flame hit the fumes, the whole place would blow up. And there would be less to salvage than last time the bar had caught on fire.

He and Michaela and their child would have nothing left to salvage. Not even their lives…

* * *

Michaela didn't know why she had come back to the Filling Station. She'd had Hank drop her back at the firehouse. But even though her truck had been sitting in the lot, with newly inflated or replaced tires, she was reluctant to make the drive home. There were no cameras in St. Paul, like the ones Braden had had installed inside the firehouse. Figuring she would be safer here, she'd gone up to the bunkroom with the intention of getting some rest. But she'd tossed and turned, unable to sleep even though she had the entire room to herself.

Nobody else was staying there. But after what had happened to Rory and then the Molotov cocktail thrown at her, she understood why everyone else would be reluctant to spend the night at the firehouse. But Braden and Trick had sworn that it would be safe, that they were keeping watch on the place through the video feed. Nothing else would happen there. But that was probably because nobody else was there for it to happen to...

Unless the saboteur was specifically targeting just her now, but she doubted that. Anyone could have come out the side door of the firehouse that night. And the bottle hadn't been thrown until Charlie had joined her. Then his bar had been broken into shortly after that attack.

It certainly seemed like he was the target now. That this was all about him and not the hotshots. She should have felt safer then, but thinking about him being in danger made her more restless and uneasy. And if the mayor really had been poisoned, it was serious danger. Someone could try to kill Charlie next.

And there was no one keeping watch on the bar for him, no one protecting him. Panic pressed on her lungs, and she jumped up. She couldn't sleep while thinking he was in danger. She had to make sure that he was okay. And she should ask him some questions, try to find out if he had any enemies, anyone who might be specifically targeting him like so many of the hotshots had been specifically targeted. But as determined as she was to get to the truth, she had to wonder what kind of investigator she would be.

And maybe she was just using checking on him as an excuse to leave the quiet bunkroom because she felt so alone. The last time she'd felt like that, she'd sought out Charlie, that first night they'd slept together.

Thankful that her truck was fixed, she quickly headed to the bar again. It was nearly 3:00 a.m., so it was closed. But there was light behind the blinds on the windows on the second story. He must have been awake. So she texted him. Then she called, but his phone went directly to voice mail.

Had he fallen so deeply asleep with the lights on that he hadn't heard his phone? Or was he just ignoring her?

Maybe he didn't want to have that conversation about the future any more than she did. She didn't want to have the fights her parents had rehashed so many years after her mom's unexpected pregnancy with her. She didn't want to fight with Charlie at all, she just wanted to see him, to ask him those questions about himself, about his enemies, but mostly to make sure he was okay.

Because she had that panicky feeling, especially when she went around back, to the door to the alley that hadn't been replaced yet. Someone had gotten inside once. It could have happened again.

He could be hurt.

She drew in a deep breath, trying to calm her nerves. And she smelled it: gas. She could even hear it whistling out of the line that went through the wall and into the furnace in the utility room on the main floor. She could also hear the faint whine of an alarm, maybe coming from a carbon monoxide detector in his apartment. Hadn't he heard it?

Maybe he had and he'd already left. Or maybe the gas had already gotten to him.

She had to get in there to make sure that he wasn't still inside. So she pounded harder with one hand while she used her cell with the other.

"What's going on?" Braden's voice emanated from her phone's speaker.

"There's a gas leak at the Filling Station," she said. "I need to get inside and make sure that Charlie's all right."

"You don't have a key?"

It was a fair assumption, given their situation, but she'd refused to take the one that Charlie had tried to give her. She hadn't wanted that whole awkward "can I have my key back" conversation when their passion fizzled out and they ended their…whatever it was. Now she wished she had one, because she was going to have to break down the door.

While she didn't have a key, she did have some of her firefighter equipment in the back of her truck. Like an axe. And her oxygen mask.

"No, I don't have a key. You need to hurry." But as she disconnected the call, she hurried to where she'd parked her truck in the alley and pulled out her gear. Then she focused on that door again. While there was a new board in the jamb, the door itself still looked warped and bent, not fitting tightly in the new wood. Obviously, he hadn't been able to replace it yet.

That was a good thing. She didn't even need the axe, she was able to kick it open, almost too easily, and she realized that someone else might have done the same thing earlier, when they'd gone inside to mess with the gas line. They'd probably only shut it again to keep the gas closed in, so she left the door open. But there were no windows that opened on the main level, so she didn't step inside until she'd strapped on the oxygen tank and covered her face with the mask. She had to protect the baby.

And now she had to find the baby's father and make sure he was safe.

She headed first toward the furnace, trying to find the gas line to shut it off. But it had been taken apart from the furnace, the same way the carbon monoxide sensor had also been taken apart. She couldn't find a shut-off valve for the gas line, but she wasted no more time looking for it. She had to find Charlie.

Grateful for the oxygen, she hurried up the stairs to his apartment. Fortunately, he hadn't locked the stairwell door tonight.

Maybe the gas line had already been leaking before he'd gone up. But she didn't find him in his living room. He was lying across his bed, fully clothed, as if he'd passed out before he'd been able to undress.

Was he just unconscious?

Her eyes burned, but since she had on the oxygen mask, it wasn't necessarily from the gas. She was scared, too, more scared than she'd been since she was a kid growing up in that house of constant arguments and fits of rage. She'd felt so helpless back then.

But she wasn't helpless anymore. She'd saved Charlie once, she had to be able to save him this time too. She couldn't be too late. Their daughter could not grow up without ever meeting her father. Pulling aside her mask, she yelled, "Wake up!"

He moved slightly and pried open his eyes. He stared up at her like he had that day in the fire in his bar, like he didn't think she was real. Then his lids dropped over his eyes again, like they were too heavy for him to lift.

They weren't the only thing that might be too heavy to lift right now. Despite the iron infusion and the food, she was still tired. Still weaker than she'd been, just like the doctor had warned her. She wasn't sure she could carry him out like she had that day from the flames.

Pulling aside her mask again, she yelled, "Wake up, Charlie!" And she lightly tapped his face, her hand shaking with fear. Then she moved her mask to his face, trying to get him some oxygen to rouse him. There was so much gas that she was as afraid for herself and for her baby as she was for him now. Because, in just that short time she'd tried to revive him, she could feel her head getting lighter and her limbs heavier. She quickly fixed the mask on her face again.

The levels were getting lethal. And Charlie had probably breathed in so much already, which was why he wasn't responding to the oxygen she'd given him. And she needed it now for herself and for her baby. She had to get him out of the apartment now, or she was going to lose him.

Here he was again, pacing the damn floor of the ER waiting room. Braden spent entirely too much time in this place. And the last two times had been because of Michaela.

She had to be okay. If only she had waited for him and Trick…

Then Charlie would have been dead for certain. Owen had said that when he'd shown up in the alley behind the Filling Station in his paramedic rig. Then he'd loaded up both Charlie and Michaela and gotten them the hell out of there because the whole area had been toxic.

And if someone had struck a match…

More than the Filling Station probably would have gone up. They could have lost half the block.

Trick had stayed back at the scene to oversee the situation so that wouldn't happen. He was making sure the gas got shut off and that the fumes dissipated enough so that the area would be safe again. And while he was doing that, they'd had the police evacuating people from all the residences and businesses in the vicinity.

The police.

Braden's stomach knotted over how much this scenario reminded him of how he'd nearly lost Owen. Someone had tampered with the gas line in his house just like this. But instead of being connected to the furnace like Charlie's, it had been the gas line to his water heater.

Supposedly, it had been Dirk Brown's widow trying to kill Owen because she thought he might have overheard something that would have incriminated her in her husband's murder. She'd wound up incriminating herself, though.

Braden had always wondered if it had actually been Luanne Brown's lover who'd messed with Owen's gas line to try to kill him. Luanne's lover, Sergeant Marty Gingrich, was behind bars now, and Luanne Brown was dead. So neither of them was responsible for what had happened tonight.

But what if...

He glanced up as Trooper Wynona Wells strode into the lobby through the automatic doors. What if she had been helping or at least covered up Gingrich's involvement in that attempt on Owen's life? Then maybe she had restaged the same event tonight.

But why? Why copycat the things that had already happened, unless maybe the would-be killer/saboteur was repeating things they'd already done.

But what could the trooper's motive be? What could she have against Charlie and Michaela?

Or was her motive the same as Luanne's and she thought

Charlie and Michaela had seen or heard something that they hadn't? Maybe that was why his bar had been broken into after the incident in the parking lot. Maybe they were worried that Charlie and Michaela had heard them or seen them. Or her...

If Trooper Wells wasn't the person behind the attempt tonight, someone else might have that same motive for going after them. Or maybe this person had no reason at all for any of the things they did.

Braden had learned over the years that some people were just bad.

Like the saboteur...

Was he or she behind this as well? But had the attempt been on Charlie's life or on Michaela's?

And maybe it hadn't been just an attempt. Maybe they had actually succeeded. Thanks to the oxygen she'd had with her, Michaela had been conscious when they'd shown up at the bar, but she'd dragged a completely unconscious Charlie from upstairs and had obviously exhausted and maybe hurt herself or her baby.

Since arriving at the hospital, they'd been back in the ER for a while now, with no one coming out to give word of their condition.

Were they both okay?

Was Michaela's baby okay?

Because Braden had been able to tell that no matter how surprised she'd been with her pregnancy, she was also happy. Maybe happier than he'd ever seen Michaela. As well as more scared than he'd ever seen her.

Michaela Momber was one of his toughest—if not *the* toughest—hotshot on his team. But he wasn't sure if she would survive if her baby didn't...

Chapter 13

Charlie awoke with a start and an urgency gripping him. He jumped up—or tried to—but something was clasped over his nose and mouth. He reached up to knock it off but realized it was an oxygen mask like the one that Michaela had kept putting over his mouth when she had needed it more.

He remembered that, remembered her being with him... in that... Or had he just dreamed she was there?

Was she here now? He peered around, but the bright lights blinded him for a moment. He was in the hospital again. The last thing he remembered clearly was going to sleep at home after lying across his bed. He'd just intended to lie there for a minute before he showered and went look-ing for Michaela. But then he remembered Michaela being there, trying to wake him up, trying to get him out.

Gas.

There had definitely been a gas leak. He drew in a deep breath of pure oxygen and tried to calm himself. But the panic pressed harder on his lungs.

Michaela.

And the baby...

He dragged off the mask. "Michaela..." He'd intended to yell her name, but it came out as a faint rasp. His head pounded as if he'd shouted, as if he was hungover. But he'd had nothing to drink the night before or for a while. The gas leak must have left him feeling this way—groggy, with a headache and a dry mouth.

He shook his head, trying to clear it so that he could focus more.

"Sit back. Rest," a woman urged him. It wasn't Michaela or even a nurse. His sister sat beside his bed, her face pale and pinched with concern. She stood up and tried to pull the mask over his face again, but he kept his hand up, fending her off. "You need this."

He shook his head again. "I need Michaela..."

She let out a shaky sigh. "Oh my God, can't you see how bad she is for you? She's brought nothing but danger into your life! All the hotshots have."

"She saved my life again," he said. "I would have *no* life if it wasn't for her." She was his angel. But God, he hoped she hadn't become one. "Where is she? I have to make sure she and the baby are okay."

If something had happened to them because she'd been trying to save him...

Valerie closed her eyes for a moment, then opened them with tears still brimming at their edges. "The baby..." She nodded. "I'll find out where she is." She pushed back the heavy curtain and stepped out, pulling it shut behind her, probably hoping that he would fall asleep again.

But he wouldn't be able to rest until he knew how Michaela was. How their baby girl was...

He swung his legs over the side of the gurney, intent on getting up and finding her himself. Then that heavy curtain moved again.

But it wasn't Valerie who stepped back into the small

ER bay with him. It was Michaela, her face pale, with dark circles beneath her beautiful blue eyes.

He rushed over to her and cupped her face in his shaking hands. "Are you all right? What are you doing up?" She needed a gurney and oxygen.

While he just needed…her.

"I'm fine," she said. Then she focused on his face, staring intently at him, and added, "And because I had my oxygen tank with me, the baby is too."

He released a shaky breath of relief. "Thank God."

"You do want her?" she asked.

"Oh my God, yes," he said, surprised she hadn't realized that. But he had been trying to be so careful with Michaela because he hadn't wanted to pressure her or overwhelm her that he might not have made his feelings clear. The baby wasn't all he wanted either. But he was well aware that Michaela didn't want anything serious, because she had made her feelings very clear from the beginning of whatever this was between them.

After his disastrous first marriage, he'd thought that was what he wanted, too, in the beginning—nothing serious. Just *her* for however long she was interested. And for however long that was, he wouldn't have to just dream about the angel who'd saved his life. He'd have her in reality.

But now it wasn't just her. She was carrying their child too.

"Are you sure you're both all right?" he asked. "Shouldn't you be getting oxygen, too, or an IV or something?"

Her lips curved into a slight smile, and she shook her head. "No. I'm fine. I had the oxygen mask on—"

"You kept putting it on me, I think…" he said, trailing off as he tried to remember.

"When I had it off, I tried not to inhale. And fortunately,

the bar is so big that your apartment hadn't filled up too much, just enough to knock you out but not kill you."

"But it would have," he suspected. "If you hadn't shown up and saved me again. Thank you, Michaela."

She shrugged off his gratitude, as she always did. "We really have to figure out who the hell is messing with us."

"Messing with us, or just me?" he wondered aloud. And if that was the case, then he was the one putting her in danger. So he couldn't tell her that he felt more than gratitude for her. Not now...

She stepped back so that his hands dropped to his sides. She studied him intently as she asked, "But why would anyone mess with you? Do you have some enemy from your past, someone who might want revenge on you? Or maybe someone who wants to intimidate you?"

He hated to think that anyone was after him, but that gas line hadn't broken on its own, not after being so recently replaced after the fire. "The mayor thinks..." He couldn't even repeat what the mayor thought, especially if it was just a delusion. But after tonight, that probably wasn't the case.

"That someone poisoned him," Michaela finished for him.

"You already heard?"

"Trooper Wells let me know," she said.

"It's true, then?" he asked, panic gripping him. "Les really was poisoned?" And if that was the case, then whoever had tampered with his gas line had probably intended to do more than intimidate Charlie. His knees wobbled a bit with the realization that someone was trying to kill him.

"I don't know if she got the test results back to confirm what it was, but the doctor believes that something must have been slipped to him too."

Here Charlie had thought his older friend might be getting dementia. He felt a stab of guilt over that, but that had been easier to believe than someone trying to kill such a good man.

"But if the mayor was poisoned, whoever did it must have set their sights on you next," Michaela continued. "But of course, you're Trooper Wells's number one suspect."

He groaned. "And why the hell would I poison my friend and myself with that gas leak?"

"Because you want the mayor's job," she said. "You're a cutthroat politician."

"So Wells checked into my past," he murmured.

Michaela tensed. "It's true, then?"

He chuckled. "*I* was never cutthroat," he said. "That was more like the other way around. My throat got cut, and I think my ex was the one holding the switchblade."

"What? She helped your competitor?"

He nodded. "By cheating and embezzling money, and nobody could believe that I didn't know. Maybe it was better they thought I was complicit than the idiot that I was."

She sighed. "It's not hard to be stupid when it comes to relationships."

He would have asked if she was talking about theirs, but he was pretty sure that, despite her pregnancy, she didn't consider them to be in a relationship. "Your ex?"

"He probably had a thing with your ex," she joked. "And I just thought he was being supportive of my career, that it never bothered him when I was gone and he was alone at home. But the thing was that he was never really alone."

"I'm sorry." He knew how devastating that was to a person's heart and to their self-esteem. The realization that they weren't enough.

She shrugged. "He blamed me for being gone and for never giving him a child."

He sighed. "My ex did the same. Said I wasn't giving her

what she wanted. That I hadn't kept the promises I made when we were college kids, dreaming big about our future."

"Dreams don't always come true," she murmured.

"No," he agreed. But his dream about her coming to rescue him had. Once again…

But at what cost?

"Or sometimes, they become nightmares," she added.

He realized then that they were both as wounded emotionally as they'd been physically over the past couple of days. And the physical injuries were easier to treat and heal.

Well, they would be, as long as nothing else happened to them, as long as they weren't hurt again worse than they'd already been.

Michaela's conversation with Charlie was cut short in the ER. His sister returned with the doctor, who decided to admit them overnight in order to monitor their oxygen levels. Though Michaela had the oxygen tank and mask, she'd kept putting it over Charlie's mouth, trying to revive him. He'd come around enough to help her get him down the stairs, but she was still afraid that she might have over-exerted herself. And maybe Dr. Smits had seen how scared and exhausted Michaela was, and that was why she'd decided to admit her, along with Charlie. Dr. Smits had also told his sister to leave and had held Trooper Wells off from taking their statements.

So Michaela actually awoke rested, with a clear head, until she noticed Charlie asleep in the chair next to her bed. Then feelings clouded her head and her heart, overwhelming her. He looked so uncomfortable, with his neck at an odd angle as his hand held up his head. He was going to be sore. But he'd inconvenienced himself to watch over her, to take care of her.

He shifted then, and a groan slipped through his lips before he opened his eyes. Their gazes met and held, and something shifted inside her. The baby…

"What are you doing here?" she asked.

"The doctor didn't want us to leave," he reminded her.

She smiled and shook her head. "Not that. What are you doing in here with me when you should be in your own bed, sleeping?"

He shrugged and grimaced as his cramped muscles protested the movement. "I just wanted to make sure nothing else happened to you."

"My bodyguard," she said with a smile.

He groaned again. "Some bodyguard. I fell asleep."

"You needed the rest, but I'm not sure you got much in that chair," she said.

"I was out cold last night when you saved me," he said. "Again. Thank you."

"I was just doing my job," she said.

"The first time," he said. "But last night…? Why did you come by?"

"Trooper Wells told me about the mayor, and I just couldn't sleep without checking on you." If she hadn't done that, he would be dead. The thought squeezed her heart so tightly that she flinched at the pain.

He jerked forward in his chair. "Are you all right?"

She wasn't, but she nodded. "Yeah, I must have just slept wrong too," she muttered. Or maybe it had been wrong to sleep at all, considering the threat to his life. And to hers?

"I'm glad you got some rest," he said, and he rubbed his neck. "You've been through so much, Michaela."

She groaned with regret. "I shouldn't have told you about my ex."

"I'm glad you did, but I wasn't even talking about him,"

he said. "I was talking about what's happened the past couple of days. The danger that you've been in."

"You've been through that too," she said.

He nodded. "I know. And I feel like *I'm* the one putting you in danger."

"That's not what your sister thinks," she said with a smile.

He sighed. "My sister is overly protective of me."

"Given what's happened to you since you came back to Northern Lakes, I can understand why she would think you need protection."

"I've had protection," he said, and he smiled too. "I've had you."

And that smile of his, which lit up his dark eyes, had her heart doing somersaults the same way their daughter must have been. She had that fluttery feeling again and pressed her hand over her stomach.

His eyes widened. "Can you feel her?"

"I don't know if you can on the outside yet," she said. "But I can feel her moving on the inside…like I swallowed butterflies…" But her stomach moved just then beneath her hand. She gasped.

"You felt her?"

She reached over the railing of her bed and took his hand, then she pressed it over her stomach. "Can you feel her?" she asked.

His dark eyes widened as her belly shifted beneath his palm. "Wow…" Then he looked up at her and murmured, "Wow…" again.

She cocked her head. "What?"

"I just… I can tell how you feel about her already," he said, "from the look that comes over your face. But I didn't know, with the career you've chosen, if you really wanted kids. When you told me you couldn't get pregnant, I didn't get the impression that you wanted to."

She remembered all too well that hollow ache she'd had for so long, that emptiness that was filled now. "It's easy to say that you don't want what you think you can't have..."

"Does that only apply to children?" he asked.

"I don't know what you mean," she said.

Was he wondering if she'd said she didn't want a relationship because she didn't think she could have one?

She knew that was the case, though. So few hotshot relationships, including her first marriage, survived.

Until recently. Now she knew a lot of people who were making it work. But that didn't mean that it wasn't without work. And without risk...

And she'd already taken too many risks. She wasn't sure she was strong enough to take a risk with her heart, especially on a man who was already in danger.

Before he could answer her, the door to her room opened, and the trooper stepped inside. With the dark circles beneath Wells's eyes being the only color on her pale skin, she looked like she hadn't slept at all.

Had she been waiting for them to wake up to question them or to try again to get rid of them? Because Michaela still had an uneasiness around the trooper. She wasn't entirely sure that Wynona Wells wasn't the threat to their lives. Or just to Charlie's?

But why?

Unless she was like that FBI agent who'd tried to kill Rory VanDam and her only motive for murder was money. But what did someone have to gain by getting Charlie out of the way? Michaela wanted to ask him that but not in front of someone she considered a suspect.

* * *

They had refused to let her question them separately since they both claimed they had nothing to hide and no secrets. Wynona doubted that. Everyone had secrets.

Even her.

"So you both saw nothing?" she asked with obvious skepticism. "Just like the other night?"

They nodded in unison.

"And you have no idea who could be after you?" she asked.

The female hotshot gave her a pointed look, while the bartender glanced off to the side, as if he was looking at imaginary suspects. "Who?" she asked him.

He shrugged. "I just… You know about the mayor…"

"Yes, I intend to ask you about that too."

"I know," he said. "You think I poisoned him for a job I'm not even sure I want."

She resisted the urge to snort. "You don't want it?"

"Not like Bentley Ford and Jason Cruise want it."

Wynona repeated back the names as if she was unfamiliar with them, even though she was very well aware who both of them were.

Michaela Momber gave her a skeptical look. The female hotshot wasn't fooled. "I live in St. Paul, and I know who they are. Ford owns most of this part of the state, and Jason is on every billboard in the area, plus every restaurant menu, place mat and refrigerator magnet."

Wynona had one of those refrigerator magnets herself. But she just shrugged. "What about them?"

"Bentley wants the mayor job to stop development and keep the hotshot headquarters close enough for them to protect his properties and his trees," Tillerman replied. "And Jason wants the job so he can develop everything that Bentley doesn't own. And they were both in my bar yesterday."

"I find it hard to see either of them tampering with your gas line," she said.

"So you do know who they are," Michaela said. "Then you must know that both of them are rich enough to hire some- one to do their dirty work for them." She gave Wynona a pointed look, like she suspected she could be on one of their payrolls—or both.

Wynona knew that she was in over her head with *every- thing*. And she wasn't sure how to handle *any* of it.

"What I do know is that you're both in danger," Wynona said.

The woman shivered then and nodded. "Yeah, we're well aware of that."

"You need to be careful," she warned them. "And trust no one. Maybe not even each other."

Tillerman shook his head as if disgusted with her while the female hotshot said, "Not even you."

"I'm trying to help you," she insisted.

Michaela snorted again.

Tillerman remarked, "Sounds like you're trying to scare us."

"You should be scared," she pointed out. "You both could have been killed last night."

And she doubted that *whoever* had made that attempt was going to stop until they succeeded.

Chapter 14

For the first time since the fire, the Filling Station was closed for the day and the night. Until the gas line could be repaired and the new security system and back door installed, Charlie didn't want to take any chances with his employees', his customers' and his own damn safety.

He could have died.

And Michaela and their baby could have died too.

He especially didn't want to take any chances with her safety. "I'm just going to grab some things," he said as he led the way up the stairwell to his bedroom. "But we shouldn't stay here."

"Why do you think *we* are going to stay anywhere?" she asked with an edge to her voice.

He had assumed that they would stick together. Maybe he shouldn't have, but he wanted to keep her safe. "Are you taking Trooper Wells seriously?" he asked. "You don't trust me?"

"I don't trust anyone," she said as if he shouldn't take it personally.

"Is that because of your ex?" he asked. He could relate to that. He never should have trusted his.

She let out a soft gasp, maybe surprised that he would bring up her ex, but then she shrugged. "Partly. But also because of everything that has been happening…"

"I've really had nothing to do with any of this," he assured her. And he hoped that she knew him better than to think he was the overly ambitious, cutthroat politician Wells had painted him to be.

Michaela nodded. "I know you didn't tamper with your own gas line. You could have died." Her voice cracked slightly, as if the thought of that bothered her.

What bothered him was that she could have died too. "But if you are in danger because of me, maybe it would be better for you to stay away from me."

She nodded. "It probably would be better for me, if we knew for certain that *you* were the target of all of these things that have happened. But everything is so random—the firehouse incident and then the break-in at your bar... and now that gas-line thing, which is similar to what happened to Owen James not that long ago." She shrugged again. "Some of these things feel like what the saboteur has been pulling on the hotshots."

"I heard about the saboteur," he said. "That some of the things that have been happening to the hotshots weren't all caused by the people who've been arrested."

"No, somebody is still out there messing with us," she admitted, "which is who I thought was responsible for what happened in the parking lot. But the saboteur would have no reason to go after you..."

"Unless they overheard me and Eric talking like you did," he said. "Maybe they don't want their favorite targets moved out of town."

"Or maybe the saboteur is one of us," she said. "But the thought of that makes me sick, which is why I didn't realize I was pregnant. I just figured I had an ulcer from all of this...danger and drama."

Concern gripped him, making him even more determined to protect her. "That is too much danger for you, especially now."

She sighed. "Because I'm pregnant?"

"Because I don't want you getting hurt," he said. "We have to figure out who's behind everything that's been happening, even if the things that have happened, like the parking lot thing and the gas-line leak, aren't related."

She nodded. "I agree. We have to figure out if we're dealing with one person who's after you and another who's after the hotshots. Braden is working hard on figuring out who the saboteur is. But *we* need to figure out if that's the same person who's after you or if there is someone else after you because of what's happened to the mayor."

"Trooper Wells certainly isn't much help," Charlie said, still frustrated that the way she'd taken their statement had felt more like an interrogation. "She can't figure out if we're victims or suspects."

"Then it's mutual," Michaela said. "I can't figure out if she's an officer of the law or an instrument of evil."

He chuckled. "That's a little dramatic."

She flinched. "I hate that…"

"What?"

"Being called *dramatic* because I'm a woman," she said, her voice sharp with bitterness and indignation.

"If you were a man and said that, I would have made the same remark," he assured her. "But I'm sorry that I said it to you. I can tell that I hit a nerve. The ex again?"

She shook her head. "*He* never said that to me."

"A different ex?"

"My dad," she said, her voice a bit gruff with emotion. "He was not happy that his only child was an overly dramatic little girl."

He sucked in a breath at the wealth of bitterness in her tone. "I'm sorry, Michaela."

She pressed her palms over her stomach, as if she had to protect their unborn child from him. "Please tell me that you won't do that to her."

"Do what?"

"Make her feel less than."

Like her dad had obviously made her feel. His heart ached for her and for their daughter, and he reached out, closing his arms around her. Against her soft hair, he murmured, "I am so sorry."

But she pushed him back slightly, her palms on his chest, and stared up at him. "Promise me," she said, her face tense and her blue eyes glistening with vulnerability.

He wished he could go back in her past and fix everything that had gone wrong for her. Everything that had hurt her.

Because Michaela Momber had definitely not had an easy life. It was all there in her eyes and her voice. The pain she'd suffered because of the men who had been supposed to love her the most.

How had her father and her ex-husband not appreciated the incredibly strong human that she was?

"I promise you that I will do everything I can to encourage our daughter and reinforce how amazing she is, whoever and whatever she becomes," he said. "But she will have no doubts. She'll know, because of her strong mama, that she is strong too. And she already is…"

Their daughter had already been through so much, and she had yet to be born.

"She's been with her mama, fighting fires and saving my life," he said.

Michaela smiled, and the tension drained from her, leaving her soft and warm in his arms. And he hoped secure, that she trusted him not just with her life but with their daughter's as well.

He leaned forward, intent on kissing her, like he wanted to do every time he was near her. But his lips just skimmed over hers when she tensed again.

He swallowed his regret that she couldn't do it yet, that she couldn't let herself trust him. But her dad and her ex-husband had no doubt affected her ability to trust anyone, just like his ex had affected his and made him unwilling to put himself out there again.

"Shh," Michaela whispered, like she had that night in the firehouse parking lot, with that same urgency and fear. Then she asked, "Did you hear that?"

He tilted his head and listened. He'd left the door open to the stairwell—otherwise, he might not have heard it. But there was a creak below, like someone walking over the hardwood floors. He'd absolutely forbidden his manager and the rest of the staff from coming to the bar until it was safe, so he knew it wasn't one of them. He leaned his head close to hers and whispered, "Lock yourself in the bedroom."

Then he drew his arms away from her and looked around the room for a weapon. There was an old oar hanging over the fireplace. He pulled that down before heading toward the stairs and to whatever danger might await him in the bar.

But there was no way in hell he was going to let that danger get to Michaela and their baby.

For a second there, Michaela had thought Charlie actually understood what her father had never been able to accept: that she wasn't the weaker sex. She wasn't a damsel in distress in need of a white knight. She wasn't the one who needed rescuing. She was the rescuer.

But when he urged her to lock herself in the bedroom, she bristled with indignation. Didn't he know her at all? Even pregnant, she could still take care of herself and him.

Then he'd grabbed the old oar from the wall and rushed down the stairs and straight into whatever danger awaited him down there. Like he had the other night, when they'd found the back door damaged.

She grabbed her cell phone and slowly and quietly walked down the steps, careful to make no noise. To not betray her presence. While she had her cell out, she wasn't going to make a call, to 911 or her team, until she knew what or who was down there.

Maybe it was just one of Charlie's employees. Or even one of her crew. She knew in the past that Braden had his brother-in-law Trick followed and protected some of the members of the team who'd been in danger.

Like Owen. And Luke. And then Trick had been in danger himself.

And after him, Ethan and Rory.

And now her?

Nobody was safe. Anybody could be in danger. And anyone could *be* the danger as well. And because of that, Trooper Wells was right, it was smarter and safer to trust no one. Not even each other.

Charlie clearly hadn't messed with his own gas line or thrown that bottle at them or broken into his own place. So she could trust him with her life. But she couldn't trust him with her heart.

Because she couldn't be sure that her judgment wasn't off again like it had been with Phil. But unlike Phil, Charlie hadn't asked for her heart. Or declared his love for her.

And when they'd first started seeing each other, he agreed that it wouldn't be anything serious. That he hadn't wanted a relationship any more than she had.

But she was afraid that her feelings were beginning to change, and she would have to work hard to make damn certain she didn't fall for Charlie. Because if she gave him her heart and started planning a future for them as a family, she knew it would destroy her if that all fell apart for her and her child.

If Charlie couldn't love her more than anyone else had ever been able to love her, he would hurt her far worse than anyone else ever had or probably ever would.

But at the moment, she had to make certain that he didn't get hurt. That, in his quest to be her white knight, he didn't lose his life.

When they'd been in the hospital overnight, it had seemed like the plan had worked. That Charles Tillerman was, at the very least, incapacitated—or, better yet, not likely to make it at all.

But then, later the very next day, he'd walked out of the hospital as if nothing had happened. As if he was totally fine…

Because of her.

Michaela Momber had been with him, walking at his side toward a vehicle that someone must have dropped off for them. She'd looked as healthy as he'd looked, even after everything that had happened to them over the past couple of days.

Clearly, it hadn't been enough to get them to back off, or to go into hiding. Instead, they'd driven back to the bar as if nothing had happened there.

As if everything was totally fine…

But it wasn't.

It wouldn't be until they were dead. And they definitely both had to die now. Because that female hotshot had a knack for showing up just in time to save him...

Over and over again.

The only way she wouldn't be able to save him was if she was dead too. Or maybe she would have to die first. Because a dead woman wouldn't be able to stop him from joining her...in death.

Chapter 15

As Charlie headed down the stairs with the oar handle grasped tightly in his hands, he heard a creak above him. He wanted to believe that it was Michaela closing the bedroom door and locking it behind her.

But he had a pretty good idea that she was starting for the stairs again. That she didn't trust him to protect himself, let alone her and their daughter too.

After how many times she'd rescued him, he could understand why. But he wanted her to worry about herself and their child more than him. He didn't want either of them getting hurt because of him.

Not that he believed she was concerned because she cared about him as much as he was coming to care for her. He was pretty sure that it was just who she was, that being a firefighter was such a part of her character that she couldn't help but put herself in danger to save other people. Any other people.

But now she wasn't putting just herself in danger.

Surely, she had to realize that.

Every time she risked her life, she risked their baby's life too.

So he had to do whatever he could to save them both. He stepped into the kitchen and peered around. It was empty.

Quiet. But on the other side of the door to the bar, he heard something. Another creak and the rumble of a low voice.

God, was there more than one intruder, like there had probably been the other night?

And would an antique oar be enough to fend them off? Not if they had a gun. Or pretty much any other kind of weapon.

"Hello?" a voice called out now, louder.

A vaguely familiar voice. But that didn't mean Charlie should trust whoever it was. The oar still gripped tight in his hands, he used it to push open the door and stepped out behind the bar.

One of the older hotshots, Donovan Cunningham, stood in front of the bar. But he wasn't alone. Two people stood behind him, almost as if they were hiding.

Charlie wasn't feeling particularly welcoming, so he coldly pointed out, "The bar's closed."

"I know," Donovan replied.

"Then how the hell did you get in?"

"That door to the alley—" the man gestured toward the hall that led to that door "—it doesn't shut tight."

"Because someone damaged it when they broke in the other night," he said.

"I know," Donovan said, and his broad shoulders sagged as if he was carrying a heavy weight.

He was one of the older hotshots, probably in his late thirties or early forties. Unlike Carl Kozak, who'd shaved off his thinning hair, Donovan wore his longer in the back, as if he was still trying to look younger or compete with the younger hotshots. He and Carl were the ones usually sitting with those young guys, Bruce and Howie.

"What do you know about the break-in?" Charlie wondered. Had Michaela told him? Or had someone else told him?

The man reached behind him then and dragged out two boys. With their pimpled, greasy faces and lanky builds, they were obviously teenagers, probably early to midteens. "These two idiot sons of mine know all about what happened."

"What do you know?" Charlie asked them. But from the way their faces flushed and their gazes shifted away from his, he suddenly had a pretty good idea.

Neither of them answered his question. Donovan must have tightened his grasp on each of their arms, because they flinched.

"We're sorry, Mr. Tillerman," the younger-looking one said. "We didn't mean... It just all got out of hand..." Then he glanced at his older brother as if he was as scared of him as he was his dad.

"Somebody...threatened us... Wanted us to break in here to steal some alcohol," the older one said.

"Somebody?" Charlie asked. "Who?"

The older boy shrugged and glanced down. "Just some kid..."

"Just some kid was threatening enough to get you to commit a crime?" Charlie asked.

"You know kids," Donovan said with a disparaging snort. "How the peer pressure gets to them. They do stupid things because of their friends."

"Actually, I don't know that," Charlie said. He had no kids and had thought that he would never have kids. But he had one on the way now.

Donovan shrugged. "You got a couple of nephews. The Boy Scout, he'll be this age soon. And that's just because us hotshots saved him from that wildfire."

Charlie's stomach twisted with disgust over the guy's manipulation. Or was it a threat? He had no idea. He just felt compelled to remind him, "My nephew was in danger because the arsonist was after the hotshots. The same reason my bar was burned down. It was collateral damage." And if Michaela hadn't saved him, he would have been too.

"I didn't think you were holding a grudge over that," Donovan said. "Although some of the guys think you are. And they think that because of that grudge, you might be behind some of the stuff that's happened."

"I've had nothing to do with any of that. And I certainly didn't break into my own bar and do significant damage to the door and the cash register, not to mention all the broken and missing bottles of alcohol," he pointed out.

"They'll make restitution," Donovan said. "They can work off the amount of the damage, after school—"

"I got practice, Dad," the older boy protested.

"Then weekends," Donovan said.

Charlie shook his head. He didn't want these kids anywhere near his bar again, and especially not near Michaela. He didn't trust them.

"Your grandfather would've agreed to that," Donovan said. "Hell, about twenty years ago, he let me and my buddy do the same thing."

So that was where his sons had gotten the idea. Not from some anonymous friend at school but from their own father.

"My grandfather was a good man," Charlie said. He'd admired him and had wanted to emulate him for so many years. Too bad he'd met Amber when he went off to school, because he'd wound up switching from business management and accounting to politics. Because of those big dreams. He realized now those dreams had never been his, though—just hers.

"Your grandfather was the best," Donovan said with a

grin, as if Charlie had agreed to what he'd proposed. "And you're just like him, everybody says."

He was often compared to his grandfather, which was a source of pride for him. Until now.

That hadn't been a compliment but a manipulation. And he couldn't help but wonder just how manipulative this guy was being.

So he held on to the oar and was so uneasy that he nearly swung it when the door behind him creaked open. But the person behind him posed no physical threat, like Donovan Cunningham and his sons might have. The person he swung the paddle toward only posed a threat to his heart.

Michaela had already been seething as she listened through the door to her team member trying to manipulate Charlie. Then, when she'd stepped through the door and Charlie jumped, she knew he felt as uneasy as she did.

He moved a bit, positioning himself and his oar between her and the Cunningham family. "Well," he said. "I'm not my grandfather."

"What are you saying?" Donovan asked, and he was tense too.

"He's saying that you haven't fooled him into not pressing charges," Michaela said. "And he intends to call the police." She wished that she already had, because the kids jerked away from their dad and Donovan's face flushed with anger. And there were three of them against her and Charlie.

Donovan snorted and shook his head. Then he turned back to Charlie, dismissing her, and scoffed, "You going to let a woman do your talking for you?"

Michaela bristled at the dismissive tone, the one that

sounded so much like her dad's. The one that implied a woman was somehow less than.

"She's not saying anything that I wasn't already going to," Charlie said. "I don't want your kids working for me. I don't hire people I don't trust."

"You just sleep with them?" Donovan asked with another disdainful snort.

His kids snickered and stared at her.

Michaela wanted to slap them all. She nearly reached for that oar.

"What kind of example is this to set for your kids?" Charlie asked. "You're not showing any humility. Any accountability."

"I brought them here," Donovan said. "I made them apologize. I told them that this would all be okay…" His voice cracked now.

"You had no right to do that," Charlie said. "They committed a crime."

"And your grandfather would have given them a break, just like he did me all those years ago," Donovan persisted.

"And I'm not sure that was a good thing my grandfather did," Charlie said. "You obviously didn't learn anything, except that you can do bad things and get away with it."

Donovan cursed then. "You're just talking like that because of her, because she wants to call the cops."

"Because a crime was committed," Michaela pointed out. "And that wasn't the only one that night." She focused on those sneering teenagers. "Did you two slash the tires at the firehouse and throw that bottle too?"

"They had nothing to do with that!" Donovan shouted before the kids could even reply. As if he hadn't wanted them to admit to that too.

"That's up to Trooper Wells to figure out," Michaela said, "and prove."

"Another overly emotional woman trying to do a man's job?" Donovan snorted again. "She won't listen to reason any more than you will. You shouldn't be a hotshot, and she shouldn't be a cop!"

The last thing she would have ever accused Wynona Wells of being was overly emotional. In fact, it was really hard to figure her out at all. Was she the protector or the threat?

"This hotshot saved my life a few times already," Charlie pointed out. "She's the best damn one on your team, and you know it."

Charlie sounded as if he really believed it, too, which made Michaela's chest swell with pride.

But Donovan just snorted again.

Charlie added, "You're just not man enough to admit that she's better at your job than you are. Just like you're not man enough to hold your kids accountable for their actions."

Donovan lunged toward the bar then, as if he was going to come over the top of it and tear Charlie apart.

But Charlie raised the oar toward him. "Stay back," he said.

"Who's the overly emotional one now, Donovan?" Michaela mused, with the same sneer his kids had been giving her.

Maybe she shouldn't have goaded him, because, as she'd already realized, she and Charlie were outnumbered. But she couldn't resist the jab. And if she had to, she would fight for her sake and Charlie's and their baby's.

Braden had been happy that Michaela and Charlie were admitted overnight. They would be safe in the hospital.

But he should have realized that once they left it, they'd be right back in danger.

He had just hoped that that danger wouldn't come from another member of his team. Donovan was the one who'd called him from the state police post. He drew in a deep breath before pushing open the door and stepping inside the building.

"Thank God," Donovan said, and he rushed forward, his face flushed and his eyes wild. "You have to help me."

"The superintendent has no authority here," Trooper Wells said. "He can't do anything for you."

"What the hell's going on?" Braden asked. That was all he wanted to know. All he'd wanted to know for a hell of a long time, but he had yet to get an answer.

Unless this was it…

Charlie Tillerman glanced up from the counter where he was signing a piece of paper. Michaela stood near him, as if her allegiance was with him rather than her team member.

And maybe it should be.

"What's going on?" he repeated. He didn't see handcuffs on anyone, but he'd been called down here to help Donovan. At least, that was what Donovan had said over the phone—that he needed Braden's help with Momber and Tillerman.

He should have made the man make it clearer what kind of help he'd wanted. But hearing their names and *state police post* had been enough for him to know that his help was needed.

"Tillerman and Momber had my kids arrested," Donovan said. "Just over some stupid teenage stuff."

"And you're damn lucky I'm not arresting you for obstruction," Wells remarked. She looked as if she was still considering it—and maybe not just for Donovan but for Braden too.

"Did you know?" the trooper asked him, her eyes narrowed with suspicion while she studied his face.

"Know what?" Braden asked. "I have no idea what's going on." And that had been the case for way too long with his team. He was the superintendent, he was supposed to know what was going on with them. But he hadn't known Michaela was even seeing anyone, let alone pregnant.

"My kids did a stupid thing," Donovan said. "They let some other kid goad them into doing something stupid. Just reckless teenage stuff—"

"They broke into Charlie's bar," Michaela said. "And they're probably the ones who slashed the tires earlier that night and threw that—"

"They didn't do that!" Donovan interrupted, his voice shaking with rage. "They didn't."

"How do you know?" Wells asked.

Donovan tensed. "'Cause I know my kids. They fessed up to the bar break-in—"

"Why?" Michaela interrupted him now. "Because you caught them with the booze they stole?"

The way his mouth fell open and his face flushed, it was apparent that was exactly how he'd caught them.

Michaela continued. "They didn't steal anything from the firehouse parking lot. You have no idea what they're capable of."

Tears flooded Donovan's eyes then, but he closed them and tensed. "Get her out of here," he growled.

Braden didn't know if he was addressing him or Charlie.

"Can we leave now?" Charlie asked the trooper.

"You've given your statements," she said. "Just remember what I told you."

"To trust no one?" Michaela asked.

"To be careful," Wells said.

But Braden couldn't help but think that both things were good advice. For them and maybe for him too. What was going on with Donovan?

Nobody said anything else until the door closed behind Charlie and Michaela.

Then Donovan let the tears flow, his shoulders shaking. "God, Braden, it's all such a mess. Michaela's right. I'm a terrible father. We're gone so much that they've been running wild. I really don't have any idea what they're capable of…"

Could the two of them be the saboteur? As kids of a hotshot, they certainly had access and knew their way around the firehouse. And maybe they even had motivation because their dad was gone so much.

Braden had never considered such a possibility. But now he realized that anyone—besides the hotshots he'd ruled out as suspects—could possibly be the saboteur.

So Michaela and Charlie shouldn't trust anyone and neither should anyone else. Not until the saboteur was caught.

Chapter 16

"You're not very happy." Charlie knew that was an understatement even as he said it, but he didn't want to make Michaela any angrier than she already was. As close as they sat, with just the console separating his driver's seat from her in the passenger seat of his SUV, he could just about feel the rage coming off her like heat waves rolling off hot asphalt. And he had a feeling that some of that anger was directed at him.

That was also why he had waited awhile before voicing his observation aloud.

Once they'd left the police post, which was nearly a half hour from Northern Lakes, he'd found a drive-thru restaurant. Fortunately, they'd eaten breakfast at the hospital, but dealing with the Cunninghams had caused them to skip lunch and dinner. He'd claimed he was hungry, which he realized was the truth when he consumed his burger and fries, but he'd really wanted her to eat and drink again so that she didn't get any more dehydrated. They'd eaten slowly, sitting in the parking lot in silence.

And when he finally got back on the road, he risked breaking that uncomfortable silence with his remark: *You're not very happy.*

"Nope," she replied. "Are you?"

"I would be," he said, "if I actually believed those smart-ass teenagers were responsible for everything that had been happening around Northern Lakes."

The kids were behind bars for the moment until their father made bail. Once he did that, Charlie doubted that he or Michaela would be safe. And chances were, after their side stop for food, the Cunninghams might have already made bail or even been released into their father's custody since they were minors.

"You don't think they are to blame for everything?" she asked.

"Do you?"

She shrugged. "I don't know. I'm not sure they would have been able to tamper with that gas line on their own."

"You think their father is helping them? He would definitely know what had happened to Owen, with that gas leak…" And he had used that same trick to try to kill Charlie. But why?

"Donovan can be a chauvinistic jerk—"

"Obviously."

"But he brought them to you to apologize," she said. "And to make restitution. So I don't know…"

Charlie sighed. "Yeah, I don't know either." And why would Donovan or his sons have gone after the mayor too? Unless Les Byers was just delusional, thinking that he had been poisoned. Hopefully, he had not been. But with his doctor thinking it was a strong possibility, according to what Wells had told Michaela…

"And Donovan is not the only chauvinistic jerk," Michaela said.

"Sounds like there are some other hotshots who think the same way he does."

"I was talking about you."

So she *was* angry with him. "What did I do?"

"After spewing all your bull about how strong I am, you tell me to lock myself in a bedroom like I'm helpless and desperately need you to protect me, and that was just over a little noise."

"That 'little noise' turned out to be three men who'd basically broken in the same way they had a couple of days prior," he pointed out.

"Two boys and an idiot are who showed up," she said. "Not three men."

"At least you're not calling me the idiot," he said.

"No, you're possibly worse," she said. "If you just told me what I wanted to hear instead of what you really feel, then that would make you a liar."

Charlie flinched at her insult. But as a former politician, he was used to being called even worse things. "I feel and think that you're a badass," Charlie said. "And when I told you to lock yourself in the bedroom, I wasn't thinking just about you. I was thinking about our baby."

She sucked in a breath, as if the comment surprised her, then murmured, "Oh…"

"You're used to rushing headlong into danger, Michaela, and I respect and admire that," he said. "But you're not in the same position to do that right now. This is what I was talking about when I told you that everything's changed. You're not rushing in *alone* anymore."

She let out a shaky sigh and touched her stomach, which protruded over her seat belt. "I know. I just… It's like an instinct…"

"To save lives," he said. Specifically, his life lately, and he was the one who kept putting her in the position of having to do that.

"I usually don't rush in alone," she said. "Usually, I have my team to back me up."

Now anger bubbled up inside him over the way Cunningham had talked to her. "But do you? Can you trust them, knowing how they really feel about you?"

"I've always known how they've felt about me," she said, "which ones support me and respect me and which ones don't. But the whole sabotage thing…"

"Makes you trust no one, just like Wells has advised?" At least, he hoped that was the case for her, that Michaela didn't trust any of her fellow hotshots, because clearly there were a few she shouldn't trust.

"Well, hopefully those kids have been responsible for *everything* and there will be no more danger."

The second she said it, he cringed. The words hung in the air between them like her anger had just moments ago. "It's like you're just tempting fate," he murmured.

She chuckled. "You're superstitious?"

"I'm cautious." And as a precaution, he glanced into his rearview mirror. Lights shone brightly behind him on a vehicle taller than his SUV. Like a truck or a bigger SUV.

Those lights were closing the distance fast between them. He pressed his foot down on the accelerator, pushing his SUV to speed up. But with all the curves on the roads around Northern Lakes, it would be difficult to keep up the pace without going off in the ditch. He grasped the steering wheel tightly in both hands, keeping the tires on the road as he rounded a corner.

"Charlie…" Michaela said as she grasped the console between them and the armrest.

"I have to go fast or—"

But he didn't think she was protesting the way he was

driving, because she was staring instead into the side mirror and bracing herself.

Then he felt it, the bone-jarring sensation of the vehicle hitting them from behind, crumpling metal and spinning his SUV out of control.

Seeing how fast that vehicle had been coming at them, Michaela had braced herself for the impact. But she still hadn't been ready for the crash, for how out of control the SUV went despite Charlie's efforts to keep his vehicle on the road. He hadn't been able to do it.

The airbag cushioned Michaela's head as she leaned over the dash. The entire vehicle was tipped forward, into the ditch. But the seat belt had held fast, keeping her from hitting anything, but that seat belt also pulled tightly across her lower abdomen. Had she kept it low enough, under her stomach, to protect the baby?

And what about Charlie?

Fear coursed through her. She had to see if he was all right. Finally, the bag deflated, and she could turn her head toward the driver's side.

Toward the driver.

"Charlie?" she called out to him, her voice cracking with the panic and concern overwhelming her.

He was turned away from her, his face toward the driver's-side window, so she couldn't see anything but the back of his head and how tightly he was still gripping the steering wheel beneath the airbag, which had begun to deflate on his side too. He'd tried so hard to keep them on the road, but the truck—or whatever it was—had struck them too hard.

Like the vehicle that had struck Trent Miles and the detective on their way up for the hotshot holiday party. But they'd wound up in a lake. Fortunately, she and Charlie were only in a ditch.

But where was that vehicle? And who the hell was copying these things that had happened to the hotshots?

She peered around, looking for the vehicle that had struck them, but she couldn't see anything but the interior of Charlie's SUV. Outside, it had gone dark, the headlights of the SUV buried in the bottom of the ditch.

Whoever had hit them could be out there…while they were trapped inside the wreckage.

"Charlie!" she called out again.

He groaned as he moved, turning toward her. His dark eyes full of concern, he asked, "Are you okay?"

She nodded but she wasn't completely sure. She didn't know how the baby was. And if something had happened to her, Michaela definitely would not be okay.

"I'm not in pain," she said. Wouldn't she be if something was happening with her pregnancy? "What about you? Are you hurt?"

He shook his head but groaned again. "My neck's a little sore," he admitted.

She would probably be sore tomorrow, after tensing up like she had when she'd seen how fast that vehicle was coming up on them. But at the moment, adrenaline was still pumping through her, making her pulse fast and a little frantic. That was how she felt too.

"We need to get out of here," she said, scared that the driver was out there and determined to make sure they hadn't survived the crash.

"We need to call 911," he said.

"The police won't get here in time."

"Time for what?" he asked, his whole body tensing up. "Are you hurt?"

"No. But whoever was driving the tank that hit us could be out there," she said. "We need to get out of here."

"I can't drive out of this ditch," Charlie said. "We need a wrecker." He fumbled around in his seat. "Where the hell is my phone?" Sticking his hand between the console and his seat, he pulled out the cell. The screen was cracked. When he tried to swipe to unlock the screen, blood beaded on the pad of his thumb.

"It's not going to work," she said. Not when he couldn't even get it to unlock without getting hurt.

"Do you have your phone?" he asked. "We need to call the police."

She patted the pockets of her jumpsuit. Because of how loose it was, the cell must have slipped out. With the seat belt cinched so tightly around her, she couldn't reach far onto the floor.

"It's around here somewhere—but even if we find it and call, the police won't get here in time if that driver is still out there," she said, and she reached across the console to grasp Charlie's arm. "They could be armed."

"We don't know that," Charlie said, as if he didn't want her to worry about it.

"We don't want to find out when they start firing at us," she pointed out.

He shook his head. "I doubt they would do it here. We're still pretty close to the police post." But he must have felt her urgency, because he was fighting against his seat belt. Finally it unclipped and he slid forward, over the steering wheel.

She shuddered as she considered what that meant. "Whoever was driving that vehicle was coming from that direction. They could have been coming from the post."

"Who are you thinking?" he asked. "That it was Cunningham and his kids or..."

"Not Braden," she said.

She trusted her superintendent. Braden Zimmer was a good man who'd suffered along with every team member who came under attack. She'd seen it when she was in the hospital waiting room with him when one of their own had been in the ER. And she'd seen it when she was in the ER and he was waiting for news about her.

"Trooper Wells warned you to trust no one," Charlie reminded her.

"I think she was talking about you," she said. "But I was talking about *her.*"

"You think she might have driven us off the road?" he asked. "But if we call 911, they'll have a record of it. She won't be able to hurt us then."

Wynona Wells was one of the few who had a record of everything that had happened to the hotshots too. If anyone was purposely copycatting those incidents, it was probably her. Or the saboteur...

So Michaela was hesitant to call for help, because she wasn't sure who she could trust. Besides Charlie. Since he was the one coming under attack, she trusted that he couldn't be behind any of these things, not even the sabotage. And she didn't want him to get hurt any worse than he already was. "I really think we need to get out of here," she persisted.

She felt so damn trapped in the vehicle, like a sitting duck waiting for the bullet that would end her life to come. And what if the driver had a gun? They were definitely sitting ducks then.

Panic pressed on her lungs, making it harder for her to breathe. She tugged at the seat belt with one hand, trying to loosen it while she fumbled with the clasp with her other hand, trying to free herself.

"I'll help," Charlie said. "I'll get you out. Then we have to find your phone."

He was right—she knew that. They needed to report the crash and get a wrecker and a police officer to come to their aid. But what if the police officer was the one who'd put them in the ditch? Wells definitely had a gun.

Charlie reached over the console. He kept one arm between her and the dash as he fumbled around for the clasp of her belt. His fingers brushed across her side and her hip.

Her skin tingled in reaction, as it always did. Even in their current circumstance, she couldn't stop herself from physically reacting to his touch, to his closeness. Maybe it was just because she was so damn happy that he was all right. If he truly was...

"Are you sure you're not hurt?" she asked as she noticed a slight grimace cross his face.

The clasp clicked and the seat belt slipped away, and she fell into his other arm. He grimaced again as he tightened his grip around her.

"You are hurt," she said, answering her own question. And now she knew that he was right about calling for help. She had to find her damn cell. She scrambled around, reaching under the seat, feeling between the console, desperately trying to find it. "My phone has to be here somewhere..."

"If we can't find it, we'll have to walk back to that fast-food place to make a call," he said. And now, instead of helping her, he turned toward the driver's-side door and shoved at it as he pulled on the handle. "I can't get it open."

Michaela focused on her door then too. But it was also jammed closed. Or maybe the doors and the SUV were just too damaged for them to open. "It's stuck too."

"They might need the Jaws of Life to get us out," Charlie muttered.

He sounded a little panicked now too. Did he have that same feeling she had? Like the person who'd run them off the road was out there, waiting for them?

Or were they coming up on their vehicle now, cloaked in the darkness that enveloped the SUV?

"We'll get out," she assured him. "We'll break the glass."

"It's too dangerous," Charlie protested. "You're going to get cut."

"I'd rather get a few scratches than be stuck in here," she said.

"Sick of my company already?" he asked, and he sounded like he was teasing, but his voice was a bit gruff with concern.

She doubted that he was really worried about that. He was probably worried about the same thing she was, that someone was out there. She definitely wasn't sick of his company. In fact, when she wasn't around him, she missed him. Too much.

More than she'd ever missed her ex-husband, which was why she shouldn't have gotten involved with Charlie at all. But now it was too late for that.

She was carrying his baby. And she just needed to make sure that nothing happened to their unborn daughter or to her daughter's father.

The driver had stopped a short distance down the road and shut off the lights to their vehicle. They didn't want to be seen by anyone. But they wanted to see if Tillerman and Momber got out of the wreck.

If they had survived.

And if they had…

They wouldn't live for much longer because the driver would run them down in the street.

Chapter 17

Before she could do it herself, as she did most things, Charlie broke one of the windows. He used his elbow to pound out the glass on his side.

"Be careful!" Michaela admonished him. "You could cut an artery or something."

Thankfully, he was wearing a heavy enough jacket that the glass wouldn't get through to his shirtsleeve, let alone his skin. "I'm fine," he said, but he hadn't considered the danger she had. At least, not about the glass…

But he felt the same way she did about how the driver of that vehicle was probably waiting around out there in the dark. To see if they'd survived? To finish them off when he or she realized that the crash hadn't killed them?

Who the hell could be after them?

"Let me go up first," he said as he broke out the last of the glass, sending it tinkling down inside the door.

"Why?" she asked. "Are you worried about the baby?"

"I'm worried about all of us," he said. But he was used to worrying about her. He had worried about her every time she left for a wildfire, and that was long before he'd had any idea that she was pregnant with his child.

She released a shaky breath and said, "Me too." And she

reached across the console and grabbed his hand. "And I think the best way to stay safe is to stick together."

Just now? Or always? He wanted to ask that question, but she'd already warned him months ago that she wasn't interested in anything permanent. And he'd assured her that he wasn't either.

But now…

Now they were going to have a child together. They would have to be part of each other's lives for the rest of their daughter's life. But first, they needed to focus on making sure their daughter had a chance to *have* a life.

Charlie slid through the window first, into the darkness that surrounded them. His shoes slipped on the muddy bank of the ditch, and he fell against the SUV, rocking it. The warmth of June hadn't dried up all the rain they'd gotten during the May showers.

"Careful!" Michaela called out. "Don't slide under the vehicle."

Or he might get trapped, like they'd been inside it, and get crushed. He knew the dangers. And it wasn't just the wreckage but the strong possibility that whoever had caused the crash was out there.

He held very still, listening to the noises around them. There were a few chirps of a tree frog and the low rumble of an engine. But it didn't get louder or quieter, like it was moving. It was idling out there. Somewhere…on the road above the ditch.

"There's someone out there," he whispered through the open window.

"I know," Michaela whispered back, and her voice was closer as she scrambled over the console. "I found my phone." The screen lit up a small circle of light around them.

"Call 911," he advised.

But she must have already dialed someone else, because a deep voice emanated from her phone. "Michaela? Are you all right?" Braden Zimmer asked.

"No," she answered honestly. "We were forced off the road after we left the police post. Are you back in Northern Lakes yet?"

"I'll turn around. I'll find you," he promised.

So that wasn't *his* vehicle out there, idling in the dark somewhere. It had to belong to the person who'd driven them off the road. Maybe their vehicle was damaged too. Maybe they hadn't been able to get away either.

But then, that would make them even more dangerous, like a cornered animal. They would definitely attack rather than risk getting caught.

Without a weapon, Charlie had no idea how to protect them. But as a politician, he'd been taught that sometimes the best defense was a strong offense.

He reached through the window and found the horn on his vehicle, hitting it.

"What are you doing?" Michaela asked, and her hands gripped his, trying to pull it back.

"You don't think that person knows where we are?" he asked. "We have to make certain that someone else knows we're here and stops to help."

So he pressed on the horn again, blasting it in bursts: three short taps, three long and then three short taps again.

He could only hope that the SOS signal would help Braden find them before whoever was sitting in their vehicle came at them again.

Braden had found them at the same time Trooper Wells showed up, flashing her lights like Charlie had been blasting that horn.

And Michaela couldn't help but wonder if Wells had been there all along, waiting for them to climb out of the ditch. On the ride back to Northern Lakes with Braden, he'd confirmed that Donovan and the trooper had left shortly after she and Charlie had—Donovan supposedly to find a lawyer and Wells to supposedly go out on a call.

Braden had been on his cell phone, talking to Sam while he was still sitting in the police post parking lot. So he'd watched them drive off but hadn't seen where Donovan or Wells had gone.

After them?

One of them might have. But Michaela wasn't sure how to prove it. All she knew was that she was damn glad she and Charlie had survived the crash, so glad that she didn't protest when Charlie asked Braden to drop them at the Lakeside Inn. They knew the Filling Station wasn't safe.

And despite Braden's and Trick's assurances, neither was the firehouse. Not with Donovan so pissed at her.

She wasn't sure the inn was safe, either, though. Ethan Sommerly had been injured there, and Trent Miles's sister, Brittney, had nearly been kidnapped. But that was months ago, and the FBI agent responsible for those attacks was dead. Still, with the way this person seemed to be imitating the horrible things that had already happened to the hotshots, maybe they would try to imitate what the FBI agent had done.

But with all the things that had happened to the hotshots over the last several months and all the places those attacks had happened, nowhere would be safe until whoever was after Michaela and Charlie was stopped. And knowing that their lives could be cut short gave Michaela a new appreciation for life and for Charlie. So she didn't argue when he booked just one room.

And she barely waited until he'd closed and locked the

door behind them before reaching for him. She slid her arms around his neck and tugged his head down as she stretched herself up his long body until their lips met. As always, at just the briefest brush of their mouths, passion ignited inside her. Then, as the kiss deepened, the desire swept through her like a brush fire devouring dried grass and fallen timber. All-consuming…

Out of control.

She nipped at his mouth and ran her fingers through his hair. Then she moved her hands down his neck and over his chest, where she tugged down the zipper of his jacket before reaching for the buttons on his shirt.

He kissed her back just as passionately until he tensed and pulled back, panting for breath. "Michaela? Are you sure?"

She laughed. She'd never had any doubts about wanting him. The desire was something she couldn't resist, he was something she couldn't resist.

That was how she'd wound up pregnant when she hadn't even thought it was a possibility. Maybe that was what he was referring to.

"I can't get pregnant again," she teased. That was what he'd asked her that night they hadn't used protection. She'd told him that it was fine, and he'd asked, *Are you sure?*

But he wasn't too upset with her over being wrong, over being pregnant with his baby. And she wasn't upset at all. She was thrilled that something she'd wanted so long and so desperately was actually a possibility. As long as she stayed alive…

Maybe she shouldn't give in to a distraction, like making love with Charlie. But with as close a call as they'd had, she wanted to celebrate that they were still alive.

"And the doctor said that having sex while pregnant will not harm the baby," she assured him.

If that was his concern…

He closed his arms around her, pulling her back against his chest. "I don't want anything to harm the baby *or* you."

Was she an afterthought? Was it really just his child that concerned him?

But she could feel the tension inside him, the rapid beat of his heart beneath her palm and how heavily he was breathing. Even if he didn't love her, he clearly wanted her.

She wanted him too. She finished unbuttoning his shirt and slipped that and his jacket off his shoulders. He released her long enough for them to drop to the ground. Then he was messing with her buttons, flinching as he did, and she remembered the cut on his thumb. So she pushed his hands aside and undressed herself, stepping out of that jumpsuit in nothing but her too-small bra and thong. She hadn't bought new underwear at Courtney's boutique.

He groaned like she'd hurt him.

"Are you really okay from the crash?" she asked with concern.

Maybe she shouldn't have refused the trip to the ER that Braden had suggested—but for Charlie's sake, not hers. She felt fine. She didn't have a scratch from the crash, and she was in no pain. Yet.

Except desire…

Which wound tightly inside her, making her desperate for a release. Desperate for him. But if he was hurt…

"You're the one killing me," he said. "You're so damn beautiful."

Other men had made comments that she was too muscular from all the working out she did. But Charlie truly did seem to appreciate her body.

And she certainly appreciated his. He had muscles, too,

lean but defined ones. And chest hair that was as soft as the hair on his head.

She reached up then and unclasped her bra, letting it fall away from her breasts. Then she slid the thong down over her hips until it dropped to the floor too.

He groaned again. Then he moved, discarding his jeans, boxers and boots as quickly as he could. But she was already lying on the bed then, her legs parted and ready for him to fill that ache inside her.

He joined her on the bed, but he touched her just with his fingertips, gliding them over her shoulders and along her sides. He lowered his head, kissing her lips before sliding them over her collarbone and down to her breasts. He kissed each one before closing his lips around one of her nipples and gently suckling at it.

She felt the tension stretch from her breast to her core like a rubber band at the point of breaking. And then he moved his mouth lower, between her legs, while he kept his hands on her breasts. He stroked her skin and rubbed his thumbs across her nipples, which were so sensitive that she nearly came then. But his tongue was doing things to her, too, things that made her nearly sob with the passion and pleasure overwhelming her.

And that rubber band broke. She cried out at the intense pleasure of the orgasm that shuddered through her, releasing some of the tension but not all of it.

She needed him for that, his body inside hers, filling that emptiness she'd felt for so long. She wasn't empty anymore because of him.

But she still needed *him*.

Then he was there, easing inside her, building the tension in her body again with long strokes and gentle thrusts. But it wasn't enough.

The release was just out of her reach.

She pushed him onto his back and straddled him, taking him deeper.

He groaned and clenched his jaw, as if he was in pain. But even in pain, he was focused on her pleasure. He reached up and cupped her breasts, and his thumbs stroked over their taut points again.

She went mad with desire, which led her to move quickly. And she rode him into ecstasy, her body nearly convulsing with the intensity of her orgasm.

He gripped her hips and uttered a guttural sound as he found his release, his body pumping inside her. She collapsed onto his chest, panting for breath, and his arms closed around her as if he never intended to let her go. She wrapped her arms around his shoulders, holding him just as tightly as he was holding her.

If only she could trust that it was her he really wanted and not just the baby they'd created…

But before she'd gotten pregnant, he'd agreed that it was smart to keep whatever they were doing secret. He'd agreed that nothing would come of it, that they weren't going to get serious. And if he'd changed his mind, it was probably only because of her getting pregnant. While she…

He was right: everything had changed for her. Because now she wanted more than the baby. She was beginning to want Charlie too. But even if he wanted her *and* the baby, Michaela would still be denied that happily-ever-after…if whoever was after them eventually succeeded in their attempts to end his or their lives.

The call came through Dispatch, pulling Wells off her self-assigned surveillance duty outside the Lakeside Inn, where Braden Zimmer had dropped Tillerman and Momber.

The new sergeant wanted to see her. Now.

Was she in trouble?

Had the hotshots convinced him that she was somehow complicit in the things that Gingrich had done? Or had they convinced him that she was responsible for the things that had happened to them after Gingrich had been locked up? It wasn't helping her that some of those things were similar to what had happened to the hotshots before, things she'd taken reports about. That was probably making them even more suspicious of her.

They had no evidence, though, only suspicions.

If they had evidence, she wouldn't have had to worry about just getting taken off the case. She would have to worry about joining her former training officer in jail.

Chapter 18

Charlie jerked awake like he had jerked when the SUV spun out of control and crashed into the ditch. There was no airbag to cushion the blow this time, but there was a soft mattress. He reached across it but wasn't surprised to find it empty now.

She was gone. Like she always was when he woke up from one of those dreams.

But it wasn't safe for her to be off on her own. Alone. She'd agreed that it was smartest and safest for them to stick together. Hell, she'd suggested sticking together. Frustration bubbled up in his throat, which he released in a groan.

"Are you okay?"

At Michaela's question, he jerked his eyes open and peered around the room. She was sitting in a chair by the window, her skin bathed in the soft hues of the sunrise. She wore just his shirt, leaving her legs bare. He nearly groaned with frustration of another kind.

"You're here," he said.

She smiled. "Yes, I'm not that dream you sometimes think I am."

"From the fire," he said. "I think that because of how you rescued me from the fire at the Filling Station like you were an angel."

She shivered. He didn't know if it was because of the

memory or because she was cold. "You were pretty out of it then," she said. "Like you were with the gas leak."

"Something else you saved me from."

"Owen nearly died that same way," she said. "Someone messed with the gas line in his house and tried to kill him."

"Dirk Brown's widow," Charlie said. "I remember hearing about that. She thought he knew she'd killed her husband and that she'd been having an affair with Gingrich. So she tried to kill him with ways that looked like accidents."

She nodded, and her blond hair brushed across her cheek. She was really beautiful. "But the gas line on your furnace—nobody even bothered trying to make it look like an accident. Maybe they wanted it to be obvious, though." Her blue eyes narrowed into an intense stare as she continued. "And so many other hotshots have been run off the road. Just recently, Trent Miles's truck was hit so hard that it went into a lake."

He shivered now as he remembered what he'd heard about that. "But that was the kid who followed him up from Detroit, the one who nearly killed him and the detective outside my bar." The one who might have started shooting up the bar if the detective hadn't handled him like she had. "Those people are gone. They can't be the ones who came after us."

"I don't know if you're in danger because of you or because of me," she said. "Maybe the saboteur is copying all the things that have happened to hotshots or…"

"Until yesterday, I didn't think you had any enemies," he admitted. "But I don't trust your team members now, especially Donovan Cunningham."

"I don't trust him either," she said. "But I'm not the only one he's mad at now."

Charlie sighed and shoved one of his hands through his hair. "I don't know…" he murmured. "Maybe I should have handled it like my grandfather would have. Let them make restitution."

"Do you really want those kids hanging around the bar?" she asked, a blond eyebrow arched over one eye.

"Because they're so young, I technically can't have them around the bar," he said. "They would have had to do something else to pay me back for the damages."

"A judge will probably have them picking up trash by the road," she said. "I doubt they'll serve much time—if any—in a juvenile detention center."

"If it's their first offense, probably not," he agreed. "But if it *is* their first offense…" Then maybe he should have been more lenient. But after the attempts on his life and on hers, he hadn't been feeling too magnanimous to anyone. And if those teenagers were actually the ones who'd done the other things…

He shook his head. "No, you're right. Turning them in was the right thing to do. But I'm just worried that *you* are the one who will wind up paying for me having them arrested for the break-in at *my* bar."

"I'm not worried about Donovan Cunningham or his kids," she said. She rose from the chair to cross the room to the bed. "I'm worried about you, Charlie. And I don't know if it's a hotshot who's been trying to hurt us or if it's someone connected to the situation with the mayor who's copying those things to frame a hotshot."

"Someone like Trooper Wells?" he asked because she was clearly suspicious of the state trooper.

She nodded. "I'm worried because I don't feel that we're safe anywhere…with anyone…"

He was worried, too, and not just because he'd had too

many close calls with death. He was worried because he was pretty sure he was falling for her. Hard and deep, and he couldn't trust that she wasn't going to break his heart.

She shouldn't have gone back to bed. Because they hadn't slept. They'd made love again. And to Michaela, it was making love now. She was falling for him.

With the way he'd defended her to Donovan and had even defended her to herself. With the way he respected her and seemed happy about the baby, Charlie had gotten under her skin so deeply that she was afraid he had embedded himself in her heart.

But she wasn't even sure what they were to each other. Not boyfriend and girlfriend. Maybe not even friends. But they were going to be future parents. Still, there were so many things she hadn't known about him. Like his political aspirations.

She lay in his arms, her head on his chest. His fingers idly stroked over the soft hair near her cheek.

"What are you going to do about the mayor position?" she asked with more than idle curiosity, although she made it seem like that was all it was. "Is it something you can really just accept?"

His body tensed against hers. "Yes, since the deputy mayor passed away, the position could go to a town council member of the mayor's choosing while he's alive."

"But if he's dead?"

"It would go to a vote with the council first," he said.

"Could that be why someone tried to kill the mayor? So he couldn't pick you?" she asked, her heart beating faster with fear for him. Because it was beginning to make more sense to her now.

He just shrugged. "I don't know," he said.

"Well, you can't take the position, then."

"But I think I have to take it," he said with something like resignation.

"Why?" she asked with alarm. "Taking it could put you in even more danger." If that was why he was in danger... and it didn't have anything to do with the hotshots.

"I'm going to take it because I don't trust anyone else to take it," he said. "Or maybe I should say that I don't trust anyone else who wants to take it."

"You really believe that the other town council members, Bentley Ford or Jason Cruise, could have poisoned the mayor and come after you?" That was what he'd mentioned to Trooper Wells, what seemed like so long ago.

"We don't know for sure yet that the mayor was really poisoned," he said, and he sounded like he didn't want to believe that was what had happened. Probably because Les Byers was his friend.

She knew that it was hard to believe that someone would want to hurt someone you cared about. She'd felt that way when that madwoman had tried to kill Hank. Like, why would anyone want to hurt someone as sweet and kind as Henrietta Rowlins?

And Les Byers was just as sweet and kind.

He continued. "But I'm going to go see him and find out if they got his blood work back yet, if they know that he was really slipped something and what it was."

"And if he wasn't poisoned?" she asked.

"Then what's been going on—the gas line, someone running us off the road—might not have anything to do with the mayor and Ford and Cruise," he said.

And everything to do with the hotshots instead. He didn't say that, but what else could it be?

Charlie didn't have any enemies that Michaela knew

about—not that she knew him all that well. But here in Northern Lakes, the only people who'd ever said anything bad about Charlie Tillerman had been the hotshots who'd speculated that he could be the saboteur.

"If you take the interim position of mayor, will you do what your sister and brother-in-law want you to do?" she asked. "Will you force the hotshot headquarters to move out of Northern Lakes?"

"They're not the only ones who want that," he said. "A lot of townspeople are upset about all the danger the hotshots have brought to town. A corrupt FBI agent just went after Rory VanDam. And someone followed Trent Miles up from Detroit to kill him out of revenge and Ethan Sommerly— who isn't even Ethan Sommerly—had paid assassins coming after him, shooting up the town. You can't say that all of that hasn't put other people's lives in danger."

"No, I can't say that," she admitted. And she did wonder if his life was one of those in danger. If it was the saboteur who'd come after him…

Maybe that person was worried he might have seen them that night at the firehouse.

While the Cunningham kids had admitted that they'd broken into the bar, they'd denied everything else. So maybe there was someone else out there, someone else who posed the real threat to his life.

And a threat to hers too.

He tipped up her chin so that she met his earnest gaze. "So, thinking about all that, can you understand that it might be in the best interests of everyone if the hotshot headquarters was somewhere else? Somewhere that isn't populated, like a forest ranger station in the middle of nowhere?"

She couldn't deny that it probably would be in everyone's

best interests. At least in the best interests of the towns-people. So she just sighed and nodded as dread settled heavily in her stomach.

If the headquarters was somewhere else, she would have no reason to keep coming to Northern Lakes, to keep coming to him.

The doubts and insecurities of the little girl whose own father hadn't wanted or valued her overwhelmed her. And she couldn't help but wonder if Charlie had another motive for moving the headquarters out of Northern Lakes.

Did he really want to get rid of all the hotshots? Or did he want to get rid of just her?

Not that he didn't have a real reason to want to protect the town and his family...

But her baby was going to be his family too. Did he want her? Or would he be like her father and come to resent them both?

Michaela knew that to protect herself and her daughter, it would probably be smartest to push him away, to reject him, before he could reject and hurt either of them.

Too many people kept getting in the way, ruining well-thought-out planning. And while opportunities had been presented to eliminate the obstacles to that planning, Charlie Tillerman and Michaela Momber kept escaping, relatively unscathed, from every carefully planned and carefully copied scrape with death.

They were still alive.

Still in the way.

They weren't the only ones—the only things—that hadn't gone according to plan. There were other problems that needed to be addressed and eliminated for good.

Then after that… Charlie Tillerman and Michaela Momber would be dealt with.

Maybe the only way to get rid of them for certain was to go scorched earth. To use a method and means to ensure that there was no way they would survive.

Chapter 19

After the second time they made love and had the strangely intimate yet unsettling conversation, Michaela wanted to go back to the firehouse. Maybe she was angry with him about taking on the interim mayor position and she needed some space.

Fear came over Charlie, nearly overwhelming him with its intensity. He was afraid that she didn't want anything to do with him anymore despite the fact they were going to have a daughter. Was it because he wanted to move the hotshot headquarters? Or was it because she was scared of getting too involved with him, too vulnerable to him? So maybe she was rejecting him before he could get too close.

She was more vulnerable without him. He was also afraid of her being at the firehouse on her own. He wanted to stick close to her, as close as he could get.

But he had no reason to stay there or even to go except to drop her off. Fortunately, he still had his sister's car, which he had Eric leave for him at the hotel the night before, since his SUV had probably been totaled. So he drove Michaela to the firehouse, and when he saw Braden and Stanley and the firehouse dog, Annie, through the open garage doors, he felt a little better about leaving her. Surely she would be safe with all of them there. Nobody would try to get to her with that many witnesses around.

And Charlie had something of his own he needed to do. He had a responsibility that he needed to accept for the town and for his child too. He had to do what was going to be best and safest for the town and most especially for his baby girl. But if he accepted the mayor position and moved the hotshot headquarters, would he lose Michaela?

Not that he really *had* her. He wasn't sure she would have a real relationship with him even if he turned down the interim position. But if he accepted, he could at least maybe use it to keep her and their daughter safe. If all the dangerous stuff happening was because of the hotshots...

But now he had doubts niggling at him that maybe he was the reason for all the danger this time. The doubts weren't just because of the kids breaking into his bar and that gas line being tampered with. He just had an uneasy feeling after he dropped Michaela off, like maybe he was the one who wasn't safe.

Maybe that was because she'd turned back before walking through the doors to the firehouse garage and said, "Please be careful."

It was too late for caution now. Or he wouldn't have invited her home with him that first night they'd gotten together. He would have known then that it was too dangerous. For his heart, at least.

And now maybe for his life.

As he drove to the hospital, he kept checking the rearview mirror, making sure that nobody came up on him fast like that truck or SUV had the night before. If getting run off the road didn't kill him, his sister surely would if he wrecked her vehicle like he had his own.

But he made it safely to the parking lot with no mishaps.

Maybe because it was broad daylight now and he would be able to see the driver, unlike last night, when he hadn't been able to even tell for sure if it had been a truck or SUV that struck them.

After checking in at the desk, he headed up the stairs to the mayor's private room. He was out of the ICU, so that was a good thing. Maybe he would be able to resume his duties himself soon if he wanted, but Les had made it pretty clear that he was ready to retire.

Why?

Because of his age or because of the constant battle in town between development and preservation, between keeping the hotshots headquarters or forcing them to leave. Town council meetings always devolved into arguments, and sometimes it almost seemed as if they would come to blows.

If Charlie took this job, he would have the influence and the power to push his own agenda. He just wasn't sure what that actually was anymore. Hopefully, Les was feeling better now and would be able to give him some advice. Eager to talk to his friend, Charlie pushed open the door. Les wasn't alone, someone stood over his bed. "Sorry," Charlie muttered. "I should have knocked."

The person wasn't just standing over the bed—he was pressing a pillow over the mayor's face.

"Stop!" Charlie yelled. Then, toward the nurse's station down the hall, he yelled, "Get security!" But he didn't wait for backup as he rushed into the room and launched himself at the intruder.

The guy shoved Charlie off, knocking him onto the floor. Then he charged toward the door. At least, Charlie assumed it was a guy, from his height and build. He couldn't see his face, though, because a large mask covered it. And while the person wore a doctor's white coat, he had a sweatshirt on under it, with the hood pulled up tight around that mask so that nothing was visible of his head or face.

Charlie jumped up from the floor, but instead of running after the intruder, he focused on Les. Was he breathing? He lay so limp against the gurney, and his face was so pale. There weren't any machines hooked to him now like there'd been in the ICU, nothing monitoring his heart to show that it was still beating.

If it was still beating…

"Help!" he yelled again. "Help!"

And he hoped like hell that someone could help the mayor and that it wasn't already too late to save him. Or Charlie would have just lost a very dear friend and witnessed his murder.

The minute Charlie drove off, Michaela had a horrible feeling. And it was nothing like the little fluttery sensation of her baby moving inside her. It was an overwhelming sense of dread. Charlie should not have gone off anywhere alone. As hard as he could try to be careful, bad things still happened. Like last night…

Getting forced off the road. And the gas leak and that Molotov cocktail.

She glanced through the open side door to where the asphalt was still scorched from the fire.

Braden was looking there too. A shudder moved through him visibly.

"I'm fine," she assured him, and she automatically touched the stitches on her temple. They would probably dissolve soon too. The ER doctor had warned that she might have a scar, though. It wouldn't be the only one or the most painful one she had. The most painful ones weren't even scars that anyone could see, just the ones that Michaela felt.

Braden smiled at her. "I'm glad. But you seem to keep tempting fate, Michaela. The crash last night and going into the bar with the gas leak. Even though you had your oxygen tank and mask, the building could have exploded. It was too dangerous."

Michaela shuddered now at the thought of all the danger she and her baby had been in. "I know." That was why she'd wanted to come to the firehouse, to tell him what they both knew: she had to leave the team. "It's really not my intention to tempt fate."

"I know none of these things are your fault," Braden said.

Despite probably being only a couple of years older than her thirty-two, Braden had a certain fatherly presence to him. Not the kind of fatherly presence her dad had had but the warm and supportive kind she'd always wanted. That she wanted for her child now. Charlie seemed willing to do that now, to protect and support her, but would he always be there for them? Or would something bad happen, which always seemed to happen...

"Did you always know that?" she wondered aloud.

"What do you mean?"

"Was I ever a suspect in your mind?" she asked.

He shook his head. "Never."

"I don't know if I should be relieved or offended," she remarked.

He chuckled. "What do you mean?"

"Like you didn't think I could pull it off—"

"Like I figured you were too honorable," he said. "You and I had the same first marriages, where we couldn't trust the person we were married to. So honesty is really important to us."

"Yes, it is." And she couldn't be sure that Charlie was being completely honest with her. As Wells had pointed out to her, he was a politician, so he was probably adept at telling people what they wanted to hear. Yet she didn't think that he'd ever lied to her.

Braden released a heavy sigh. "I probably sound like a hypocrite saying that after I kept some stuff from the team," he acknowledged.

"You wanted to find out who the saboteur was without tipping him off," she said.

"But it put you all in danger."

"We're hotshots," she said. "We're in danger with every fire we fight."

He moved his shoulders again and grimaced, like he was either in pain or a chill was running down his back.

Michaela suddenly realized what was really bothering him. Braden Zimmer was legendary for having a sixth sense for when a fire was about to happen. He'd often predicted when one was coming before the call even came into Dispatch. That was probably why he kept looking outside, and not just at the asphalt that was already scorched—he was checking the sky for smoke.

She breathed in deep, but all she could smell was the wax that Stanley had used on the trucks and Annie's doggy scent. The overgrown puppy needed a bath, or maybe she'd gotten wet when Stanley had washed the trucks.

He probably shouldn't have bothered washing them if Braden's sixth sense was right and a fire was coming.

"You feel it, don't you?" she prodded.

He clenched his jaw and nodded.

"Hopefully it's something small," she said and gestured toward the parking lot. "Like that."

"You still got hurt from that," he said. "Doesn't matter how small a fire is—it can still cause a lot of damage."

"Too true," she agreed.

He tilted his head and closed his eyes for a moment. "But this…"

"It doesn't feel small," she finished for him.

He shrugged. "I don't know. I'm probably just imagining things. We've been living on edge for so long. I want to say that's why Donovan talked to you the way he did."

"He didn't say anything I didn't already know, about how some of the guys feel about me," she said. "Like I don't belong." They would be happy when she was gone, maybe that was why she still hesitated before giving Braden her notice to go on medical leave.

But while he had his sixth sense, she had that fluttery sensation inside her. Her baby.

She had to do what was right for her. She had to leave for now, and maybe she would stay gone. Maybe she would stay with her daughter and find a whole new career, one that she could know she'd chosen for the right reasons and not just to spite her father.

"You belong, Michaela," Braden assured her. "You're one of my best."

There was that fatherly praise she'd wanted for so long, that acceptance, that pride in her abilities—in her. But she'd given up on getting it long ago. And while she might have started out in her career to spite her father, she had stayed because she loved the work and even most of her team.

Giving it—and them—up wouldn't be easy.

Maybe that was why she couldn't spit out the words. Or maybe, knowing about Braden's premonition, she was just concerned that there might be one more fire she needed to fight before she went on leave. Because with everything that had been happening lately, Charlie would probably be in the middle of it.

Charlie Tillerman was once again in the middle of one of her investigations, and Wynona couldn't help but wonder why. Was it just bad luck on his part?

Or was *he* the bad luck?

"So you can't tell me anything about the man who tried to kill the mayor?" Wells asked the man whom she, along with a nurse and a town hall official, had just witnessed get sworn in as the mayor.

"It wasn't me," Tillerman said, as if he'd sensed her skepticism.

"It wasn't Charlie," Les said, his voice raspy and weak. He was alive, but after two attempts on his life and officially passing his job over to his successor, he was fragile and tired.

That was why her sergeant had called her last night for a special meeting. Not to reprimand her but to let her know the results of the tests on the mayor's blood and stomach contents. Les Byers had been poisoned, because she doubted that the mayor, at his age, had knowingly taken the high dose of ecstasy that had been found in his system.

How would he have even come across what was known as a club drug?

There was a club in town, but not many of the locals were customers of it. They were loyal to the Filling Station instead. Loyal to Charlie Tillerman.

"But your *friend* here is now the mayor, at least until the election. So doesn't that give him a motive to get you out of the way?" she asked the older man.

Les chuckled softly. "I offered him that position months ago. I've been ready to retire for a while now. I have no intention of running again. Charlie wouldn't have had to kill me to get my job. He could have just accepted my offer all those months ago."

"Why didn't you?" she asked Tillerman.

He shrugged and sighed. "A few years ago, I promised myself I wasn't going to get into politics again."

After all the research she'd done on him, Wynona could totally understand why. His opponent had found a hell of a lot of dirt about him. Well, mostly about his wife—former wife now. "But you are a town council member," she pointed out.

He shrugged again. "That was a seat I pretty much inherited from my father when he and my mother moved to Florida."

Something else she knew.

"You didn't have to accept it."

"No," he agreed. "But Northern Lakes is my home, and I need to do what I can to protect it. That was why I didn't immediately rule out running, with everyone trying to encourage me to become mayor." He sighed, then smiled at his friend. "And that's why I've taken your position, but just until you come to your senses and realize you want it back."

"I wouldn't have any senses to come to if you hadn't shown up when you did," Les said. "You saved my life."

And why would Tillerman have done that if he was the one who'd put Les's life in danger? Wynona had to eliminate him as a suspect. But now that he'd just been sworn in as the acting mayor, she was very concerned he might become the next victim.

"Okay," she said, "but if either of you remember anything else about the suspect, please let me know." She wouldn't hold her breath until they called her, though. Clearly, they'd told her all that they knew.

At least the mayor had.

She wasn't sure about Charlie Tillerman.

She stepped outside of the mayor's room and waited for Tillerman to come out.

"You're not done with the hot lights yet, Trooper Wells?" he asked when he found her leaning against the corridor wall.

"No hot lights," she said. "Just a warning that you need to be very careful now, Mr. Tillerman. Because whoever has gone after the mayor and you and Ms. Momber will probably be even more dangerous now."

Chapter 20

More dangerous...

Trooper Wells's last words kept replaying in Charlie's mind. This person, who'd gone after the mayor twice, was going to be more dangerous. Was it the same person who'd already gone after him? To keep him from accepting this position?

If he hadn't been so worried about Les, Charlie would have chased the suspect out of the hospital room and tried to catch him. But he'd been more concerned with helping his friend at that time than with catching a would-be killer.

He now wished that it had been possible to do both. Because this person had to get caught before anyone else got hurt, especially Michaela.

Was she even a target, though? Or was everything that happened all about him? About his involvement in politics again? Something he'd sworn he wouldn't do after his last campaign destroyed his marriage...

But he hadn't had to campaign for his current seat on the council or this interim position as mayor. No wonder Trooper Wells suspected he might have been involved. But surely after the things that had happened to him, too, she had to know that he'd had nothing to do with the attempts on the mayor's life or on Michaela's or on his own.

He was a damn fool for giving in and accepting the position. But after nearly losing Les twice, he'd wanted to make sure that his old friend wouldn't be in danger anymore. But now *his* life was even more at risk, because Wells was probably right about this person getting more dangerous now.

For him and for whoever was around him.

He needed to keep his distance from Michaela. That would probably be the easiest way to keep her and their unborn baby safe.

And the rest of his family…

As he was leaving the hospital, he noticed he'd missed some calls from his brother-in-law. Probably about his sister's car. No doubt Valerie wanted her vehicle back, so he headed toward the Veltema house to return it.

And to warn her and Eric.

They would be thrilled that he had accepted the interim mayor position. At least, they would be until they realized how dangerous it was.

Was he doing the right thing?

Or was he needlessly putting himself and others in danger? Others he cared about, the way he cared about Michaela and their baby…

He hadn't even talked to his sister yet about what had been going on with the mayor, about Les's offer. And they'd only spoken briefly about his being the father of Michaela's baby, the bombshell he'd dropped on her that day in the bar. So much had happened since then.

So many bad things.

And some good things too. He and Michaela had been close for a while, with the potential of maybe getting closer. But he couldn't take the chance that he wouldn't put her and the baby in danger. He couldn't take the chance with their lives that he'd taken with his own.

He turned into the driveway with the sign hanging from

the mailbox that said Veltemas. His brother-in-law was sitting in his truck, exhaust rolling out of the tailpipe. He hopped out the minute he saw Charlie.

"Park Valerie's car over there," he said, pointing to an open space in front of the garage. "We have to get going."

Valerie was standing on the front porch of the two-story farmhouse-style home. Her arms were looped around each of her sons' shoulders. Their faces looked pinched, and they didn't smile or wave or rush toward him like they normally did.

"What's up with them? Are they going to go get shots or something?" Charlie asked.

Eric shook his head. "Nothing's up for them. But it is for you and me. We have to get going."

"'We'?" Charlie asked, confused. "Where?"

"The captain of the volunteer squad said he tried to call you, but you didn't pick up," Eric said.

"I—I was tied up for a while," he said. There had been a couple of missed calls from a number he hadn't recognized and a voice mail he hadn't played. But there had been more calls from Eric, whose number he had recognized.

"We have to go to a fire," Eric said.

He groaned. That was the last thing anyone needed right now. No wonder the kids looked so upset. Valerie looked pale and shaky, too, when she was usually so tough. "Where's the fire?"

"Forest." Eric grimaced. "Not far from where the kids were trapped."

"What about the hotshots?" Charlie asked, his heart pounding fast and hard as he thought about Michaela—as he *worried* about Michaela.

"They're already out there," Eric said. "But it's big, and they need backup."

He could smell the smoke then, even before he noticed the haze on the horizon. He'd been so preoccupied with what had happened at the hospital that he hadn't noticed the smoke before. But then, he wasn't a real firefighter—just a volunteer. And a reluctant one at that.

But Michaela…

This was what she did, who she was. Was she out there? Despite carrying their baby girl, was she battling this blaze with people who'd already proved to her that she shouldn't trust them?

He shouldn't have dropped her off at the firehouse that morning. Hell, he shouldn't have let her out of his sight, not with the danger they'd both been in the past few days.

The danger she was probably in right now. He quickly parked the car and jumped into Eric's running truck.

"Hurry up," he said.

"I grabbed your gear already," Eric said, pointing into the back seat of his quad-cab pickup truck. "All the rigs are already out there with the hotshots. We have to meet them there. They're leading this. We're just there as backup."

He nodded. He was going to be backup, all right, but just to one particular hotshot.

"Hurry up," he said again. He had to get to her before anything happened to her.

If he wasn't already too late…

Michaela understood how Stanley felt now when he watched them leave for a fire call and had to stay behind in the empty garage, waiting and wondering how everything was going. If they would be all right…

If all of them would come back this time…

Braden's premonition had come to pass again, like it had so many times before. And the fire was big, just like he'd feared. Fortunately, it was outside town and would hopefully be contained before it caused much damage.

Guilt over the fact that she hadn't gone out with them weighed heavily on Michaela. But she'd wanted a baby for too long to knowingly do anything that might risk her pregnancy. And even with the oxygen mask, she risked inhaling some smoke, and with being anemic, she probably wasn't strong enough to lug around the heavy equipment. As well as trusting her team to have her back... These were all things she knew she shouldn't risk.

Some of her team had stared at her as they'd rushed in, reporting to the firehouse to suit up for the fire call Braden had put out. They'd probably wondered why she wasn't going out too.

Maybe they assumed it was because of the wound on her head. Or some might have known about her baby already. She'd told Hank, but she hadn't told any of the others, unless they'd overheard it that night at the bar when Charlie had told his sister.

The smirks from the younger guys, Bruce and Howie, suggested they probably had. And then there was Donovan Cunningham.

He hadn't even looked at her. Out of shame or anger? Probably anger. She doubted he felt any shame for the things he'd said and the things his kids had done. And what had he done?

Was he the one who'd driven them off the road the night before?

She'd been smart to not go out on the fire, because Donovan had more allies on the team than she did. More people would have his back than hers. Fires were dangerous enough with the support of her team. If she didn't have it...

But still that guilt persisted, probably exacerbated by

waiting around the empty firehouse. She should leave, go to the bar and check on Charlie. Make sure that he was still safe…

But as she started toward one of the open doors, a woman rushed in, a certain dark-haired, wild-eyed woman. Michaela tensed with dread over what was probably going to be another unpleasant interaction with Charlie's sister.

"You're here," the woman said.

Michaela nodded.

"You didn't go out on the fire?"

She shook her head as her hand automatically slid over her stomach.

"Charlie thinks you went out there," she said.

"He doesn't have to worry about me," Michaela said. "I wouldn't risk it."

"The baby," Valerie said and nodded. "That's why you're here."

"Yeah, I'll go over to the bar and let him know I'm not there."

"He isn't there," Valerie said. "The volunteers were called in as support."

Michaela shook her head. "They didn't come through here." Or she would have seen him. She would have stopped him. He couldn't trust anyone out there any more than she could. Maybe less…

He certainly seemed to be the target of these attacks more than she was. He was the one in the most danger. Especially now, in the midst of a blaze.

"They were told the hotshots had already taken out all the rigs and just to report to the fire, so Charlie rode with my husband out there."

"Then why are you here?" Michaela asked, and that dread gripped her again.

"Because Eric called me," Valerie shared, and tears sprang to her eyes.

Michaela reached out then and gripped her shoulders. She was seeking comfort more than offering it, though. "What happened?"

"He doesn't know. They got separated. He said Charlie just disappeared into the fire."

He hadn't disappeared, and it probably wasn't the fire that was the danger—it was whoever was in it with him.

"Eric can't find my brother, Michaela," Valerie said. "And he can't get anyone else to listen to him and help him look for Charlie."

Michaela would go. She had to. She couldn't sit back here and wait for someone else to save Charlie's life. That was her job.

Scorched earth had definitely been the right way to go. Especially after the close call in the hospital earlier that day.

They'd come so close to getting caught then.

To Charlie Tillerman catching them...

He'd been in the way too many times.

But now flames rose up, burning bright and hot all around them. All around the gas that had been poured around the forest, around Charlie Tillerman.

Soon those voracious flames would consume Charlie Tillerman alive...

Chapter 21

The flames were all around Charlie, like they'd been that night his bar had burned down and he'd nearly lost his life. But there was no angel coming to him through the smoke this time. A short while ago, there had been someone else, though. Because the smoke was so thick, he hadn't been able to tell if the hat and jacket they wore was the black of the volunteers or the yellow of the hotshots. He hadn't even been able to tell if they were a man or woman, because of the oxygen mask strapped over their face.

He didn't think it was Michaela, though, because of the build of the person. Definitely taller and broader than she was. But even Trooper Wells was taller than Michaela, so it could have been a woman.

But the mask had reminded him of the guy in the hospital who'd nearly killed Les, because it had almost felt more like a disguise even though it wasn't the same kind of mask. This was an oxygen mask. So the person had all the equipment of a firefighter. Not like the killer, who'd just been wearing the doctor's white coat, along with that hoodie and jeans.

Charlie didn't know why he kept thinking of the killer. Maybe it was because he hadn't had time to process what had happened earlier. What could have happened…

Or maybe it was because the fire was reminding him all too well of his own mortality.

Charlie had an oxygen mask too. Because of the masks and the roar of the fire, Charlie hadn't been able to hear what the other firefighter might have said, not that they'd seemed to be saying anything. Instead, they'd just made some hand gestures, pointing Charlie toward another section of the smoke-filled woods.

Why?

Was the fire shifting again? Would it be safer here, or was he needed here? Or was the rest of his crew here?

He'd lost Eric. That had probably been Charlie's fault, though, because he'd rushed off ahead of his brother-in-law. He'd been looking for the hotshots, actually for the one hotshot in particular whom he cared about the most.

Michaela.

Would the oxygen mask be enough to protect her and the baby? Would they be okay?

Or was this going to be too much for them?

And for him?

As he headed deeper into the woods, he just saw more smoke and flames but no other firefighters. Then he realized that the person who'd led him here might not have been a real volunteer firefighter.

Maybe he'd just gotten his hands on some gear, like he had with that white coat at the hospital. Maybe that hadn't been a firefighter at all but a killer instead, the one who'd tried to get rid of the mayor and Charlie.

But this time, his efforts might prove successful because Charlie couldn't see his way out of the flames. He couldn't get out of the nightmare.

He didn't want Michaela risking her life to come to his rescue like she had in the past. He didn't want her and their baby in danger because of him. He had to figure his own way out of the fire without endangering the person who meant the most to him.

He should have told her that, he should have told her that he was starting to have feelings for her.

Deep feelings…

But he hadn't wanted to scare her away with a commitment she wasn't ready to make. After what she'd been through, with not just her ex but also her father, he could understand her fear. Hell, he'd felt it too. That was why he'd been fine with their casual arrangement.

But it hadn't stayed casual to him for long.

And now he was the one who was scared, scared that he might never get the chance to tell her or to see their child.

Michaela kept the mask tight over her nose and mouth, breathing in the oxygen while blocking out the smoke. But just like the flames, it was all around her.

Thick and impenetrable.

Where the hell was Charlie?

Once Valerie had told her he was missing, she rushed out to the scene to find him. She'd bypassed the staging area where the superintendent was, knowing that Braden wouldn't allow her out here on the search and rescue. She was too close to the person who was missing.

Too close and yet not close enough.

So she'd called Charlie's brother-in-law, who'd met her on the street, and then he'd led her to where he had seen the bar owner last in the woods—or at least, where he thought he'd seen him last.

"Somebody else was out here then," Eric Veltema said. "And Charlie rushed off after them. I figured that he probably thought it was you."

"This other person was in hotshot gear?" Her heart beat harder and heavier with fear. Donovan was probably even angrier with Charlie than he was with her.

Eric Veltema shrugged. "I don't know for sure. I couldn't see anything clearly because of the smoke." He coughed now, choking on the smoke because he'd lowered his mask, probably to make sure she could hear him clearly. "And Charlie was closer to the person. Then he was just gone."

No.

Charlie could not be gone. He had to be out here. Somewhere. He had to be alive.

She couldn't lose him now, and she definitely couldn't lose him to a fire. Not after having rescued him from the one in his bar.

"Go back and find the hotshot superintendent," she said. While they used radios sometimes, it was often hard to get a frequency out in the field, especially somewhere as remote as the forest they were in now, so she couldn't tell him herself. "Let him know I'm going after Charlie."

Braden had probably already sent out a group of hotshots to search for him. But she didn't know whom he would pick—and if they could be trusted to save Charlie or if they would put him in more danger.

"I want to help you look," Veltema insisted.

She shook her head. "You'll help more by letting Braden know where I am."

And that she and Charlie were both out there, in the fire.

Braden, more than anyone else, would realize how much danger they were in, because he knew how determined someone was to hurt them. He'd been there for the gas leak and for the car crash. And after this, she probably wouldn't have to debate with herself about whether or not to return to work after her medical leave, Braden would undoubtedly fire her for going off on her own.

But Braden, more than anyone else, should realize she couldn't trust *anyone else* to find Charlie. She couldn't trust anyone else...*but Charlie.*

He wasn't a danger to her. But he was definitely *in* danger. And she couldn't stand around and wait for Charlie, for the father of her child, to be found. Not when she was the one who always found him.

And she had always found him in time.

In the fire in his bar...

And with the gas leak...

She had to find him this time too. She had to find him alive. And hopefully, in better condition than she'd found him those other times.

But this fire was big, the smoke thickening even here where the fire had already swept through the area. She took a deep breath of the oxygen pumping out of her mask. She would be okay, this would keep her and the baby safe from the smoke.

But the fire wasn't completely out either. She rushed now, bypassing the flames that flickered over the already blackened trees and scorched ground. Even as they began to die out, they crackled and spit sparks at her as she passed them.

The volunteers wore black, so it might be hard to distinguish Charlie from the smoke and the already burned ground.

If he was lying down...

If his oxygen had already run out...

Or if whoever had lured him out here had already gotten rid of him. Because she had no doubt that this fire had been deliberately set, and maybe to kill Charlie Tillerman.

And if she wasn't careful, it might kill her too.

* * *

Son of a bitch...

Braden cursed as he tried to figure out what the hell was going on. This wasn't some accidental fire, started from a poorly extinguished campfire or a cigarette carelessly tossed out the window of a passing car.

This thing was a beast intent on consuming the acres of woods where it had been set. And probably intent on consuming some people as well.

Charlie Tillerman and Michaela.

He stared hard at the man who'd rushed up to tell him that Charlie had gone missing. He'd already heard that a volunteer firefighter had disappeared. He just hadn't known which one, but he'd had a suspicion it might have been Charlie.

And now Michaela was missing too.

He'd left her safely back at the firehouse. And he'd been convinced she would stay there.

But she must have heard somehow that Charlie was the one missing. And she'd gone off to find him. Charlie's brother-in-law had rushed up a short while ago to tell him that.

And now Braden had sent off his team to find them. That was the priority. To rescue them.

If they could be rescued...

Maybe they were both already dead. And maybe that was the intent of whoever had set this fire, because it was definitely arson. He didn't need his wife to tell him that. He could see it in the way the flames burned like hot rainbows from the gas fumes rising up from the ground.

Someone had provided the fire with fuel, with the gas splashed all around the weeds and onto the trees. The arsonist had wanted to make damn sure this fire would take off and spread, that it would become uncontrollable.

But the thing with an uncontrollable fire was that sometimes the person who'd set it got trapped in the flames too. So he'd advised his team to be careful—and not just of the fire but of a potential killer.

Chapter 22

Charlie should have known that she would be the one to find him. At least, he thought it was Michaela wearing the yellow hat and jacket with the oxygen mask over her face.

But was it her or the person he'd seen earlier? The person who had surely tried to lure him deeper into the fire? It kept springing up everywhere he went, as if it had been set in a circle all around him. There was no way out of the circle unless he walked right through a wall of fire.

Had she come in that way?

She must have.

Walking through fire to get to him, to rescue him like she had before. Like that night in his bar.

But they weren't in his bar now, though it smelled like it had that night. Like gasoline...

This fire had definitely been set. To take him out? Had that been the plan?

Or to take her out too?

He lowered his mask and tried to talk to her. "Michaela? Is that you?" He coughed and sputtered on the smoke that burned his nose and throat.

She shook her head.

Wasn't it her?

She tapped her mask, which she, thankfully, didn't lower.

He pulled his up, breathing in the oxygen, but the tank on

his back didn't seem to be pumping as much into his mask as it had before. Was he running out? If he was, she might be as well. Were they running out of time to escape?

Then she pointed, and he saw the others. They were surrounded, and not just by flames.

They were surrounded by hotshots, all wearing the yellow hats and the masks covering their faces. And he knew there was at least one among them that they couldn't trust. Maybe more than one. Donovan Cunningham had made it clear that he wasn't the only one who didn't think Michaela Momber belonged on the team.

But maybe that was because he knew, like the others, that she was better than them. She had been the one who'd found him first.

Just like she had before.

And even though the others had shown up, he had no idea if they were being rescued or if they were in even more danger than they were from the fire. Standing in the middle of that circle of flames and hotshots, Charlie felt like he'd stepped inside the pages of *Lord of the Flies*, like there were no laws or rules out here.

Like the hotshots were a law unto themselves, with their motivations and secrets and vengeances.

He stepped between Michaela and the others, desperate to protect her and their child. Desperate to make sure that he didn't lose them. But he had no weapon on him. Nothing to battle the blaze or the hotshots. Nothing to save them.

He thought she'd saved him. That was what Charlie told her when they'd walked out of the fire. But Michaela wasn't sure that they would have made it through the flames without the help of her team. And they had acted as a team to get them all out unscathed.

Yet she was in the hospital again—just to get checked out and make sure the baby was fine, not because she was hurt. She would only be hurt if something was wrong with the baby. Or with Charlie...

She'd been so scared when his sister had said he was missing. Scared enough to risk her and her baby's life to find him. And she had, but she suspected they both would have died had her team not shown up when they had.

And for a second, she'd been as distrustful of them as Charlie had when he stepped between her and the others. She'd wondered, too, if they'd come to rescue them or to make sure that they didn't make it out of the fire alive.

But then she'd recognized Hank, who'd been her best friend for so many years. And Trick had been there. And Trent Miles and Ethan Sommerly, Wyatt Andrews and Cody Mallehan. Together they'd all worked to clear a spot in the flames so they could get safely out. And while they'd worked, Rory VanDam had flown a plane over, dropping water onto the fire.

By the time Owen had taken her to the hospital in his rig, most of the fire had been extinguished. Her team had been there for her, had saved her and Charlie, because she knew she wouldn't have been able to do it without them this time. She wouldn't have gotten herself and Charlie out of that fire without her team. She didn't have to be as alone and independent as she'd tried to be all these years. She had people she could count on.

She had friends. Real friends.

But she wanted more. She wanted Charlie too. She wanted him to be someone whom both she and her daughter could count on. But he couldn't be that for them or for anyone else if he didn't survive. Because while she had friends, he had enemies—at least one who was determined to get rid of him.

Because she'd smelled gasoline, she knew that fire hadn't been an accident. And by the way the flames had sprung up around Charlie, trapping him inside an ever-narrowing ring, he had clearly been the intended target. He had come to the hospital, too, but instead of getting checked out, he was sitting beside her bed, staring intently at her.

"I'm fine," she said.

"You shouldn't have been there," he said, as if he was admonishing her.

"I wouldn't have been if your sister hadn't told me that you were missing," she replied with a pointed look.

He frowned. "You weren't there already with the rest of the hotshots?"

She shook her head. "No." She touched her belly that strained against the T-shirt she'd worn beneath her uniform. "I'm not taking any chances."

"But you did," he said, his voice gruff, and maybe not just from the fire. There were tears glistening in his dark eyes, too, or maybe that was from the fire.

"I want our daughter to meet her father," she said, but her pulse quickened as she realized she hadn't felt that little flutter for a while. She didn't know if the baby was really all right. Now tears stung her eyes.

What if…

Charlie reached over the railing and covered her hand with his. Beneath their entwined hands, her belly moved as the baby shifted and kicked inside her.

Michaela released a shaky breath of relief. "She's still there." She'd been so afraid of losing her and of losing Charlie too.

"She kicked?" he asked, his voice cracking while his eyes lit up.

She nodded.

His breath came out in a shaky sigh, like he'd been holding it. Clearly he wanted this baby as much as she did.

Until this moment, she hadn't been certain. And she'd wanted her daughter's father to want her so that she wouldn't feel as unloved as Michaela had. She nodded, and a tear spilled over, running down her cheek.

Charlie used the thumb of his free hand to wipe it away. "Thank God," he murmured. "But we need to make sure that you're both all right." He glanced toward the closed curtains as if willing someone to appear.

His words moved through her, warming her heart. Both? He wasn't just concerned about their baby, he seemed genuinely worried about her too.

Like she was about him.

Had she fallen for them both?

She was afraid that she had, and she was even more afraid to believe that she could have and keep them both, that she could be happy. Because whenever she'd been happy in the past, it had never lasted. Something or someone had always ruined it.

And there was someone out there, someone who wanted Charlie dead. She swallowed hard to get rid of the lump of fear in her throat. "You took the interim mayor position?"

He grimaced but nodded. "I... I am so sorry. I know this is all my fault. This danger you and our baby have been in..."

"You can't know for certain that the fire had anything to do with you." But she suspected it had, that it had been set to get rid of him.

"When I showed up at the hospital to talk to the mayor, someone was trying to suffocate him with a—"

"Is he all right?" she asked.

He nodded. "Yeah, whoever it was knocked me down

and ran out of the room, and I got help for the mayor. He's going to be fine."

"You don't know who tried to kill him?"

He shook his head. "He was wearing a mask. I couldn't see his face, just like I couldn't see whoever gestured at me in the fire."

"Your brother-in-law suspected you saw someone, that you were following someone," she said. "He figured that you thought it was me."

"I'm not sure if it was a hotshot or a volunteer," he admitted. "But I am sure of one thing, Michaela…" His hand cupped her face again as he stared into her eyes.

Now she held her breath, her lungs burning from the pressure while her heart thumped quickly.

His throat moved as if he was struggling to swallow now. Then he began, "Michaela, I…"

"You're back again," the doctor said as she ducked inside the curtain. She glanced at Charlie. "And you are too."

Charlie held up his hands. "I'm fine. Just, please, make sure they're all right."

The doctor smiled. "Of course." She pulled the curtain farther aside for the ultrasound machine a nurse was wheeling into the space with them.

And then, moments later, their little girl appeared on that screen with her perfect little profile and her squirmy little body and her very strong heartbeat.

"She looks good, Mama," the doctor said.

Michaela released the breath she'd been holding.

With all the equipment and people in that small space, Charlie had gotten squeezed out a bit. He was far enough away that Michaela couldn't touch him, and for some reason, she really wanted to. She wanted to hold his hand. She wanted to comfort him because of how he looked as he stared at that screen, how awed and maybe even frightened he was.

"I'm going to get a nurse to get some blood from you, just to check your iron levels, and if everything's good, you'll be able to leave," the doctor assured Michaela. Then Dr. Smits turned back to Charlie, whose handsome face was soot-stained and intense. "Are you sure you don't need to get checked out?"

He shook his head. "I'm fine..." But his voice was even gruffer now, like he was being strangled.

Instead of arguing with him, the doctor smiled and slipped out. But she'd left the ultrasound machine on with their daughter's picture on the screen.

While he didn't move any closer to the machine, or to Michaela, he stared at that screen as if he couldn't look away. She kept glancing at it, but he held her attention the most right now. "What were you going to say to me?" she asked.

He shrugged. "I... I just don't want you or the baby getting hurt again because of me," he said. "I'm going to figure out who's doing this and stop them."

She'd wanted to do the same thing, wanted to find the saboteur and whoever was after Charlie. But she knew, all too well, how hard it was to investigate—and how damn dangerous as well. She shook her head. "You're not a cop, Charlie."

"No," he agreed. "But I am the mayor now. And this town's safety is my responsibility."

"The fire's out," she reminded him. "The town is safe now."

"Because of the hotshots," he said. "But I might have been the one who put it in danger this time. Who's been putting *you* in danger."

She shook her head. "I am a hotshot," she reminded him.

"I'm used to danger." Much more than he was. He was scaring her right now, with as determined as he seemed to put himself in more danger.

"But you didn't go into that fire until you knew I was in it," he said. "You risked your life for me, Michaela. More than once. And now…"

"What?"

But she knew.

He was going to do the same for her. Or for their baby. Or for the whole damn town…

She wanted to stop him. But before she could pull off the blood pressure cuff wrapped around her arm and the oxygen sensor from her finger, he was gone.

To try to catch a killer on his own.

Trick felt Henrietta's pain, mostly from how hard she'd been squeezing his hand while they waited for the doctor to check Michaela out.

"What if something happened to the baby?" she asked. "She wanted a child so badly but was convinced she would never be able to have one."

Trick wanted to reassure his fiancée that her best friend was fine. But he didn't know.

The fire had been smoky and hot, and he had no idea how those conditions might affect a pregnancy. But he actually wanted to learn, in case he and Henrietta decided to have kids someday.

Right now, they'd determined they were happy to be an uncle and an aunt to the baby his sister was having soon and to Michaela's child. But maybe, once the saboteur was caught, they might change their minds.

Still, the thought of bringing a child into their situation right now…

Hell, he didn't want a niece or nephew coming into this. He hadn't had to have Braden confirm it to know that the forest fire had been deliberately set.

And stoked...

Had the arsonist been trying to hurt the hotshots? Or had someone else been the specific target?

Charlie Tillerman?

There'd been that break-in at his bar and then the gas line tampered with, like what had been done at Owen's place. Charlie had come out of the ER a while ago, but the trooper had made a beeline for him before anyone else could talk to the bar owner.

Not that the trooper's presence necessarily made Charlie safe...

There was just something about Trooper Wells that made Trick uneasy. Suspicious. Like she had her own agenda concerning the hotshots...

Or Northern Lakes.

Or maybe she was helping someone else carry out their agenda. Like Gingrich, even though he was behind bars. Or...someone else...

After a corrupt FBI agent had tried to kill Rory VanDam, it was clear to Trick that anyone could be bought. For the right price.

Did Wells have a price?

Was that her deal? Was she a gun for hire like those assassins who had tried to kill Ethan?

Then the door to the waiting room opened again with someone coming out of the ER. Henrietta gasped and rushed forward, throwing her arms around her friend. Then she jerked back and asked, "Are you all right?"

"I'm fine," Michaela said, but she seemed distracted,

looking around Hank to the rest of the people in the room like she was searching for someone.

Henrietta lowered her voice and asked, "And the baby?"

Michaela looked at her then, and a smile spread across her face—a wide, bright smile—and she nodded. "She's fine too."

"A girl?" Trick asked now. "Are you going to name her Henrietta?"

Henrietta gasped again. "God, don't do that to her. Name her anything but that."

"I have some ideas," Michaela murmured as she stepped around Hank and gazed around the waiting room.

The other hotshots, who'd been able to get to the hospital and weren't still at the site making sure the fire didn't flare back to life, rushed forward now and hugged her. But she kept pulling away from each one, looking around them for someone else.

She could have been looking for one of the hotshots who'd stayed behind. Like Braden. But the superintendent had stayed back at the scene to await the arrival of a certain arson investigator.

Or she could have been looking for Donovan Cunningham. The guy definitely owed her and Charlie Tillerman an apology. But more so Michaela, for the way he'd lashed out at her. But was he genuinely remorseful about that?

Trick wasn't sure.

But he was pretty sure he had a good idea who Michaela was looking for, even before she confirmed it with, "Where is Charlie?"

Trick smiled and pointed in the direction where Wells had pulled the bar owner aside. But when he turned that way, he saw that they were gone. Both of them. "He was just there with Wells."

She released a shaky little breath. "So he's not rushing off alone, then…"

"Alone to do what?" Trick wondered.

"He's determined to find out who's been responsible for the things that have put us in danger," she said. "And I was worried he was going to put himself in danger to do that."

But if he'd gone off with Wells, Trick wasn't sure he was actually safe.

Michaela must have suspected the same thing, because she asked him, "Can you help me find him?"

Trick nodded. "Yeah, of course."

He just hoped that he did before it was too late. Before Charlie found that danger.

Chapter 23

Could he trust Trooper Wells?

Charlie wasn't sure. But the officer had sworn she was checking into all the other council members, seeing who'd had the motive and the opportunity to go after the mayor. And after him…

He wasn't worried about himself, though. He wasn't worried about Les anymore either. There was no reason for anyone to go after the former mayor anymore. The man was too beloved to have any enemies. The only motive anyone had to go after him was to take his job.

Since Charlie had that job now, he would be the target. But he had to make sure that he was the only target, that Michaela and their unborn baby didn't get hurt because of him.

Maybe, with the way he'd left her alone at the hospital, people would believe that they weren't really in a relationship. And they really weren't.

But he'd nearly told her that he loved her. That he wanted to be more than a father to their child—that he also wanted to be a husband to Michaela. But seeing their little girl on the screen, seeing how small and helpless she was, he'd been compelled to do whatever he could to protect her.

Even walk away…

But the only way to really keep her safe was to find out

who was after him and stop them. So after having Wells drop him off at his sister's house, he borrowed Valerie's car again. She wasn't home, but he didn't have to ask her permission, since the keys were still in the ignition. Instead of heading back toward town, he headed toward the fire because he was pretty sure someone had used it to try to kill him.

When he'd shared that suspicion with Wells, she'd acted like he was paranoid or delusional. He'd pretty much acted the same way when the mayor had told him he'd been poisoned, though. Maybe it was better to think one person was delusional than that another was evil.

Police vehicles blocked off the area, so he couldn't get very close to the scene of the fire, which seemed to be just lingering smoke now and no flames. But he parked alongside the road and started toward the area where Braden Zimmer had set up his command center. As he passed the other parked vehicles, he took notice of the company name on a few of the pickups' doors.

It wasn't the US Forest Service, although there were several of their trucks present too. The logo and the name that caught his attention was for BF Wood Products. *BF*, for Bentley Ford. And the man himself started down the street, wearing the black hat and coat of the volunteer fire department.

Charlie hadn't been the only town council member who'd answered the call for more volunteers for the fire department. Bentley Ford and Jason Cruise had become volunteers even before Charlie had.

Was Bentley the same height and build as the person who had gestured for Charlie to go deeper into the forest fire? He couldn't be sure, not with all the smoke that had been there then. But he could see pretty clearly now. And the guy in the hospital room, who'd tried smothering Les, had been the same height and general build as Bentley Ford.

"It was you!" Charlie shouted, and he launched himself at the guy like he had in the hospital room.

But Bentley didn't run. He stood there while Charlie slammed his hands against his chest. "What the hell are you talking about?" he shouted back at him.

"You tried to kill Les earlier today, and then you tried to kill me just a little while a—"

"You're nuts," Bentley said. "I was here." He gestured back at the charred trees.

"Yeah, I know. You set it. You tried to kill me here."

Bentley shook his head. "Now I know you lost it. Why the hell would I do that?"

"Because you know I took the interim mayor position, and you want it for yourself."

Bentley nodded. "Yeah, sure, I'd like that power." Then he raised his voice and shouted, "But not enough to burn down my own damn property!" He shoved Charlie back.

He stumbled a bit before regaining his balance. Then he focused on the area around them. "I thought this was state land."

Bentley shook his head. "No, it's mine, damn it. Acres of trees that were just getting big enough to use." He cursed again. "It's going to take too long to bring this land back. So I guess Jason Cruise is going to get his way."

"His way about what?"

"I'll sell it to him. He's got some client that's been after it for a hotel and shopping plaza."

"That won't happen," Charlie said. They'd been keeping out the big chains to protect the small business owners and the integrity of the town.

"I'll vote for it now since it'll make my now-worthless

piece of property valuable again. And then it'll pass…if you and the mayor aren't around to stop it," Bentley said.

"Are you threatening me?" Charlie asked. Maybe he hadn't been wrong about him.

"Not me," Bentley pointed out.

And Charlie realized who the real threat was. He had to call the trooper again, make sure she focused her attention on Jason Cruise so that she could find the evidence to arrest him. To eliminate that threat…

Because Charlie wasn't going to be safe—or safe to be around—until Jason was behind bars.

After her calls to him had gone unanswered, Michaela opted to go to the bar to look for Charlie. Despite everything else going on, he had a business to run. And he loved the bar so much that he'd rebuilt it as quickly as possible after it had burned down the first time. She suspected he'd done it to honor his grandfather, who'd obviously meant a lot to him.

But the Filling Station was still closed, according to the sign on the front door. She'd been able to get inside through the damaged back door to the alley.

"Charlie?" she called out. "Charlie? Are you here?"

Where else would he have gone?

Or maybe he hadn't gone anywhere. Had Trooper Wells taken him somewhere? She must have, because he had no vehicle. A chill chased down her spine as she remembered how Wells had locked her in the back seat of that SUV and she'd wondered then what the law officer had really intended to do to her.

Just question her?

Or did she have some other agenda where the hotshots were concerned? Could she be the saboteur who kept hurting the hotshots in some of the same ways that Charlie had nearly been hurt?

And what about Charlie?

Could Wynona Wells have it out for him for some reason? Maybe he'd flirted with her and broken her heart, like Michaela had been so afraid he would break hers?

So afraid that she hadn't told him how she really felt about him. That she was falling for him despite all her efforts to protect herself.

She wished now that she'd done that, because she had a horrible feeling that something was going to happen to him. It was nearly as intense as Braden must feel with his fire premonitions. The superintendent had been right again. But Michaela really hoped she was wrong.

Maybe he was just upstairs, in the shower or something. "Charlie!" she called out again, and then she started toward the bar, intending to duck behind it to step into the kitchen.

But someone was standing there in the shadows of the dim lighting. Someone tall, but a little leaner than Charlie. And even in the dim lighting, she could tell that his hair was brighter. He was blond.

"Hello?" she called out to him now.

Was it a bartender?

Then he turned and smiled at her, that patented salesman smile that made her back teeth ache at the sugary superficialness of it. Jason Cruise had always reminded her of her ex-husband—all charm but no substance.

"Moonlighting?" she asked him.

His toothy grin got even wider. "Something like that."

She felt that little shiver of unease now. How had he gotten inside? She stepped behind the bar, too, and pushed open the door to the kitchen. "Charlie!"

"I don't think he's here," the Realtor remarked with a

heavy sigh. He stepped from behind the bar to the front, but where he'd positioned himself kept her behind the bar and away from either of the exits.

That shiver rushed over her again.

"Someone said he left the hospital with Trooper Wells," she said.

"Do you think she arrested him for poisoning the mayor?" he asked, and his smile slipped out again as if the thought pleased or amused him. "I'm shocked he would go so far to get that position. But I guess he didn't want to risk losing again like he did last time he ran for office."

"I don't think Charlie wanted the job that badly," she said, "if at all."

The Realtor shook his head, then quickly touched his hair as if to make certain that not a strand had slipped out of place. "Oh, he definitely wants it. And I expect his first order of business will be to get rid of the hotshots." He watched her face as if checking to see if she would get upset.

She had when she'd first heard that was Charlie's intention. But after everything that had happened because of the hotshots, she could almost see his side of it. Especially when she worried about her child or Charlie being in danger because of the saboteur too. Maybe it would be safer for the townspeople if the hotshots moved headquarters somewhere that there were fewer people, fewer innocent bystanders to the danger that seemed to befall them whether they were responding to a fire or not.

Choosing her words carefully, she said, "I'm not sure what his first order of business will be."

"Bail." The Realtor chuckled.

"I really don't think Trooper Wells arrested Charlie." She was worried about what else the officer of the law might have done to him, though.

"Not even if she found the ecstasy that was used to poison the mayor around here?"

"Ecstasy?" Charlie hadn't told her about that. Did he even know?

And if he didn't know, how did Jason Cruise know?

Because he was the one who'd slipped the ecstasy to the elderly mayor?

He must have been. And if he had attempted one murder, there was no doubt he was responsible for the other stuff that had been happening to Charlie. That must have been why he was there.

And was Charlie here somewhere? Hurt and needing her help again? She couldn't just run out, she had to make certain that she got him help.

And that she figured out how to help herself and her unborn baby out of the situation as well.

But then Jason cursed and pulled out a gun, pointing the barrel directly at her head. "Damn it. Damn it! I slipped up, didn't I?"

He wasn't the only one. She'd slipped up, too, because he must have seen her reaction—her realization that he was a killer.

Jason Cruise was smart. He could figure out how to spin this to his advantage as he kept the gun trained on Michaela Momber's beautiful but pale face.

There had to be a way to frame Charlie for her murder, just like Jason had intended to frame the bar owner for the mayor's death. Then that case would have been closed with Charlie's death.

Tillerman was supposed to have died in the fire on Bentley Ford's property. But the damn hotshots had saved him.

She had saved him.

More than once.

"You just keep getting in my way," he said, grinding out the words with his frustration. "That's why I wasn't going to fight him wanting the hotshots to move headquarters. If you hadn't been here that night his bar burned down, he would have already been out of my way. He wouldn't have been a threat to the plans I have for this town."

"What plans?" she asked. "What do you want to do with Northern Lakes?"

He was surprised she couldn't figure that out, it was so simple. "I want to make money off it," he said matter-of-factly. "I want to expand the town onto some land I already bought. Bringing in new business and more tourism will also raise the value of the other properties I already own, and when I sell everything, I'll have enough money to retire early."

That was the dream. And it was within his grasp. But he had to deliver, or the developers he was talking to would lose interest and go somewhere else, somewhere people weren't so opposed to growth and improvement.

"You're too young to retire," she said with an almost flirty smile. Or it would have been, if not for the fearful look in her blue eyes as she kept glancing at the gun, as if to see if he was still pointing it directly at her. "What will you do with yourself?"

"Lay on the beach, drinking mai tais," he said with a smile of his own. He considered for a moment if he could see her sitting next to him. But he didn't think money mattered much to a woman like her. She'd chosen a hard profession that couldn't pay nearly enough for the risks it posed.

This probably wasn't one of those risks. She would have been more likely to die in a fire than from a gunshot wound.

If only the others hadn't shown up while they were out in the forest...

Then he could have gotten rid of both her and Tillerman in the fire on Bentley Ford's property. And when the drugs were found in the bar—the drugs Jason had just planted— no more investigating would have been done.

He would have been in the clear. A door creaked open, light from the alley shining down the hall into the bar. He tightened his grip on the gun even as he started to shake.

"Who's there?" he called out.

Who else was he going to have to kill so that he didn't get caught?

"It's me," Tillerman said. "I assume I'm who you're looking for, that's why you're here. To kill me."

"Yes."

Relief eased the tension in him. A murder-suicide. That was what he would make it look like. Hadn't that idiot Gingrich tried to do that with Luke Garrison and his estranged wife?

Jason had been using some of the stunts that the former lawman had pulled on the hotshots. But none of Gingrich's efforts had paid off the way he'd wanted. Still, Marty Gingrich hadn't been smart enough to carry them out. Even the other people who'd gone after the hotshots—like the kid who'd run Trent Miles off the road and the FBI agent who'd taken shots at the reporter and Rory VanDam—hadn't been able to finish the job. Not like Jason was about to do, because he was smart.

He was so much smarter than all those other people. That was why he'd done the things he had, copying the things that had happened to the hotshots, so that people would think this was all about the hotshots and never connect it to him.

It was nearly over now. He was so close to pulling this off, to making the money he wanted—that he needed—and to getting away with murder.

Not just one murder either.

But two.

Charlie Tillerman and his hotshot girlfriend were about to die.

Chapter 24

Charlie often dreamed of Michaela. But usually, she was rescuing him in his dreams and in his reality. It wasn't the other way around.

Until now.

If he could figure out some way to rescue her...

But the way that Cruise had the gun barrel pointed directly at her head had Charlie feeling like he was in a nightmare that wasn't going to end how he wanted it to. He wasn't going to wake up from this to a happily-ever-after.

He needed to get Cruise to point that gun at him, not Michaela. So he moved closer. "Jason, I don't understand why you have the gun on her when I'm the one you want to kill."

Jason snickered like a giggly little kid. Maybe it was nerves, or maybe he was about to break from reality. "You know damn well why. The only way I'm going to be able to actually kill you is if I get her out of the way first. Or she'll rescue you like she has over and over again."

"That must have been frustrating for you," Michaela said, as if she was commiserating with her would-be killer about how hard she had made killing for him.

What she was going to do was set off the man and make him pull the trigger faster. To stop that from happening, Charlie rushed forward, and his sudden movement had Jason swinging the gun toward him.

But Michaela must have moved, because then it swung back toward her. Charlie moved again, easing through that opening to get behind the bar. He had to get between them, had to make sure that Michaela didn't take a bullet that was really meant for him.

"She's not part of this," Charlie said. "You don't have to kill her."

Jason snorted. "Yeah, because she'll keep quiet about everything after I blow your head off?"

He flinched from the fear pumping through him. This was so damn dangerous. All Jason had to do was squeeze that trigger, and it would all be over for Charlie and probably for Michaela too.

"No," Charlie said, in reaction to his awful thoughts and to Jason. "She'll say you did it, but you can say that she did instead. Press the gun into her hand after you fire it. Say that she did it because she was so upset about me wanting to move the hotshot headquarters out of Northern Lakes."

"And she would kill you over that?" He snorted.

"We're in a relationship," Charlie said. "She's pregnant with my kid, and I won't marry her or support her. I'm denying paternity, and she's emotional and furious with me. You got here just too late to save me."

Jason snorted again. "If I thought it would work…"

"It would work," Charlie insisted. "People are going to believe your word over hers. You're a big shot in this town, Jason. You're respected. She's just one of the hotshots who's always causing trouble."

"They are always causing trouble," Jason said. "But she's caused *me* the most trouble, always saving your ass, Charlie. You would have been out of my way over a year ago if she hadn't dragged you out of the fire the arsonist set here. And then I could have snapped up this corner for something big, like a fast-food restaurant or chain drugstore instead of you rebuilding the same old eyesore of a building that had been here for too damn long already."

Charlie flinched again as indignation jabbed at him. The Filling Station was revered and respected and of historical significance to Northern Lakes.

Jason sighed. "So while I will definitely use your excuse for the reason she shot you, she'll have to turn the gun on herself afterward...before I could get it away from her. She's so overwrought and emotional due to the pregnancy hormones that she lost her mind once she saw that she'd killed the man she loved."

Charlie chuckled. "You think anyone is going to buy that? That one of the bravest hotshots around is overwrought and emotional?" Or in love with him? He wanted to believe that, but he hadn't done a whole lot to earn her love. Even now, she kept moving around behind him, probably trying to jostle him aside to play his heroine once again.

But he wanted to save her and their baby, even if it cost him his own life to do it.

Fury bubbled up inside Michaela. She hated the way that Jason and Charlie were talking about her, with the same dismissive, condescending tone her father had.

Like just because she was female that she was overly emotional. Unlike her father, she could always control herself. Even now, as much as she wanted to pull Charlie down behind the bar and protect him, she used him as the distraction she needed.

Not that she was sure her plan would work. It was risky. But it was their only shot to not get their heads blown off, the way Jason Cruise intended to kill them.

She snorted derisively and criticized their plan aloud. "You guys are idiots," she scoffed. "That's not going to work." But hopefully, her plan would.

Jason turned that barrel toward her again, and his cold eyes narrowed. "What do you mean? Of course it will." There was an edge of desperation to his voice, like he was afraid that she was right.

"Wells is going to bring in a crime scene unit to check out the scene," she said. "Unless…"

"Unless what? That they take my word for what happened?" he asked hopefully.

"Unless she's on your payroll," Charlie said, voicing her concern aloud.

Jason chuckled again.

That chill raced down Michaela's spine again. He hadn't confirmed or denied how involved the trooper was in his scheme or if she was involved at all.

"Even if she is," Michaela said, "Braden doesn't trust her. He'll insist that someone else lead the investigation. He knows me too well to buy your story. And when he brings in an expert, they'll see that you were too far away when you shot me for me to have fired the gun myself."

Jason let out a soft gasp. "Uh, then I'll just have to get closer to you when I pull the trigger."

That was what she was counting on.

"Or you could flip it around," Charlie suggested. "Shoot me in the head, make it look like I killed her and then myself because—"

"Because you tried killing the mayor and know you're going to get caught," Jason finished for him.

"He planted the ecstasy he used to try to kill the mayor somewhere in the bar," she warned Charlie. Just in case she didn't make it out of this.

"Yeah, yeah, that could work," Jason said. "Get out here." He pointed the gun toward Charlie.

She would have rather he kept pointing it at her so that if it went off, Charlie wouldn't get hurt. But she didn't want to get hurt either. The only person she wanted to hurt was Jason. But if her plan didn't work and he started firing...

Charlie was going to get killed for certain. She had to do something. Or they didn't have a chance in hell of surviving. So when Charlie started walking away from her, she flicked the lighter and started the end of the bar rag on fire. Then she tossed the bottle full of barely legal moonshine over his head at the man holding the gun.

And just as she'd feared, the gun went off. The blast echoed off the hardwood floor just as the bottle ignited and the fire started.

She realized she'd made a horrible mistake—that if the gunshots didn't kill them, the fire probably would. But the biggest mistake she'd made was not telling Charlie that she loved him.

Because now she might never have the chance...

Shots fired. And a fire...

Wynona Wells cursed as the call came through Dispatch. She didn't even have to hear where it was. She knew.

Charlie Tillerman's bar.

He hadn't left the investigation up to her like she'd told him to.

And now, just as she'd warned him, he'd probably gotten himself—and maybe Michaela Momber too—killed.

Chapter 25

A week had passed since his bar caught on fire again. While Charlie was out of the hospital now and at town hall, he had spent that past week in the hospital, recovering from the gunshot wound to his shoulder.

He was lucky it hadn't been his head. Trick McRooney had told him that after he and the other hotshots had rushed into the bar. Trick had found him, per Michaela's request, just as Charlie had been about to walk into the bar. They'd realized quickly that Michaela wasn't in there alone and that she was in grave danger.

Trick had wanted Charlie to wait until they called for backup or Trooper Wells. Uncertain of whether or not to trust her, they'd decided to call in Braden, Owen, Trent, Ethan and Rory instead. But Charlie had refused to wait until they arrived. The last thing he'd wanted was to be standing outside if a gun went off and ended the life of the woman he loved, the mother of his unborn child.

He'd been more than willing to risk his life for hers, just as she'd done for him over and over again. She was someone he could rely on—someone he could trust—and she was worth every risk, to his heart and his life.

She'd risked her life for his that day. While he'd kept Jason talking, she'd been making a cocktail behind the bar—a Molotov cocktail. She'd tossed it at the Realtor just as he'd been about to shoot Charlie. While he had still pulled the trigger, his aim had been off.

And then Jason had gone down, set on fire from the pure alcohol inside the bottle. The others had rushed in, putting out the fire while Owen got Charlie to the hospital. Jason hadn't made it there. Knowing that it was all over—or maybe in excruciating pain—he'd turned that gun on himself.

And Michaela…

She was all right. At least, that was what Trick had assured him, and a few of the other hotshots who'd visited him that week had sworn the same thing. But she hadn't visited him. And he'd worried that she wasn't all right.

Or that something else had happened.`.`.

That she'd realized she didn't want him in her life or their daughter's life. And she'd left town.

Would she show up here?

From his podium, he stared out over the expansive auditorium used for town hall meetings, like the special one he'd called as interim mayor of Northern Lakes. He'd requested her presence, via text and through Trick and Hank and Braden. It was important that Michaela come because he had a couple of proposals for her. But since she hadn't even checked on him in the hospital, he didn't have much hope she would be interested in either of them.

"We really should get the meeting started," Les prompted him. The former mayor was doing so well that he'd agreed to take Charlie's seat on the town council. They had another one open too: Charlie had a couple of possible nominees for Jason Cruise's former seat.

"Yes," Bentley Ford agreed, his tone short. He still

wasn't happy with how Charlie had suspected him, but he'd at least visited him in the hospital.

Charlie looked out once more over the group of people gathered in the auditorium. Despite all the seats, there were still some people standing in the shadows in the back. Michaela stepped out of them with Hank beside her, their arms linked. They approached the last row of seats, and Trick McRooney and Donovan Cunningham sprang up and offered their chairs to her.

Wasn't she all right?

Had everyone lied to him?

Or was it that she was all right but she'd lost the baby?

He wanted to talk to her, to ask, but everyone was staring at him, waiting for him to start the meeting that he'd called.

Les cleared his throat. "It's time, Charlie."

He nodded and flipped on the microphone that was mounted to the podium. They'd done a sound check earlier, he knew it worked.

"Thank you all for coming," he said. "And thank so many of you for the well-wishes and cards you sent while I was in the hospital." He peered out into the crowd, trying to see Michaela's face. But people jumped up, applauding and blocking her from his view.

"Thank you, thank you," he said, as emotion rushed over him. He hadn't expected that reaction. "I am very grateful for you all." He cleared his throat. "I am especially grateful to our town heroes, the Huron hotshots, for putting out the fire Jason Cruise set. They saved the town and my life twice that day."

"So are you still going to run them out of town?" Bentley tossed the question at him from where he sat in the front row.

"No, I'm not," he said. "As I, painfully, came to realize,

it isn't the victim's fault when bad people try to hurt them. And I think that's what I and some other people in town have been doing." He sent his sister, who sat in the front row, a pointed look. "Instead of blaming the bad elements for trying to hurt our heroes, we were blaming our heroes. Instead, we all need to unite to protect them and to celebrate them." Then he stepped back and began to clap for the hotshots.

The people in the crowd, still on their feet for him, clapped along, turning toward where most of the twenty-member team sat in that back row with some other members standing behind them. "I would also like to extend an invitation for one of the hotshots to take an open seat on the town council. Maybe Braden Zimmer or Owen James would be interested."

They'd both grown up here in Northern Lakes like he had. They were town heroes even before they were hotshots.

Whistles pierced the air in approval of the suggestion.

"And I am also going to create an official position in the mayor's office for another hotshot to act as a liaison between the town and the hotshots. And I would like to offer that position to Michaela Momber."

There was a bit of a pause, a brief silence, and then the applause started up again. But he still couldn't see her. He wasn't even sure she was still there or if she'd slipped out behind all those people who now stood in the aisle.

When the people finally took their seats again, his suspicion was confirmed. She was gone.

So he didn't get the chance to make his other proposal to her. And if she wasn't interested in the first position, he doubted she would have any interest in the second one.

The disappointment hit him about as hard as that bullet had. But instead of missing, like the bullet had, it struck him directly in the heart.

* * *

Michaela sat alone in the dark. Except that she wasn't completely in the dark anymore. She knew that Charlie had changed his mind about her team, he wanted them to stay. And what about her?

Would he have offered her that job if he hadn't wanted her, specifically, to stay as well?

Or had he just extended that offer so that she wouldn't keep trying to work as a hotshot and risk losing their baby?

She had nearly lost her that day in the bar, which was where she sat now, in the dark. Everyone had come back here after the meeting, celebrating the reopening. But just like at the auditorium, she'd tried to stay out of his sight. And she'd waited in the ladies' room while he closed up the bar and shut off the lights.

She could hear him still in the kitchen and see the light beneath the door. But then the light went off. And she thumped her fist on the bar, using that Morse code he'd used with the horn the night they were run off the road.

Jason Cruise.

He'd done all of it. Or so it seemed.

Hopefully, Wynona Wells hadn't been involved, but nobody still knew for certain that she was innocent of all wrongdoing. Or if she was as complicit as so many of them suspected.

The door opened and lights flashed on, nearly blinding Michaela. She blinked and squinted, then focused on the man standing in the doorway brandishing an antique oar like a baseball bat.

"And here I thought I was the one up to bat," she mused.

He blew out a breath and sagged against the jamb of the open door. "God, you scared me!"

"Now you know how I felt when you got shot," she said,

her voice breaking like the fear had nearly broken her in that moment.

She'd thought she was going to lose him and that it was because of her—because he'd been trying to save her—that he was going to die. Even wounded, he'd tried to get her out of the fire, but the hotshots had rushed in at the sound of the gunshot, and they'd quickly extinguished the flames.

He set the oar down, leaning it against a wall, and walked over to the bar. "Really?" he asked, and there was skepticism and bitterness in his tone and in his dark eyes.

She nodded. "Yes."

"You never even came to see me," he said, and now there was pain.

Her heart ached with it too. "I was there."

He shook his head. "No, don't lie to me."

"I was in the hospital too."

He jumped over the bar then so that he was standing next to her, and then she was in his arms, held tightly against his madly pounding heart. "They told me you were okay. That you weren't hurt. Oh God, is it the baby? Are you okay?"

She reached up and pressed her fingers against his lips. "Shh, slow down…"

"Michaela—"

"I'm fine now, and she's fine too," she assured him. Then she eased back and put one of his hands on her belly, which shifted and moved beneath his touch.

Charlie let out a chuckle of delight and relief. "Then what happened? I don't understand. You didn't get shot? Or burned?"

She shook her head. "No. I got so scared, though, when he shot you. I thought I lost you, that he got you in the heart. It was so close." And her heart had broken then—or at least, it had felt that way. "My blood pressure went sky-high, and to keep it under control, I had to go on complete bed rest."

He bent over and slid an arm around her legs, and then he picked her up. "You should be off your feet now." But he grimaced too.

"Your shoulder," she protested. He was still healing.

He shook his head and held tightly to her. "It's fine. And I want to be the one to carry you now." Instead of putting her down on a stool or even the bar top, he carried her around it, through the kitchen and up the stairs to his apartment. "I want to be the one who takes care of you now." He carried her through the living room to his bedroom, then gently laid her down on the four-poster bed.

"I'm fine," she assured him. "I really am. Clean bill of health now. As you got better, so did I. My blood pressure is completely back to normal. So are my iron and glucose levels and everything else they kept monitoring. Even the doctor made a remark about how my recovery coordinated with yours." She had never realized it was possible to love anyone as much as she loved their baby and him.

"I'm so mad that everybody lied to me," he said, "that they kept telling me you were fine."

"I made them do that," she said. "And they were all so worried about me that they would have done anything I asked." She was truly lucky to have friends like the ones she had—loyal, loving, trustworthy friends. "I needed you to get better."

"And I needed you," he said, his eyes glistening with emotion.

"As your liaison between the mayor's office and the hotshots?" she asked.

"That's really just an offer I'm extending to you out of

nepotism," he said with a grin. "The role I really want you to fill is as my wife. My partner for life."

Warmth flooded her heart, making it beat harder but stronger. And she could almost feel the baby's heart beating just as strong. She smiled and teased, "So you're offering me two jobs?"

"Would it be a job to marry me?" he asked. Then he groaned. "I guess it would be, with as much as you've had to save my ass over the past year or so."

She grinned. "I'm so glad I did." Her smile slipped away as she relived those terrifying moments a week ago. "And I was so scared I didn't when you got shot."

"I'm fine," he said. "Or I will be once you put me out of my misery and accept my offer."

"Yes," she said, and held up a hand when he reached for her. "I will be the liaison between you and the hotshots."

He grunted, but a slight grin turned up the corners of his mouth. He knew…

"And I will be your partner for life, Charlie Tillerman," she said. When he reached for her again, she held her hand firmly against his chest yet, holding him off. "As long as you're not just proposing because of the baby."

He snorted. "You think I'm an honorable man who wants to do the right thing?"

She laughed. "Yes, I do. But the right thing is to give a baby two parents who love each other and don't feel trapped and resentful."

His mouth dropped open as he nodded with sudden understanding. "You were worried that I would be like your dad, that I would resent our baby—or you?"

She sighed but nodded. "I know that I shouldn't have. That not everybody is like him. But I haven't had much luck with love. I blamed myself for that, that my judgment was lousy, and so I was determined to just stay single. To be independent. But I realized I need people. That I don't want to be alone. That I want to love someone and be loved in return."

"I love you, Michaela," he said. "I love you so much, and I am so in awe of how strong and smart you are. The way you handled Jason, the way you handle everything life has thrown at you." Tears sprang to his eyes again. "I am just blown away that you would even consider my offer."

She shrugged and teased, "It is kind of a shitty job. I bet the pay is really lousy."

He chuckled. "Yes, it is. But the benefits…"

This time she didn't hold him back when he pulled her close and lowered his mouth to hers. He kissed her deeply, passionately, and desire caught fire inside her. She eased back, panting for breath. "Yeah, the benefits might make it worthwhile."

"And I promise that this will be the last time you save my life," he said.

"What do you mean? I'm not saving you right now."

"Yes, you are," he said. "You're saving me from a broken heart if you'd rejected me."

She knew how painful rejection could feel, and from his failed first marriage and first campaign, he must have felt it too. "I can't resist you, Tillerman," she said. "At first, it drove me crazy—*you* drove me crazy. But I know now that was just me fighting the fact that I was falling for you."

"I fell for you the first time you carried me out of a fire," he said. "You've been my angel ever since."

She gasped as the baby kicked hard, and then she put his hand over her belly where the little foot was still sticking out. "I think that's her name."

"Angel." He grinned. "Yeah, I think it is right to name

her after her fierce mama, who fought so hard for her safety and for the safety of our family."

That was what they were, everything Michaela had ever wanted: a loving family. "I love you."

"I love you." He kissed her again like he would kiss her for the rest of their lives—deeply and passionately and with such love and devotion.

And Michaela had never felt as safe and protected or as loved.

"So, are you taking the job?" a deep voice asked, drawing Braden's attention up from his desk to the man filling the doorway to his office.

"What job?" he asked.

And how the hell did this man already know about it? Had he been in the auditorium and yet, despite his size, somehow been invisible, like he seemed to be? He'd showed up in town months ago and had saved Rory's life, but nobody had seen him.

They only really knew he had been there because Rory was alive and that crooked FBI agent wasn't.

"I'm talking about the town council job," the man replied, "but you know that."

"I just didn't know you knew." The offer had just been extended a couple of hours ago. And he hadn't even known Mack McRooney was in town.

"So, are you taking it?"

Braden leaned back in his chair. "That depends. Are you taking the open spot on my team?"

Mack McRooney, the younger one—Braden's brother-in-law, not father-in-law—stepped inside the room and closed the door with his broad back. He didn't need to lock it, nobody was getting around him.

And Braden was pretty sure that nobody would.

"Yeah, I'm taking the job," Mack said. "It's about damn time to figure out who the hell this saboteur of yours is and stop him or her."

"It's way past time for that," Braden said with a heavy sigh. "If we don't stop them, I'm afraid someone's going to die because of them." And he didn't want to lose another member of his team.

Mack nodded in agreement. Unlike his dad, whose head was shaved, this Mack wore his dark hair in a buzz cut. He was military. Something. Or CIA. Nobody really knew for sure what he did, just that he was damn good and that he spent more of his time somewhere else than anywhere around his family. But he was here now in Northern Lakes.

And until the saboteur was caught, Mack McRooney was a hotshot. On Braden's team.

But Braden had that feeling he sometimes got, which wasn't always about a fire. It was a feeling that something bad was about to happen.

And he couldn't help but wonder and worry that, despite all the other things Mack had done and dangerous places he'd been, Northern Lakes and being a hotshot might be his most dangerous mission yet.

* * * * *